The Ghost and Mrs. McClure

"Part cozy and part hard-boiled detective novel with traces of the supernatural, *The Ghost and Mrs. McClure* is just a lot of fun."
—*The Mystery Reader*

"[The] enigmatic townspeople come alive in this quirky mystery, and readers will eagerly anticipate future installments—and the continuing easy banter and romantic tension between Jack and Penelope."
—*Romantic Times*

"A charming, funny and quirky mystery starring a suppressed widow and a stimulating ghost who is attracted to her even though they can only meet in her dreams. He is hard-boiled in the tradition of Phillip Marlowe, and she is a genteel Miss Marple; yet the two opposites make an explosive combination. Alice Kimberly definitely has a hit series if the first book is anything to go by."
—*Midwest Book Review*

"A deliciously charming mystery with a haunting twist!"
—Laura Childs, author of
The English Breakfast Murder

"This is such a well-written cozy . . . a fabulous first mystery. I highly recommend this book! You won't want to put it down."
—*I Love a Mystery*

"Ms. Kimberly has penned a unique premise and cast of characters to hook us on her first of a series."
—*Rendezvous*

"What a delightful new mystery series! I was hooked from the start. . . . I adored the ghost of Jack. . . . Pairing him with the disbelieving Penelope is a brilliant touch."
—*Roundtable Reviews*

The Ghost
AND THE
Dead Deb

ALICE KIMBERLY

BERKLEY PRIME CRIME, NEW YORK

THE BERKLEY PUBLISHING GROUP
Published by the Penguin Group
Penguin Group (USA) Inc.
375 Hudson Street, New York, New York 10014, USA
Penguin Group (Canada), 90 Eglinton Avenue East, Suite 700, Toronto, Ontario M4P 2Y3, Canada
(a division of Pearson Penguin Canada Inc.)
Penguin Books Ltd., 80 Strand, London WC2R 0RL, England
Penguin Group Ireland, 25 St. Stephen's Green, Dublin 2, Ireland (a division of Penguin Books Ltd.)
Penguin Group (Australia), 250 Camberwell Road, Camberwell, Victoria 3124, Australia
(a division of Pearson Australia Group Pty. Ltd.)
Penguin Books India Pvt. Ltd., 11 Community Centre, Panchsheel Park, New Delhi—110 017, India
Penguin Group (NZ), Cnr. Airborne and Rosedale Roads, Albany, Auckland 1310, New Zealand
(a division of Pearson New Zealand Ltd.)
Penguin Books (South Africa) (Pty.) Ltd., 24 Sturdee Avenue, Rosebank, Johannesburg, 2196,
South Africa

Penguin Books Ltd., Registered Offices: 80 Strand, London WC2R 0RL, England

This is a work of fiction. Names, characters, places, and incidents either are the product of the author's imagination or are used fictitiously, and any resemblance to actual persons, living or dead, business establishments, events, or locales is entirely coincidental. The publisher does not have any control over and does not assume any responsibility for author or third-party websites or their content.

THE GHOST AND THE DEAD DEB

A Berkley Prime Crime Book / published by arrangement with the author

PRINTING HISTORY
Berkley Prime Crime mass-market edition / September 2005

Copyright © 2005 by The Berkley Publishing Group.
Cover design by Elaine Groh.
Cover illustration by Catherine Deeter.
Interior text design by Stacy Irwin.

ISBN: 0-425-19944-4

BERKLEY® PRIME CRIME
Berkley Prime Crime Books are published by The Berkley Publishing Group,
a division of Penguin Group (USA) Inc.,
375 Hudson Street, New York, New York 10014.
The name BERKLEY PRIME CRIME and the BERKLEY PRIME CRIME design are trademarks belonging to Penguin Group (USA) Inc.

PRINTED IN THE UNITED STATES OF AMERICA

10 9 8 7 6 5 4 3 2 1

ACKNOWLEDGMENTS

Sincerest thanks to literary agent John Talbot
and Senior Editor Christine Zika for their valued support—
an intangible yet invaluable commodity
in making ghosts come to life . . .
and making this sort of living.

Thanks also to Kimberly Lionetti
for the all-important start.

And very special thanks to
Major John J. Leyden, Jr. (Ret.),
former field operations officer, Rhode Island State Police,
and Corporal Michelle Kershaw,
detective bureau, Rhode Island State Police,
for helpful answers to procedural questions.

AUTHOR'S NOTE

Although real places and institutions are mentioned
in this book, they are used in the service of fiction.
No character in this book is based on any person, living or dead, and the world presented is completely
fictitious.

CONTENTS

I did not lead a very wise life myself, but it was a full one, and a grown-up one. You come of age very often through shipwreck and disaster, and at the heart of the whirlpool some men find God.

—*The Ghost and Mrs. Muir* by R. A. Dick
(a.k.a. Josephine Aimée Campbell Leslie)

PROLOGUE

I'm licensed as a private detective. . . . The police don't
like me. The crooks don't like me. . . . My ethics are
my own . . . and I'll shoot it out with any gun in the
city—any time, any place.

—Race Williams in *The Snarl of the Beast*
by Carroll John Daly, 1927
(cited as the first hard-boiled private detective novel)

New York City
July 19, 1946

"PACKED AND STACKED," muttered Jack Shepard, gazing down at the sweltering Manhattan rush hour. Cars,
trucks, taxis, and people—swarms of them. Pouring out of
buildings, spilling down avenues, racing back to Cracker-
jack apartments and cramped rowhouses, smoky bar cars,

and roomy Victorians in the suburban north, land of do-right guys and fair-play Janes, chubby-cheeked kids, and manicured shrubbery.

"Excuse me, but are you Jack Shepard?"

The perfume reached him before the words. Not cheap and obvious, like his gum-chewing secretary's, but subtle, delicate, and dripping with pedigree.

"Look at 'em," said Jack, still staring out the window. "Most of 'em hungry and tired and crazy to get out of the summer heat. All of them, from this height, small enough to swat like flies."

"One of them did get swatted," said the dame. "That's why I'm here."

Without turning, Jack rubbed his neck. Beneath his thin dress shirt, shoulder muscles rippled. His sweat box of an office was no place for a jacket. He'd tossed it hours ago, loosened his tie, rolled up white sleeves. His rod stayed where it was, strapped in a holster, just under his arm.

Checking his watch, he turned to his desk, slid open a drawer. Like an old friend, the liquid gold greeted him. He pulled out one glass, poured two fingers.

"Quitting time," he said, flat as a pancake. The week had been a long one. He'd done the job he'd been hired to do, but he hadn't liked it. Or himself for doing it.

"Does that mean you want me to return on Monday?"

Slowly, Jack glanced up. When the world went bad, a man had two means of escape. A bottle. Or a dame. The sight of this one matched her sound and smell—cultured and subtle in a pink polkadot halter and white gloves, her golden locks upswept beneath a wide-brimmed hat. She looked to be in her late twenties, had a long white neck, and smooth, firm shoulders.

"Stay awhile," said Jack, nudging the glass. It slid a few inches across the battered wood.

She stepped forward, slowly took off her gloves—a

blue-blood striptease. She picked up the glass. Jack reached in the drawer for another.

Her big brown ones studied his muscular forearm as he poured his own, then her long, blonde lashes slowly lifted and she took in the V of his torso, the narrow waist and broad shoulders, the dagger-shaped scar across the flat, square chin, and the gunmetal gray eyes, staring down her own with sharp interest.

She swallowed nervously, put the shot glass to her glossy pink pout, and tentatively sipped. A delicate eyebrow rose in surprise—no doubt at the high quality of the hooch. It made no sense with his battered wooden desk, davenport of cracked brown leather, and old metal file cabinets. But Jack wasn't cheap where it counted.

"Thanks," she said softly. Her teeth were right and straight, white and perfect.

Jack knocked back his own in one gulp and pointed to a wooden chair across from his desk. "Take a load off."

She did. Pulling up her skirt, she crossed million-dollar gams in strappy sandals, giving him a happy glimpse of bare skin. One long limb swung nervously.

With a sigh, Jack moved to his worn leather chair and sat down, putting a mile of desk between them. This rich, blonde honey may have flowed easily through his door, but honey wasn't always sweet. Sometimes when you reached for a taste, you got stung.

"You look as though you're having a bad day," said the dame from across the wide, brown desert of his desktop.

"What are you? My bartender?" Jack's lips gave a wry little twitch. His eyebrow arched a fraction. "I'm the one pouring."

The dame studied Jack's face, took another genteel sip. "I don't believe men really tell bartenders anything."

"Why's that?"

"Because men don't like to reveal their weaknesses to

other men. In my experience, men are more likely to tell women what's vexing them."

"*Vexing*. Now there's a two-dollar word. Barnard? Or Sarah Lawrence?"

"Vassar, actually."

"That was number three on my list."

"Come now, Mr. Shepard, I'm sure my higher education is not what's vexing you." This time it was her eyebrow arching, her own wry smile teasing.

"Tracked down a clipster running a con on a suit," Jack found himself confessing. "Only the con turned out to be minor, fifty bucks even on a check-bouncing grift—and the clipster just a little old guy down on his luck after losing a legit job. The suit hires me. Easy for him, 'cause he's sitting on wads of dough, but he got his ego bruised, you know, the kind who's mortified to be smarted out of one dollar, let alone fifty—so he pulled some strings with his judicial buddies after I bring the old man in. Now gramps is gonna do hard time."

"But this con man person was guilty of a crime, no?"

"The old guy was so scared he pulled a gut-ripper on me. Pathetic little switchblade. I had to rough him up to keep him from running. I didn't like it."

The dame took another long look at Jack's acre of shoulders, his boxer's nose, his muscular forearms. "It was your job, no?"

"Frail old guy. Did his bit in the first war. Gave up the con racket a decade ago—till his legit job let him down. Hard time in Sing-Sing. It'll be the end for him."

"That's not your business, though. You did your job. You should be proud."

"Yeah. Sure." Jack poured another one, knocked it back. "So who's your fly, honey? The one that got swatted?"

"My sister. And if you don't help me, Mr. Shepard, the next fly that gets swatted will be me."

CHAPTER 1

The Princess Ball

> The girls I know do not like real life. When it roars in
> for a landing in their backyards, threatening to fly
> them from dance class to dorm room, beach chair to
> office, bar stool to altar, they race for the underground,
> looking for shelter. After all, why be neurotic when
> you can be numb?
>
> —Angel Stark, *Comfortably Numb*

Quindicott, Rhode Island
Today

"ALL THE PLAYERS were in place. The lights were up,
the stage was set for a tragedy worthy of the bard . . ."

Crisp paper rustled through the warm July air of Buy the
Book's Community Events room, a space so packed with
people, the store's modest air-conditioning unit had been

rendered irrelevant. At the carved-oak podium, a slender young woman with long copper hair and triple-pierced ears had paused from her reading to slowly pour water into a glass. The audience, packed elbow to elbow, waited with reverent patience for the young author to sip her drink.

I, Mrs. Penelope Thornton-McClure, thirty-something widow, single mother, and co-owner of Buy the Book, leaned forward in my folding chair, joining my customers in their anticipation—an atmosphere of breathless expectation as artfully created as I'd ever seen.

After swallowing deliberately, Angel Stark gave a little smile. The daring, corset-laced bodice of her green and pink Betsy Johnson sundress alone could have held the room's attention. But she'd come to my small Rhode Island town for a reading, not a fashion show, so she cleared her throat and finally returned her attention to the open book.

"No, perhaps good William is not the appropriate model for our tawdry little tale," she read. "Perhaps the story of Bethany Banks's final moments more mirrored one of those lurid Jacobean tragedies by John Webster, where the adulteress is punished by cruel torture and horrible death for her carnality. Of course, every tragedy, even a tawdry one, is unique. This tragedy, my tragedy, unfolded in a gilded beux arts mansion by the sea, under glittering lights that twinkled from high crystal chandeliers like a billion beckoning stars of the northeast. The Newport players were coifed and manicured young women and affluent and mannered young men. Like the cast of an A&E movie, they smiled and chatted as they waited in regal finery for the un-crowned, yet silently acknowledged, queen of our courtly crew to arrive.

"Before something could happen, really *happen*, Bethany Banks had to put in an appearance. That's the way things worked—at the annual parties, the sorority, those week-ends in the Hamptons or Cap Antilles. Bethany was our diva and our queen, our Simon Says . . ."

From the folding chair beside me, I heard a familiar *tsk-tsk* of disapproval. I frowned at the pale, slender man in tailored slacks, a crisp, white short-sleeve button-down, and bow tie.

"Simon Says?" he whispered when he saw my raised eyebrow. He shook his head in dismay. "Good lord."

I sighed, not entirely surprised at Brainert's critical reaction to Angel Stark's prose. J. Brainert Parker (the J was for Jarvis, a first name to which he'd refused to answer since the age of six) was an assistant professor of English at nearby St. Francis College. In his thirties, well-read, acerbic, and gay, Brainert was one of Buy the Books' most loyal customers—and one of my oldest friends. He never missed an opportunity to voice his opinions about the books I stocked or the authors I brought in for readings. In Angel Stark's case, he'd dismissed her work the very day her publicist had phoned to accept my invitation to appear at Buy the Book.

I myself had been delighted that the author of the acclaimed best-selling memoirs of her years of depression, addictions, and therapy—and now a controversial true crime tale—would come to our quiet little town, and I immediately rolled out the welcome mat. But when Brainert Parker had heard the news, he'd been less than impressed.

"Angel Stark!" he'd cried. "You mean that silly girl who wrote *Comfortably Numb*. Every angst-ridden teenager in America had to have a copy, which made her the darling of the New York literary set for two afternoons in a row."

"Lighten up, Professor," I'd replied, feeling that as a bookstore owner I should stand up for the honor of any and all authors.

"Forgive me, but I'm speaking as an educator," Brainert had informed me with a sigh. "It's a genre now, you know, 'Prozac-Girl-Interrupted-in-a-Bell-Jar,' and I found nothing redeeming in her contribution to it or the influence of any of it on my impressionable, if not downright gullible, students. She has a lazy, self-indulgent style, glorifies anti-depressant cocktails, and, in my opinion, the most disturbing 'affliction' she displayed in her story was her addiction to the letter 'I.' Whatever possessed you to ask her to appear at a *mystery* bookstore?"

There'd been no need for me to answer. My seventy-three-year-old aunt Sadie, and my partner in Buy the Book, had been locked and loaded.

"The subject of Ms. Stark's new book is *true crime*," Sadie had sharply informed Brainert as she polished the glasses that dangled on a chain around her neck. "It's all about the Bethany Banks murder. Angel Stark was there, and apparently knew the victim quite well. I hear the book is a real tell-all. So why don't you listen to my niece—and lighten up already on Ms. Stark."

(What Sadie actually said was *Miz Stahk*. The "Roe Dyelin" accent can vary from light to heavy as you travel our state—the tiniest in the Union—but it's murder to write out phonetically. To wit: *Car*, *pasta*, *letter*, and *chowder* would look more like *cah*, *pahster*, *letta*, and *chowda*. So, you'll forgive my going with the conventional spellings here.)

"Hmm," Brainert had replied to Sadie, clearly intrigued in spite of himself. "I concede you have a cogent point."

An understatement if ever there was one since the Bethany Banks murder and subsequent investigation were the biggest scandals to rock the Newport jet set since Klaus von Bülow was accused of injecting his obscenely rich wife with enough insulin to send her into a coma until the twenty-second century. And when I'd heard that some of the chic book emporiums in Providence and Newport had refused to consider an author appearance by Angel, I'd immediately issued an invitation for her to come to Quindicott. Miracle of miracles, Angel—or her publicist, at least—had accepted our invitation, and here she stood in our packed Community Events room.

I would have turned my attention back to Angel's reading just then, but my thoughts were suddenly interrupted by another voice. The one in my head—

In my day, dames with money from well-heeled families hired me to help them duck scandal on the QT. The last thing they'd ever do was write a book about it and tart it up in front of a ham-handed audience for applause.

The booming, masculine voice was either Jack Shepard—the ghost of a private detective who'd been haunting Buy the Book since his murder here more than fifty years ago—or a delusion of what would have to be my half-demented mind.

Which was true?

Take your pick.

"It's a different world than the forties, Jack," I silently replied, not a little annoyed that the ghost—who, so far as I knew, only I could hear—broke our agreement that he'd stay silent on evenings of important author appearances.

I liked my world better, Jack shot back. *The uptown crowd kept their trashy messes in the back alley, not on their bookshelves.*

"Shhh!" my thoughts insisted. "I want to listen to Ms. Stark's reading."

"Bethany was our radiant star," Angel continued from the podium, "and like moths to a flame we circled her, even though at times our wings got burned."

Brainert *tsk-tsked* again.

I glanced his way.

"Moths to flame?" he whispered. "Forget the Banks girl, these cliché's are killing me."

I shushed him, too.

"In medieval times, songs would be sung about a young maid's beauty, her wisdom, her virtue. Bethany, like all my other pretty friends, lacked an intellect, an original mind, but no matter. Of her beauty much was written—in the gossip columns and fashion magazines, the Internet fan sites and fawning letters—for Bethany had beauty enough to be envied by all, not to mention a PR flack with a fat Rolodex. Her line of handbags, created by a ghost designer, was sweeping the world. Her face was used to sell magazines. 'Bethany,' the new fragrance by an exclusive cosmetics company, was just hitting the market.

"In a life so short, Bethany Banks had possessed it all. But a perfect face, a perfect figure, perfect teeth, a perfect trust fund, and a perfect life were at least one perfect too many for someone. Clearly, that someone had decided that the only experience Bethany lacked was to be brutalized."

Listen, babe, I'm getting the drift—there's a big chill unsolved here.

"Yes," I said. "This is a type of book we call in the book business 'true crime.' Most books of this type recount the murder, the apprehension, and the trial. This one covers the crime, but it's still unsolved. And the author was a friend of the murdered girl."

So, the author's got the inside scoop?

"Yes."

Then who are her suspects?

"She hasn't gotten around to naming them yet."

Well, she better get to it soon, 'cause all this overblown yammering is putting me to sleep.

"Jack, if you don't settle down, neither of us is going to hear a thing!"

Take it easy, doll. Don't get your panties in a twist.

I could feel the heat on my face and just knew my pale complexion was reddening. "I wish you wouldn't use that phrase, Jack."

His response was a deep laugh—and a whisper of cold air to cool off my flaming cheeks.

"Bethany wore a spotless white gown the night of the New Year's Ball, the night of her murder—a radiant white so pure she appeared ghostly under the heavenly gleam of the chandeliers. When she floated down the stairs, all eyes followed. Then she paused to girlishly wave her gloved hand at us, her closest circle of friends, a group that, incredibly, held a person capable of murdering Bethany before the clock struck twelve midnight. Of course, at that dazzling moment of arrival under the thousand-bulb chandeliers, our princess was not dead. Not yet.

"All Newport balls are resplendent, and this one was no exception. The Gilded Age mansion gleamed in polished marble and gilt-edged moldings. The army of waiters in white-jacket uniforms carried brimming silver trays. The bejeweled women and turned-out men were there, obeying the black-tie command printed in gold ink on the crisp parchment invitations. And, as usual, everyone appeared captivated by Bethany's angelic beauty. But let's be frank, since we're telling the truth here. Not even Ms. Banks's fiancé would describe her character as angelic, not with a straight face—for God knows, there wasn't much virtue left inside that perfect shell. No, by this time, Bethany Banks had filled her mortal vessel with almost every vice imaginable . . ."

Back to the trashy mess again, Jack complained. *Is she ever gonna get to the suspects?*

"You're trying my patience, Jack," I silently scolded.

"Still," Angel continued, "Bethany had a way of diminishing the rest of us, of banishing us to bit parts, walk-ons—shadow players in our own lives. Here stood I, a literary light with a best-selling book and film adaptation on my resume, yet the fire that was Bethany Banks shone so much brighter.

"For Georgette LaPomeret—pathetic, eager to please, eating-disordered Georgie-girl—it was her absurd dream that her grotesque couture would become a runway sensation."

Okay, finally, the first suspect.

"Beyond her sad illusion of fashion immortality, Georgie lived for two things—the pharmaceutical fortune she would one day inherit, and copious amounts of a snowy powder distilled not in her family's New Jersey factory, but South of the Border down Cartegena way. That habit—like all bad habits—was actively encouraged and enabled by Bethany Banks. Then there's Henry 'Call me, Hal' Mc-Connell, who lived for love, not that he ever got any . . ."

Second suspect.

"Hal was the sweet, clueless man-boy who had pined since elementary school for the girl next door Bethany Banks, the beauty he could never touch. The irony here was that 'hands-off Hal' Bethany had done more than touched so many others. . . . Katherine Langdon used the breezy, approachable nickname 'Kiki' as a façade to disguise her cold-as-ice interior."

Number three.

"In a world of old money and old reputations, Kiki put the *stiff* in 'stiff upper lip.' With the calculated strategy worthy of Mary, Queen of Scots, or Catherine the Great, she became Newport's Princess of Wales, another lady in waiting who would only have to wait a little longer.

"And last but not least, there was the uncrowned king of our little fiefdom: Donald Easterbrook, Jr.—'*Le* Donald.' The Prince who escorted the Princess to the ball, only to discover that his lady-in-waiting had not waited for him."

That makes four.

"Of course, Donald shouldn't have been too surprised. On that particular night, at that particular ball, Bethany Banks was not waiting for anyone. In fact, the Princess was fleeing her assembled subjects without leaving so much as a glass slipper behind.

"It was midnight when Bethany Banks hurried out of the main ballroom and down the back stairs. Reality was stalking our heroine, you see. Adolescent no more, her debutante days behind her, Bethany was fast approaching the one true thing that none of us could deny or avoid. Soon Bethany would relinquish her belle-of-the-ball status to her little sister, her sorority presidency to an underclassman, her key to the 'special rooms' at Manhattan and Hampton nightspots. Adulthood loomed, and real life was closing in.

"Now, the girls I know do not like real life. Anything close to reality sends them packing for underground shelters. As I've often been quoted, my saying still applies: 'Why be neurotic when you can be numb?'

"Bethany Banks ducked underground often—'slumming' in the Depression-era parlance of her Chief Justice grandfather. Like a Roman noblewoman cavorting with gladiators, on the last night of her life, Bethany Banks descended dark and narrow stairs to a dank hole in the wall, a workspace occupied by the peons who served her drinks and prepared her foods and tended her gardens and, as it turned out, fed her addictions to sex, to drugs, to popularity.

"You see, Bethany Banks led a secret life. For her, low life and high life were interchangeable. She slummed with the best of us, too often (as we have seen) behaving like the worst of us. And the next morning she woke up, combed out her hair, pulled her clothes over her head, and went back home to Ma and Pa's mansion to sleep it off. Seemingly untouched by the orgy of self-indulgence, and incapable of an orgy of self-recrimination, Bethany moved between the worlds with an impunity others were not lucky enough to possess. Bethany used drugs, but never became a slave to them—rather, she used the power of illegal drugs to enslave others.

"Bethany swam in a sea of available young men, taking on lovers and dropping them as quickly and easily as last year's fashion, and came away unscarred by abortion and unpolluted by STDs."

STDs? Jack queried in my head.

"Sexually transmitted diseases," I silently informed him.

Ah . . . Neat little abbreviation. In my day, the lingo wasn't quite so pretty.

"What was it?"

Jack whispered it in my head, and my face flamed again. Suffice it to say, I'm too much of a prude to repeat it.

"After so many successful escapes, evasions, and near misses, Bethany must have felt herself immortal. How could she know that on this night, the precious, privileged, pampered Princess of Newport would face the consequences of her actions? How could our Duchess of Malfi know that one of the princes in her life—perhaps the very prince she came to meet in secret rendezvous—had shed his human guise and become a werewolf?

"Perhaps the realization came after her gown had been hiked up, her panties removed—at the moment the leather belt wrapped around the tender marble-white of her throat and squeezed the life out of her.

"Did Bethany know the hands that murdered her? Did she understand who she had wronged, and why the end had come? Or did she laugh as if it were a prank, until the leather noose tightened and silenced her laughter forever?

"What were Bethany's final thoughts as her lips turned blue, then purple? Before her green-flecked eyes grew dim, who did Bethany see? When her tongue turned almost as black as her sins, did Bethany know—did she really understand—why it was that she had to die?"

And that makes five, said Jack.

"Five?" I whispered in my head. "Who's the fifth?"

Who do you think, doll? Angel Stark herself.

The slender young woman at the podium employed a lengthy pause, then loudly and emphatically closed her book, signaling to the audience that she had finished her reading.

CHAPTER 2

Dying for Applause

While von Bülow saved himself for an exclusive interview with Barbara Walters, his mistress did a saturation booking on the television shows ... and told friends she was writing a miniseries based on the trial. Von Bülow made plans with his publisher for his autobiography and, according to one friend, made arrangements for a face-lift.

—Dominick Dunne, *Fatal Charms and Other Tales of Today*

MY AUDIENCES AT Buy the Book could always be counted on to provide genial applause. But the intense emotions stirred by Angel Stark's true tale of murder among the yachting class released a tide of screaming cheers and zealous hand-clapping I hadn't heard outside of a rock concert.

I have to admit, the noise level startled me, and I resisted the urge to slap my hands over my ears. After all, I thought to myself, how would it look?

Who the hell cares? This racket's giving me a headache. And I haven't had a head for fifty years.

Pointedly ignoring the ghost, I put my hands together in a polite show of unity with my enthusiastic patrons.

Author Angel Stark blinked her animated brown eyes, then tossed her long copper hair behind her shoulders. Her full lips tipped slightly and she cocked her head in poised acceptance of the ovation. The din continued, loud enough it seemed to blow the elfin wisp of a girl off the small portable stage.

I turned to Brainert. He was applauding, but only mildly.

"Well," I fished, "her delivery was certainly dramatic, don't you think?"

"Dramatic?" Brainert replied. "Try indulgent."

"At least you can admit that Angel Stark knows how to play to a crowd," I argued.

Brainert frowned and shook his head. "Showmanship does not an author make."

"On the contrary," interrupted Fiona Finch, sitting directly behind us. "An author knows how to tell a story. And her story is quite fascinating."

As the applause died, I could hear the metal chain on Fiona's large falcon-and-falconer brooch clink as she leaned forward to speak in my ear. Fiona herself was a small, brown-haired, wrenlike person whose most memorable characteristic, besides her compulsion for eavesdropping, was her colorful collection of bird pins—hundreds of them were in her possession, and she was forever on the yard sale hunt for more.

"A wonderful choice for your author event," she gushed with a sincere smile as she patted me on the back of my cream-colored linen pantsuit. (I usually dressed more casually for work, especially on a warm summer day like this one, but this was a major author event, so I thought looking the part of a co-owner appropriate.)

"A very interesting reading," Fiona complimented.

Brainert snorted.

Fiona was also Buy the Book's number-one purchaser of true crime books, so this event was right up her proverbial dark alley.

"Too many books about crime and criminals are written by journalists or police investigators," Fiona continued. "It's refreshing to have an eyewitness and friend of the victim write a book—much more intense and immediate. The excerpt she read was . . . fascinating."

Brainert rolled his eyes and mumbled something about "book review adjectives."

"Really, Fiona. Any good thespian should be able to read the phone book and make it sound *fascinating*," Brainert said. "And Ms. Stark certainly is a capable showman, as I graciously conceded. As for the quality of her prose . . ."

Brainert raised one brown eyebrow above his straight brown bangs and shook his head in the perfect expression of an underwhelmed English professor. As the applause finally died completely, Brainert leaned toward me. "Shouldn't you get up there and introduce the question-and-answer session?"

"No, the author's instructions were quite specific," I whispered. "Angel's publicist is handling everything beyond my introduction and a nice send-off at the end of the event. So I get to sit this one out and enjoy the show."

"What is there to enjoy?" huffed Brainert.

Even as he spoke, an elegant, thirtyish Asian woman, wearing a tailored, pinstripe suit with a surprisingly high hemline, approached the podium, clapping like the others and beaming a big smile to her client. This was Dana Wu, Angel Stark's publicist.

Angel took a step backward as Dana stepped before the microphone.

"Ms. Stark has graciously agreed to answer as many questions about her new book, *All My Pretty Friends*, as she has time for . . . so I give you Angel Stark."

When Dana stepped back and Angel moved forward again, I relinquished my seat to one of the many standing-room-only audience members and moved through the thick crowd to the back of the events space. The book signing would begin soon, and I wanted to make sure our copies of *All My Pretty Friends* were on the floor because it looked to be a sellout crowd.

On my way to the exit, I surveyed the audience. I was disappointed that one of our most loyal customers, Bud Napp, owner of the town's hardware and plumbing supply store, whose favorite sleuth, surprisingly enough, was Miss Marple (whom Sadie said he'd discovered while trying to get his mind off his wife's fatal cancer a few years ago), hadn't made the reading, although I noticed that his handsome nephew, Johnny, was seated in the back wearing his typical outfit of baggy jeans and black T-shirt.

I'd only met Johnny once or twice, and he seemed like a nice young man—quiet and very intense with a muscular build and the kind of dark good looks that could have cast him in a Rat Pack movie—big brown eyes and a dimpled chin. I doubted that Bud's nephew was here for Angel Stark—more likely he came to meet our clerk, Mina, for an after-work date.

I was also pleased to note that this was a very different demographic from the usual attendees of Buy the Book's author events. For one thing, this crowd was much younger—college-aged and decidedly female, by a margin of about ten to one. And this was an affluent audience, too. Many drove in for this event from Brown University or the Rhode Island School of Design, and as far away from Yale and Harvard, if the decals and bumper stickers on the Volkswagens, BMWs,

Volvos, Jaguars, Saturns, and Accords parked along Cranberry Street were any indication.

The visitors had been assembling since late afternoon, grabbing all the rooms at the Finch Inn—Quindicott, Rhode Island's, only bed-and-breakfast, run by Fiona Finch and her husband, Barney—and filling the Comfy-Time Motel, which had opened up recently on the highway. They'd been tying up traffic and jostling the locals off the sidewalks since early afternoon, gathering in clumps around the diner, and crowding the commons in the center of town.

Yet few Quindicotters complained, because these visitors were also spending lots of money—at the Seafood Shack, Cooper's Bakery, Koh's Market, Franzetti's Pizza, Gilder's Antiques, and, yes, our bookstore. It was the kind of economic activity unknown in these parts just a year ago, and I was proud of my own small part in revitalizing this formerly sleepy little Rhode Island rest-stop of a town.

As I tried to push through the packed aisles to the back of the room, I nearly collided with another Buy the Book regular. Seymour Tarnish, avid collector of pulp magazines, was moving through the crowd, searching in vain for a seat, even as he surveyed the audience. By day, Seymour was our local mailman. On evenings and weekends, Seymour became a purveyor of frozen treats, dispensed from an ice cream truck he'd purchased a few years back with part of the money he'd won on *Jeopardy!*

"Hey, Pen, good crowd," Seymour said, grinning. "If you told me the title of Angel Stark's book was *All My Pretty Young Half-Naked Friends*, I might have gotten here sooner!"

As he spoke, Seymour scanned—wide-eyed—the sea of attractive, college-aged young women packed into Buy the Book.

"Not funny," I said to the forty-year-old avowed bachelor who lived in his late mother's house with a middle-aged male roommate and their huge collection of valuable pulp magazines.

Seymour noticed that I was wringing the life out my hands—one of the nervous habits I sometimes exhibited during author signings. My aunt Sadie has always maintained that nerves of steel were essential commodities in the always-volatile book business. Lacking same much of the time, I relied on my aunt, and co-owner, Sadie to keep an even keel.

Me? I did all the fretting—more than enough for both of us.

Seymour continued to relish the view. "Wow! I haven't seen this many navels since I got a bag of oranges from my retired uncle in Miami."

"Didn't you volunteer to work store security tonight?" I asked, changing the subject.

"Your aunt gave me the night off. Says your author has a publicist that's handling everything. But I'm here to help out if you need me."

"Stick close," I replied. "I don't anticipate trouble, but this is the largest crowd we've drawn in quite a while—and the youngest."

Seymour spied a space between two young women— twins—with curly, honey-gold hair. When he was gone, I looked up in time to hear the first question from the audience, posed by a heavy-set young woman who rose when she spoke, even though she was clearly nervous. Despite the warmth in the crowded room, the questioner wore a long-sleeved Brown University shirt.

"How has Bethany Banks's murder affected you and your friends?" the coed asked shyly and quickly sat down again.

Angel nodded to acknowledge the questioner, then stepped close to the microphone to answer.

"In *Comfortably Numb* I spoke about emotional fallout—a term I coined—and how toxic such fallout can be.

I wrote my first book to purge myself of toxic emotional fallout caused by my abusive home, my clinical depression, my promiscuous behavior, and my dependency on illegal drugs."

This is still a tough pill to swallow, Jack complained. *You're telling me this dame wrote this dirt about her own life. Wrote it herself and* wanted *it published?*

"Yes, Jack," I silently informed him. "It's quite common. These days it's encouraged, often celebrated."

Jack grunted his dismay.

"Bethany's murder caused a ripple effect," Angel continued. "Georgette LaPomeret took her own life, for example . . ."

There goes suspect number one.

Angel paused, gazing out at the audience. "Was it emotional fallout that drove her to suicide? Was it a kind of Post-Traumatic Stress Disorder response to the murder?"

Brainert leaned toward me and whispered, "Or did she kill herself because of your book?"

I scowled. Not from Brainert's comment but at the idea that the comment itself could be on the mark.

"Or," continued Angel, "perhaps Georgette knew something about the killing—a secret that has gone to the grave with her. I wrote in my book that I believe Georgette was secretly in love with Bethany's fiancé, Donald Easterbrook. This, of course, is understandable, because Donald was Newport's leading lothario and he'd secretly been sleeping with some of Bethany's closest friends."

Hmm, murmured Jack, *if that's true, could be Bethany caught fiancé Donald cheating, flew into a rage, threatened or attacked him, and he killed her.*

Gasps of surprise were heard, and the audience leaned forward, waiting to hear more. But instead of elaborating further, Angel pointed to another audience member with a hand raised.

This time a young man with longish brown hair and a

fuzzy brown soul patch under his lower lip stood up and asked Angel the question that was probably on everybody's mind. "Do you really know who killed Bethany Banks? Was it the dude they charged and later freed? Or was it one of her friends?"

Angel cautiously scanned the room like a scout in front of a wagon train. "Are there any *lawyers* present?" she asked at last. "If so, please leave."

Her mock inquiry was greeted by laughter and applause. When the response died, Angel seriously addressed the man's question.

"I have my suspicions, of course. And if you read my book, you'll see what I think. I can only say that I am absolutely positive that the young man who was arrested was innocent, and that someone close to Bethany Banks is the real murderer—and that's the person who framed the catering worker. You see, there wasn't any physical evidence linking him to Bethany's murder, only his belt around her neck, which the killer could have easily taken with gloved hands from the worker's unlocked locker . . . which is why they couldn't prosecute him.

"All the defense would have had to show was physical evidence that pointed to other people having been in that room with Bethany near the time of her murder, which there clearly were, and sufficient motive, which I amply reveal in my book, and they would have created a shadow of a doubt that would have easily meant an acquittal for that young man. Therefore, I believe, and most everyone who examined this case believes, that Bethany *knew* her killer, and that she left the ball to rendezvous with the person who murdered her."

Of course she knew her killer, said Jack. *That murder was a crime of passion. Without a doubt.*

The young man with the soul patch called out a follow-up. "So why haven't the police solved it?"

"Two names: O. J. Simpson and Martha Moxley. As in

the Simpson case, the local cops botched their handling of the physical evidence. They pinned all their expectations on a confession from the catering worker, and allowed the wealthy crowd to flee without being questioned or searched." Angel shrugged. "After that poor catering worker was released, the case just became another example of the very rich successfully retreating behind their attorneys and high hedgerows—as teen Martha Moxley's killer had done for decades before Mark Fuhrman broke that in *Murder in Greenwich*."

Next, a woman wearing tight jeans, a belly shirt, and a nose ring rose to speak.

"Ms. Stark, it seems that you condemn Bethany Banks for the life she led—for the men she slept with and the drugs she consumed. But as a feminist yourself, don't you feel you should be defending Bethany Banks's right to choose whatever lifestyle she wished to live, regardless of the moral and ethical strictures placed on women by the double-standards of a sexist society?"

Angel Stark listened to the question without even a nod. When the girl sat back down, Angel wet her lips and spoke. "I think you all know the kind of lifestyle choices I've made, since I've written about them ad nauseum—"

Sly laughter from the audience.

"My problem with Bethany was that she hid her true self behind a mask, as if she were ashamed of the men, the drugs, the partying. No one should ever sin and then feel bad about it. Either don't sin, or don't feel bad. Anyway, I've always believed that guilt is something best left to working-class churchgoers, nuns, and old ladies. Of course, I realize this is a cutting-edge, postmodern philosophy that flies over the heads of a population stuck in the past."

Sheesh. This dame really thinks she's class on a stick, but I've got news for her. There's nothing new about her attitude. In my day, she's what was called a "debutramp."

"A what?" I was trying my best to ignore Jack and listen to the author I was hosting, but that last comment got me. "Come again?"

Debutramp. Walter Winchell's shorthand for a wild, amoral society girl.

"Whose shorthand?"

Walter Winchell! Jack said in a tone that showed he was clearly astonished and annoyed that I didn't recognize the name. *Vaudeville man turned* New York Evening Graphic *and* Daily Mirror *gossip columnist? Scandal sheet hound turned radio personality? Walter . . . Winchell . . .*

"Uh . . . sorry . . ." I replied.

Aw, forget it.

I turned to Seymour. "I guess everything is under control here—"

Everything except the broad at the podium—

I ignored Jack. "Seymour, have you ever heard of Walter Winchell?"

"The newspaperman from the twenties and thirties? Sure, Pen, who hasn't?"

I blushed and changed the subject. "So I'm going to make sure we're ready for the author signing." Then I raced to the front counter on the selling floor where Aunt Sadie was assisting a few locals now staring with open curiosity at the laughing, youthful crowd overflowing from the events room. Mina Griffith, our part-time clerk, worked the cash register.

"Angel Stark is still answering questions, but she'll be done soon. Are we ready for her?" I asked, still giving Lady Macbeth a run for her money with my hand wringing.

Sadie reached out and gently pushed my arms to my sides. "Nerves of steel," she reminded me, finger raised.

"Is the table—"

"All set up and ready," Aunt Sadie declared. Like me, she'd dressed for tonight's event, abandoning her usual casual slacks, loose T-shirt, and open denim shirt for a new, powder-blue dress. She'd even stopped by Colleen's Beauty Shop to get the gray rinsed auburn and those "Shirley MacLaine" strawberry-blonde highlights put in.

"And the books?" I asked.

"Stacked and ready to go, Mrs. McClure," Mina said with confidence.

I smiled at the girl. A tall, slender St. Francis College student with flyaway light brown hair and freckles, Mina was a sweet, quiet kid who devoured books and hoped to one day become a librarian.

I exhaled with relief. "Looks like you two have got it covered. So, I'll just—"

"Go back inside and relax," Aunt Sadie insisted. "You've earned it, dear, setting up this whole shindig in the first place. Believe me, everything's under control."

Before going into partnership with me a year ago, my aunt had never attempted author appearances like this one. I was the one who'd urged her to agree to the store's complete remodeling, an inventory overhaul, and the addition of the new Community Events space. But whether it was Sadie's years in the book trade or just her seventy-three years on earth, the lady's nerves were clearly tempered into firmer stuff than mine.

Just then I heard a woman's hysterical shouts echo out of the events room. I froze, trying and failing to make out what she was saying.

A second later, Seymour Tarnish, ashen-faced, burst out of the room and ran toward me. "Better call the cops!" he called. "You've got a riot on your hands!"

CHAPTER 3

Accuse Me?

> Not only could she spit a curve in your eye, but she
> could cuss for minutes at a time without repeating.

—Walter Winchell, *New York Evening Graphic*, 1929

SEYMOUR'S FRANTIC PLEA was followed by a loud cry,
then the clatter of a metal folding chair as it struck the hardwood floor. Before I realized I was moving, I raced across
the length of the store and into the packed events room.

Most of the audience members were still seated. But
many were on their feet, especially those seated in the
first few rows where, apparently, the trouble had started.
Near the center of the third row, I spied the overturned
chair. Standing next to it was a petite young woman, her
straw-blonde hair tied into a tight ponytail. Her eyes were
bright as she shouted and shook her fist at Angel Stark—
or rather, at Angel's publicist Dana Wu, who had thrown

herself between the ranting young woman and her client.

"Lies! Lies! I hope someone makes you pay for your lies," the woman cried, her voice strident and full of rage, yet trembling as if she were fighting back tears. "You're smearing Bethany's name. You and your stupid books and your filthy lies. Why did you come here? No one wants you . . . No one wants you anywhere near us, you bitch! Why don't you just die and leave us all in peace!"   .

Despite the harsh emotion, that twisted the young woman's face, she possessed a gangly, adolescent beauty. She wore no makeup and her casual clothes were typical of a college freshman—a Brown University T-shirt and cargo shorts.

I tried to approach the woman, intending to calm her even as I escorted her out. But so many people were on their feet and filing out of the row of chairs that I found myself swimming against a human tide. I saw Brainert, watching the whole scene with a bemused expression.

Meanwhile, hands tugged at the woman, trying to pull her back, away from the podium. Two women, roughly the same age as the heckler, were attempting—so far unsuccessfully—to mollify the distraught woman.

One of the two was at least a head taller than the heckler. Dressed in a black tank top and lowrider jeans, her shoulder-length raven hair contrasted starkly with her pale skin, and her pierced lower lip was curled into a frown. She had grabbed the ranting woman by the shoulders and was attempting to speak to her.

The other woman was dressed in a pink sundress and sandals and was compelled to push back long, red curls that danced around her flushed face as she gamely tried to drag her friend away from the confrontation.

I was hoping Brainert would do something, but he seemed stunned by the action. Then Seymour appeared at my shoulder. Arms raised, he made a valiant effort at taking control of the audience. "Everyone! Calm down!"

With chaos whirling around me, and visions of lawsuits dancing in my head, it was definitely not the time for the ghost of Jack Shepard to speak up.

So of course he did.

What a hairball! Sounds like a speakeasy raid.

"Not now, Jack."

Then take my two cents and give that little girl the bum's rush solo, before your big-draw, money-in-the-bank author takes it on the chin.

"Butt out," I told Jack as I pushed past Seymour.

It occurred to me that I'd spoken out loud when Seymour faced me. He had the hurt expression of an abused puppy.

"Hey, Pen . . . I was just trying to help . . ."

"I wasn't referring to you, Seymour. I . . . I mean the troublemaker," I lied.

As it turned out, no more help was needed. The girl's companions had calmed her. Clinging to her girlfriends, the young woman allowed herself to be led away. The crowd parted as the trio moved to the door. The young woman, tears streaming down her face, muttered apologies to her companions as they moved up the aisle.

Like the others, Seymour stood aside to let them pass, even as I exchanged looks with the woman's two companions.

"Can I help?" I asked. The tall girl with the short black hair and the pierced lip shoved me aside with a strength that surprised me.

"Get out of the way, bitch," she hissed, glancing over her shoulder at the podium. Her words evoked gasps from those within earshot.

I threw up my hands in surrender and backed away. As the trio made their exit, all eyes watched them go.

A pale, frowning Dana Wu was still clutching the microphone stand, legs braced as the eyes returned to the stage. The publicist seemed determined to protect her client until the rabid young woman was out of the building.

Then I peered over Dana's shoulder, into the bright brown eyes of Angel Stark. She didn't seem disturbed in the least by the ugly scene—even though some of the heckler's angry words bordered on criminal threats. She seemed almost pleased. Obviously, this was an author who loved to shock her fans. And she'd wowed them again. But I couldn't share her enthusiasm.

As members of the crowd took their seats and waited for the Q & A to resume, I hurried toward the exit, intent on tracking the troublemaking trio. But before I passed through the archway that led from the large Community Events space to the main bookstore, I noticed that one woman, near the side of the room, had not reclaimed her seat.

The tall, thin woman with light blue eyes, long, straight blonde hair, sunken cheeks, and a small, pointy chin had remained on her feet to fire poisonous eye daggers directly at me. Our gazes locked—as if she expected me to recognize her. Or was she challenging me to approach her?

I was concerned enough to comply, but was interrupted by the amplified screech of our public address system. Angel Stark was trying to speak, but her words were lost in electronic distortion. I turned from the dagger-staring blonde and rushed toward the microphone box to fix the problem.

Bud Napp's nephew, Johnny, who'd just joined a local band and understood the vagaries of feedback, moved to my side after a few seconds of my own inept adjustments and helped me fix the mike to eliminate the screech. When the sound was stabilized, Angel smiled at Johnny's big brown eyes and dimpled chin, then nodded. Finally, she faced the crowd.

"Well, the critics have spoken, and I can only say that a

certain inscrutable reviewer at the *New York Times* was far less kind. My conclusion therefore is simply this—that chick needs to have her meds adjusted!"

There was a burst of laughter, and a ripple of applause. Still, an undertone of nervous tension remained in the room. Angel simply tossed her long copper hair.

"Any more questions?" she asked breezily.

A dozen hands shot into the air. Angel pointed to someone who proceeded to compare Angel's previous book to the work of the number-one purveyor of gonzo journalism, the late Mr. Hunter S. Thompson himself.

"Well, unlike Mr. Thompson, I don't travel armed."

More laughter followed, and as the debate continued, Angel seemed to enjoy the comparison.

Satisfied that order had been restored, I moved toward the exit again. On the way, I searched for the statuesque young blonde with the pointy chin and ice chip eyes who'd glared at me from the side of the room. But like the mysterious heckler and her companions, the stranger was gone.

In the main store, I could sense the "emotional fallout" from the coed's outburst had reached the checkout area. Aunt Sadie had witnessed the trio's exit, but she didn't appear bothered. She smiled and chatted up the customers as if nothing were amiss. By her side, however, Mina seemed tense as she rang up purchases and bagged them.

Outside, the streets were dark, but the summer heat had not dissipated. Seymour came through the front door and approached me.

"They're gone," he said quietly. "All three of them piled into a black sedan and drove away. That girl seemed pretty upset with your author."

"Did you speak with her? Find out who she was? Why she was here?"

Seymour threw up his hands. "Hey, you're talking to a confirmed bachelor. I wasn't going near her. Women's tears scare the heck out of me." A sudden burst of applause from the events room interrupted him. When the cheers died away, Seymour shrugged and added. "Anyway, I've got to admit, this was the most exciting author appearance since Timothy Brennan croaked at your podium last year."

CHAPTER 4

Guilty Pleasure

I'm a lousy writer; a helluva lot of people have got
lousy taste.

—Grace Metalious
(author of *Peyton Place*, the blockbuster best-seller
that spawned television's first prime-time soap)

AFTER ANOTHER HALF-HOUR of questions and answers, Dana led Angel Stark to a chair and a table stacked
with copies of *All My Pretty Friends*. Her fans lined up to
have their purchases autographed. To my surprise, Brainert
had taken up a position near the end of the autograph line,
one copy of Angel's hardcover tucked under his arm and
another wide open in his hands.

"I thought you weren't impressed," I said.

Brainert looked up from thumbing through the book's
pages. "Fiona had to get back to the Inn. Apparently your

guest is lodging there. Anyway, she asked me to get her copy autographed."

"That explains one copy. Who's the other copy for?"

Brainert raised his eyebrow. "Guilty," he replied. "Actually I thought tonight's intermission was more exciting than the main event. Exciting enough to get me curious, so I started breezing through it."

"Speaking of curious, did you notice a tall, blonde Paris Hilton clone standing along the side of the room. I think she's gone now, but—"

Brainert nodded and began flipping pages. "Right here," he said, holding the book open. My eyes skimmed down the page, past two small before-and-after photos of Bethany Banks—in one, she was smiling and alive at the New Year's Ball, waving her gloved hand. In the other, she was lying on a dingy floor, a belt around her neck, her arms at her sides, fingers bent in rigor mortis. I shuddered and my eyes continued down the page. The photo at the bottom depicted the woman in the audience.

"Katherine Langdon," said Brainert. "Kiki to her friends . . . One of the principals involved in the Bethany Banks murder."

"I wonder what she was doing here?"

I also wondered why she was staring at me, though I didn't mention that to Brainert.

"That got me wondering, too," Brainert replied. "From some of the passages I've read, I doubt that Kiki Langdon and Angel Stark are on speaking terms, let alone friends."

"Maybe she came here to confront Angel also, and that other girl beat her to it. Any clue as to the distraught co-ed's identity?"

Brainert shook his head and snapped the volume closed. "Not yet. But I haven't really read the book, just began to skim it."

I noticed that Sadie was alone at the counter and I excused myself to help her check people out.

"Where's Mina?" I asked.

Sadie peered over her glasses at me, then jerked her head toward the couches and stuffed chairs I'd placed at the other end of the store. Mina was there, next to Johnny Napp. They were holding hands and speaking in whispers, their heads nearly touching.

"Ahhh, that's sweet." Aunt Sadie sighed as she slipped a copy of Angel's book into a plastic Buy the Book sack and passed it to the customer. "You remember what it was like to be young and in love, don't you, Pen?"

"No," I replied, ringing up the next purchase.

ANGEL HAD FINISHED signing books and was chatting with a few holdovers—specifically a pair of enthusiastic female fans who couldn't tear themselves away from their favorite author. It was nine—our usual Friday night closing time.

Aunt Sadie and Mina were still ringing up customers, and I stood in the corner wringing my hands. With a theatrical sigh, Dana Wu sidled up to me.

"Rough night?" she asked.

"At least nobody was murdered," I blurted out, remembering our store's first ever author appearance, the one Seymour had mentioned, which the author hadn't survived.

Dana stared at me blankly for a moment—clearly it wasn't a response she'd expected.

"Oh my goodness," I told her instantly. "Please forget I said that."

"Why?" she said. "It's pretty much how I feel about most of my author tours."

Now it was my turn to stare—until we both burst out laughing.

I'd liked Dana from the moment I'd met her. Now that I'd seen her in action, I was also impressed. I invited her to sit down in one of the comfortable corners set up in the main bookstore.

"Wow, you've really transformed this place," said Dana, pausing to study a framed picture of the old store hanging near the register.

"Thanks," I said, trying not to beam too much.

I truly was proud of saving this old store, which my aunt had run for decades and was about to close when I'd swept in the year before. Using the money from my late husband's life insurance policy, I'd revitalized the inventory, done away with the ancient fluorescent ceiling fixtures and old metal shelves, and brought in an eclectic array of antique floor and table lamps and oak bookcases. I'd had the chestnut-stained wood plank floor restored, and throughout the stacks I'd scattered overstuffed armchairs and Shaker-style rockers to give customers the feeling of browsing through a New Englander's private library.

"Can I get you something? Coffee, tea—bottled water?" I shuddered ever so slightly at the mention of the bottled water, considering its role in Timothy Brennan's death the year before.

"No thanks . . ." said Dana, scanning the nearly empty Angel Stark display and table. "It looks like you sold most of your books."

"We did. We'd ordered a lot of copies, but I was afraid we'd run out before the end of the night."

"Don't worry about that when I'm around. I have fifty copies in the trunk of my car, just in case."

"God, you are amazing," I gushed, remembering some of the high-handed publicists I'd had to deal with when I was a publishing professional. In my experience, most were primarily good for forgetting to wear bras when chaperoning male authors to television appearances, cutting cakes for executive birthday parties, and planning their weddings on company time, before giving notice that they were quitting to marry that investment banker who made high six figures. "How did you ever get hooked up with a character like Angel Stark?"

Good God, I'd just insulted her author, I thought, the second I'd said it. Now I was two for two. "No offense . . ." I quickly added, deciding maybe I was too hard on those braless publicists. From the way I was sticking my foot in my mouth, I could probably use one.

"No worries," Dana said with a wave. "Actually, I'm a freelance publicist these days, and Angel only belongs to me until her book tour ends next month."

"You don't work for Angel, or the publisher?"

"I'm the go-to girl when the hard cases come along."

I must have looked confused, because Dana kept on explaining things.

"When a publisher has a problem client—like a certain beloved children's writer who had to be reminded to bathe and be *nice* to the little children, or the world-famous literary author with the obnoxious trophy wife—I get the job. But I have to admit, Angel is a special client to me."

"You *are* brave."

"It's nostalgia, mostly," said Dana. "I was a publicist at Saul and Bass when Angel published her first book. I had just been promoted from ad assist to junior publicist, and my first assignment was Angel. I wouldn't have gotten the job except that nobody thought her book had a chance, and absolutely nobody thought it would end up on the bestseller list for nineteen months."

Dana sighed. "Angel was a pill—and if you read *Comfortably Numb*, you know she *took* a lot of them, too. I'm pretty sure she's cleaned up her act since then, though—at least on that score—but Angel is still careless. . . ."

"Careless? What do you mean?"

Dana shrugged. "Angel is careless in the way a lot of wealthy people are careless. The way John F. Kennedy, Jr.

was careless when he got into that airplane. Their money cushions them from the true impact of things, and sometimes their judgment is off where real consequences are concerned."

"I follow. You mean, careless like Jay Gatsby's Daisy. Yes, I've actually had some experience with people like that myself."

"Well, sometimes it's more than just careless. Sometimes, I think Angel's simply mean."

I knew something about that, too, but I didn't say it. Of course, in my head, Jack said it for me—

You're thinking about that rummy late husband of yours. The overeducated, over-pampered, trust-funded depressive who found fatherhood and husbandhood a bore, verbally abused you, stopped taking his medications, and threw himself on the mercy of the Upper East Side concrete—from thirty stories above it.

"Right," I silently replied. "Now be quiet, Jack. Please."

Dana rubbed her eyes. "I shouldn't say that . . . She's never been mean to me. Or cruel to her readers . . ."

I saw my opening, and took it.

"That scene tonight . . . Does that kind of thing happen often?"

Dana laughed. "Last week, actually. A pill-pushing New York doctor she practically named in her book is facing charges now—he confronted Angel at a bookstore on Fifth Avenue. Turned out to be a lot of yelling and screaming, that's all."

Then Dana grinned as her professional instincts took over. "It wasn't a total downer. Got a nice mention in the *New York Post.*"

On the other side of the room, Angel finally stood up and shook hands with her two remaining fans—Goth girls in black lace skirts, black midriff T-shirts, and matching navel rings. When they exited, she stretched and yawned and headed for the front door.

"Girlfriend," Dana called to Angel, "can I get you anything?"

Angel shook her head. "I signed all the books in the store. I'm just going outside for a smoke and some fresh air."

"Don't get lost," Dana said, rising. I stood up, too.

"God," Dana whispered. "In the old days, when Angel said the word *smoke*, I had to check to see if there were any policemen around—there were states in this country I couldn't take her back to when she was using. Felony states like Texas. Now you know what I mean when I say careless. Fortunately she can afford people like me to take care of things when they get out of control."

"So . . . any clue who that girl was who confronted Angel tonight?" I asked quickly, before Dana got away.

"I think it was someone from Bethany Banks's family. So far, the Bankses have been pretty quiet—but just between you and me, the publisher fully expected to fight a lawsuit. And the press has been stirring the pot, trying to start a feud between Angel and the Banks family. In the end, though, all publicity is good publicity because it's good for the bottom line . . ."

I was about to ask Dana another question, but I never got the chance. From outside, we heard angry words, a loud scream, then the squeal of tires on pavement.

"Gee-zus. Not again," Dana Wu cried as she raced to the door.

CHAPTER 5

Hit and Run

I shall tell you a great secret, my friend. Do not wait
for the last judgment. It takes place every day.

—Albert Camus

BEFORE I'D REACHED Buy the Book's front door,
Johnny Napp was already through it, running outside. Dana
Wu bolted after him, with me on her heels and Aunt Sadie
and Mina on mine.

Outside, in the middle of the otherwise desolate street,
Angel Stark lay sprawled on the concrete, the gauzy skirt of
her Betsy Johnson neon-green and hot-pink sundress flutter-
ing in the night like a downtown distress signal. In his baggy
blue jeans and black T-shirt, Johnny Napp knelt over her. But
Angel wasn't moving, and I feared the worst—until she began spewing an outraged string of obscenities.

Obviously, the girl wasn't dead.

Dana raced into the street and to her client. But the elementary school crossing guard programmed into my head through years of motherhood made me pause and check for traffic before stepping off the sidewalk. All eyes were on Angel, but when I turned my head, I spied a car careening up Quindicott's main street, its scarlet taillights receding in the distance.

The sedan was a black Jaguar. Unfortunately, with only Cranberry Street's brand new faux-Victorian streetlights as illumination, and because I've read far too many novels late into the night, my eyes weren't up to deciphering the license plate, though I did notice a white and blue bumper sticker of some kind—but on the left side of the *trunk*, not the chrome bumper, where one would expect such a sticker.

"Son of a bitch!" Angel Stark yelled as the vehicle vanished around a corner. I turned to find Johnny Napp and Dana trying to help Angel to her feet. Pale and out of breath, Angel had lost one of her shoes, which gentleman Johnny quickly retrieved, and her corset-bodiced sundress was disheveled and dirty. Otherwise, Angel Stark did not seem any worse for wear, though her face was florid and her classic features folded into an angry scowl.

I was still on the sidewalk as Mina and Sadie caught up to me.

"Oh, my," Aunt Sadie muttered, and I noticed she was wringing *her* hands now. But as I've tried to tell her many times before, bookselling is murder these days.

"Damn it! Is everybody in this cracker burg a critic?" Angel yelled, pushing her hair back and tugging on her pump.

Dana reached for Angel's arm. "Let's get off the street. Get you inside—" But Angel Stark fended her off.

"I'm fine. I can walk!" Angel insisted, even as she grasped Johnny Napp's muscular, barbwire-tattooed bicep for support. In fact, once her shoe was in place, Angel wrapped both of her shapely, health club–toned arms around his waist.

I glanced back at Mina. In the soft night breeze, her fly-away brown hair was dancing about her freckled face. Her brown eyes were flaring, her expression pained.

"What happened?" Aunt Sadie whispered.

"I think someone tried to run Angel down," I replied. "I saw a car—"

Dana Wu whirled and faced her client. "Is that what happened?"

"No! God no," Angel replied, too quickly. "It was just some low-rent asshole who made a rude comment about my book. I guess I should be used to cheap shots by now, but I'm tired, and *it really pissed me off!*"

Angel screamed the last few words in the direction of the Jag, now long gone.

I wondered what sort of "low-rent asshole" drove a hundred thousand dollar car. Clearly Dana Wu wasn't satisfied with the author's characterization of the incident, either.

"Listen to me, Angel," Dana said, grabbing Angel's shoulders. "You have to be straight with me, kiddo. Tell me exactly what happened."

Angel stepped back, then ran her fingers through her long, copper hair. Finally, she turned away from us and, with both hands, adjusted the corset-laced bodice of her dress, nearly exposing her breasts. After that she leaned against Johnny for support—which seemed rather odd to me because, a moment ago, Angel was strong enough to stand on her own two feet—and screamed bloody murder.

"What happened, Angel?" Dana asked again.

"It was like I said," Angel replied, calmer now—and more guarded. "Some creep pulled up in a car, rolled down the window, and told me my books suck. I grabbed the door handle and told the jerk to come out of the car and say that again because I had a few things to say back, and the driver took off—I lost my balance and fell facedown in the street."

"Man or woman?" Dana's eyes were hard as she asked the question.

Angel dodged the woman's eyes, suddenly busy brushing the dirt off her filmy skirt. "What difference does it make?"

After a long silence, I spoke to Dana. "Maybe you should report the incident to the police? Ms. Stark is a celebrity, and this could be a stalker incident, and we all know stalkers can be dangerous. At the very least Angel should file a police report in case it happens again."

It was an intelligent and logical response—and exactly the *wrong* thing to say.

"No way!" Angel blasted. "Don't you get it? I'm the one exposing the incompetence of how their brothers in blue over the next hill completely botched Bethany's murder investigation." Angel vehemently shook her head. "No police. No way."

To my surprise, Dana Wu agreed.

"Angel's right. This is too close to where it all happened. In my opinion, Angel's got no friends among the local authorities. And nobody wants this story to turn up in the newspapers."

Something in me expected to hear Jack's voice at that moment saying, *Hmm, apparently not all publicity is good publicity, all of a sudden.* I reached out with my thoughts anyway. "Jack?"

But the ghost was nowhere near me now, because I had stepped beyond the fieldstone walls of my bookstore. Why had Jack's spirit been imprisoned inside the store since his death? I had my theories, but I still didn't have any real clues.

Suddenly, to everyone's surprise, Angel Stark did not return to the store. Instead, she slumped down on the curb next to a battered rust-red pickup truck with "Bud Napp's Hardware" emblazoned in black on the side panels.

"I still need that smoke," Angel announced. "Then I'm going back to that lace-doily inn up the street and shutting down for the night."

As she spoke, Angel produced a thin brown cigarette from a hidden pocket, then fumbled for something to light it with. There was an embarrassing pause, for none of us smoked.

A sudden toot from the car alarm sounded as Johnny unlocked the cab of his uncle's Napp Hardware pickup truck and reached into the glove compartment to retrieve a Ronson lighter, which he opened with a snap.

"Thanks," Angel said as she took a drag.

Johnny looked ready to walk away when Angel smiled from the curb and touched his hand. "Hey, I want to talk to you . . . Thank you for what you did out there."

Standing in the shadows, Mina watched as Johnny hesitated for a moment, then crouched down in front of Angel.

Aunt Sadie saw the hurt look on Mina's face and nudged the girl's shoulder. "Shouldn't you take care of your boyfriend?"

Frowning, Mina called, "Hey, Johnny. Are you coming?"

Johnny turned. "It's okay, Mina. Go on back in and finish your shift. I'll hook up with you later, like we planned."

Her eyes narrowing, her hurt turning to anger, Mina spun and marched back inside.

Dana took my arm. "I think the show is finally over for tonight." Politely but firmly, Dana pushed Aunt Sadie and me back into the store, too.

Sadie moved behind the counter, while Mina headed back to the events room. After that, the rest of the evening was a blur. Dana gave me the heads up about some of the hot author tours she knew would be barreling down the tracks, but had not yet been announced.

Meanwhile, my aunt tallied up the day's receipts and counted out the cash in the registers, and from the Community Events space I could hear metal chairs banging and clanging loudly. I assumed that Mina was using the task of breaking down the room to vent her angry frustration with Johnny's playing along with Angel's flirtations.

I considered talking to the girl, but I knew it was something that had to work itself out. Young love is nothing if it isn't volatile—which has got to be the oldest story in any bookstore.

Near the end of my conversation with Dana, we realized we had a few mutual acquaintances in publishing, holdovers from my days in New York. Dana was happy to fill me in on the latest gossip. Time slipped by and I didn't notice that Mina had left for the night, or that Aunt Sadie had retired to the apartment above the store—the home we both shared with my son, Spencer, since my husband's suicide a little over one year before.

"Oh, wow, it's after midnight," Dana cried. "I really have to run."

I rose and escorted her to the front door, which my aunt had locked after Mina left. Dana and I said good night, and she promised to drop by again before she returned to New York City the next afternoon.

Then, dead on my feet, I yawned and locked the door. My eyes dry and red from wearing contact lenses for hours, and the start of a headache throbbing at my temples, I turned out all but the security lights and activated the burglar alarm.

Just then, a tapping on the front door startled me. I peered through the window and saw my slight, young employee standing on the dark sidewalk. I deactivated the alarm, unlocked the door, and Mina Griffith stepped inside.

Mina's freckled face appeared flushed. "Sorry to bother you, Mrs. McClure, but I need to use the phone. My cell battery died and the pay phone in front of Koh's isn't working."

I ushered her inside. "Who do you need to call? Are you stranded?"

Mina nodded. "I can call Rebecca, my roommate. She drove me to work today, and she can pick me up. Johnny was supposed to meet me at Frenzetti's Pizza and give me a ride, but he's an hour late and they're closing up . . ."

Her voice faded, and I felt a stab of pity for the girl.

"Look, maybe there was a plumbing emergency or

something and his uncle needed him," I said. "Maybe he's trying to call you and your cell is dead."

Mina nodded listlessly.

"Why don't I drive you home myself?" I offered.

"No," Mina replied resolutely. "Rebecca can get me."

I could see how upset Mina was, and I suspected she needed to pour her heart out to her roommate as soon as humanly possible. Twenty-five minutes later, Rebecca was pulling up, honking lightly in her Toyota, then Mina was gone.

AS I LOCKED up, set the alarm, trudged upstairs, and fed our little orange striped cat, Bookmark, I sincerely hoped Johnny Napp would turn up in the morning on Mina's doorstep with a fistful of daisies and a good excuse—one that didn't involve Angel Stark.

I checked on Spencer, and found him asleep. I gently kissed his tow-headed bangs, untangled his legs from the sheets and pulled them over his torso, then slipped back out the door.

I was sorry that I hadn't spent much time with Spencer today. I had been busy getting ready for the author appearance, and he had day camp, so he'd been gone all morning until late in the afternoon. Then came Angel Stark's appearance and I had to manage that.

Usually Spencer enjoyed the author appearances, but this time I felt that the R-rated nature of Angel Stark's true crime book precluded a nine-year-old attending. Fortunately, Spencer willingly agreed to remain upstairs, most likely because Friday night was *Cop Show* night on the Intrigue Channel, and Aunt Sadie and I had stocked the freezer with all his favorite treats. (Thank heaven for cable and Hot Pockets.)

In my small bedroom, I stripped off my linen pantsuit, kicked off my slingback heels, and undid the French braid from my shoulder-length reddish-brown hair. Then I took out my contact lenses (worn for special occasions like author appearances), placed them next to my black, rectangular-framed glasses on the small wooden nightstand, crawled into bed, and clicked off the lamp.

For some reason, I couldn't stop thinking about Dana Wu's assertion that Angel Stark was careless. It was that damn Jag, I guess, dragging her through the street then peeling off without a backward glance.

I thought about that big yellow car in *The Great Gatsby*. How the rich and careless Daisy on a carefree lark of a drive from the Plaza Hotel to a Long Island mansion had run down that poor Queens woman on the wrong side of the Fifty-ninth Street Bridge—and never even slowed her pace. Just ran her down and kept right on going. How Gatsby had covered up for her, took care of her mess . . . which led to more than a few bullets through his brain.

I might have dismissed Fitzgerald's novel as pure fiction except my late father had been a Quindicott police officer, and I'd grown up hearing plenty of stories of the wealthy kids around the region getting into trouble—from prankish vandalism to drunk driving and date rape—only to have charges dropped when things were "taken care of " through payoffs to victims or connections with authorities.

I myself had struggled to get a half-scholarship into a top university, paying for room and board through work-study and the auctioned sale of my late father's old *Black Mask* magazines—at the time, through Sadie's store. I remembered my own earnest approach to classes and grades, remembered the shock of seeing a certain segment of the "smart" set look-ing down on my seriousness, taking pretty much nothing seri-ously themselves, blowing off classes without a thought.

Of course, to be honest, back then, I'd had stars in my eyes about the moneyed class, fancied the dream-life of be-ing a part of their afternoons on the yacht and evenings at the country club. As a part of that world, Calvin immediately appeared polished and aloof and intellectual and desirable.

My reality check came after I'd gotten accidentally pregnant with Spencer. My late husband and I had married right out of college, and I was instantly thrown under the thumb of his new family. A family with money—lots of it. And used to always getting their way.

And because Calvin's wealth had made life perpetually easy for him, I found out too late that yes, he may have been intelligent and introspective and had all of those sensitive qualities an impressionable college girl wants in a romantic college boy, but he had a limited capacity for the things that actually mattered in a real-world marriage: patience, tolerance, strength, the capacity to compromise and make hard decisions, or even the discipline to make a consistent, continuous effort.

The ease with which he'd been able to breeze through the years of his life had done nothing to build his character. His father's early heart attack and his mother's incessant coddling—accompanied by pulling strings attached to his money when it suited her—left the man a moral weakling.

Of course, that's my perspective now. Then, I'd been too caught up in it all to understand what was happening in my marriage and why.

It's been said that anything coming close to accomplishment, achievement, invention, or discovery emerges from an ability to overcome obstacles and roadblocks . . . from a willingness to endure pain. Too late, I deduced that Calivn didn't actually ascribe to this philosophy.

After years of making excuses for my husband in my own mind, I was forced to admit the bald truth. Calvin had grown so accustomed to letting his family sweep in and solve any childhood difficulty, that the first sign of any roadblock in his adult life sent him off every path he'd begun to travel.

He dropped out of law school, quit job after job with which his mother's friends had hooked him up. He'd started writing probably two dozen novels and plays, but never wrote past page forty on any one of them. He took to smoking cigarettes and staring out windows. He wasn't a man who could even muster the requisite vigor to enjoy partying, clubbing, or any other vice, for that matter—having had his fill of them all through his high-society teen years.

The most interest Calvin showed in anything was his own analysis. For five solid years, he sought daily appointments with therapists, but he never kept the same one more than six months. Each, eventually, would be labeled a "quack." Then, during one stretch, while ostensibly "searching" for a new one, my late husband stopped taking his medications.

And where was I during all of this?

Right there with him, trying to raise a young son whom Calvin took little interest in. Trying to deal with in-laws who refused to see Calvin as deeply troubled. Yes, right there with him . . . to absorb his verbal abuse and mood swings, to take it all because I told myself that my husband was ill and in need of help, right up to the day my hand turned the door knob to our bedroom, just in time to witness his attempt to fly—

Hey, baby. Wanna talk?

"Jack," I whispered into the dark. "You there?"

I'm always here, sweetheart. Cosmic joke, remember? City slicker forced to spend eternity in cornpone alley.

I smiled. A year ago, I'd forbidden Jack to hang around in the upstairs ether. He told me I couldn't lay down house rules to a man with no body. An uneasy truce followed. For the most part, he gave me my privacy upstairs, but occasionally, on nights like this one, he'd make his presence known.

Just remember this, Jack added. *In the scheme of things, nobody's got it as bad as yours truly. For me, this isn't a bunch of gag lines.*

"Well . . . look at the bright side," I told him, fluffing the pillow behind me, "a Rhode Island bookstore in July really isn't that bad. There are much *hotter* places you might have been sent."

Hit me below the belt, why don't ya?

A long minute of silence followed.

The room had cooled off with Jack's arrival, but now I felt the summer's cloying warmth seeping back into the bedroom air.

"Jack?" I silently called, sitting up. "I was just teasing."

The silence was getting to me. "Jack, please answer. Don't go."

Has it ever occurred to you—because it has to me—that this is my eternal punishment?

"No," I said falling back against the pillow again, "and do you know why? Because it's beyond insulting."

What?

"You're suggesting the fire and brimstone of Satan's inferno is less of a punishment than running an independent bookstore?"

Lead pipe cinch.

"You really can be infuriating, you know?"

Okay, so we're back in Miss Prissland, are we?

"Can it, Jack."

That's better.

"I don't want to fight."

For once we agree.

I sighed.

So what's eatin' you?

"What Johnny did to Mina was pretty hard to witness," I told him. "The kid obviously ran off with Angel tonight and left Mina high and dry. I always liked Johnny, but what he did tonight was pretty rotten. It makes me angry at Angel, too . . . but I'm also sorry for the girl. And furious about that Jag dragging her through the street and then taking off without a backward glance, and all because she dared tell the truth about her privileged circle of friends—one of whom likely committed murder during a party then tried to frame a member of the catering staff.

Yeah, like I told you earlier, the Banks girl knew her

killer, all right. I don't agree with your author on much—
but I agree on that.

"Maybe you should read her book."

You're just determined to doom me to some sort of pun-
ishment while I'm here, aren't you, dollface?

"I could tell you weren't impressed with her reading."

Theatrics do not impress me. Real detective work does.
You want some true crime stories, try reading through
some of my case files.

"I have, after a fashion. I've read all the Jack Shield
novels, and Tim Brennan based all of them on your cases."

That bloated barstool raconteur stole my files after I
was shot to death in this damn store, but he barely touched
the cases with the most juice. I noticed his son-in-law fi-
nally sent over my files for you to look at, but you haven't
gone through them yet.

"I will . . . I just haven't had time . . ."

Sure, honey, sure . . .

"What's that tone? You don't believe me?"

No.

"Why?"

You don't want to make the time—because you're afraid.

"Of what?"

Of what you'll find in those files. Things you'll find out
about me . . .

"Ridiculous."

You're a smart dame, sweetheart, but when it comes to
people you care about, seems to me you're more comfort-
able with your glasses off . . . and keeping those edges as
blurry as possible for as long as possible . . .

"Don't be insulting."

Don't be naïve. You did it with that worthless late hus-
band of yours—

"Don't, Jack."

A long silence followed.

"What is it you think I should know?"

Your little Angel's act with Johnny Napp tonight reminds me of a case I took back in '46, after the war. I couldn't go back to being a cop—leg wound left me with a slight limp on bad days—so I set out a shingle as a licensed P.I.

"What was the case?"

Vassar grad in her mid-twenties comes in on a Friday at six, looking to hire me to save her life from a blackmailer she claimed already gave her sis the big chill. Class clash. He was an indoor aviator—

"A what?"

Elevator operator. And she was the well-heeled uptown type. There's a special kind of velvet-lined skirt gets bored with the expensive fabrics, likes to look for something a little rougher against the skin. Not for long, but for a while. That's my guess on your Angel going after the Johnny kid.

The trouble comes when the little lady's ready to toss away the rough goods. Not always easy. Cheap goods too often leave a stain when you rub them the wrong way.

"Johnny's usually a nice kid. I don't think he'd actually hurt anyone."

"You hardly know him, doll. And from what you've told me, he's already hurt that tall, freckled thing, Mina—"

"He hurt her emotionally, I'll grant you, but not physically. That's what I meant."

Baby, trust me when I say, you like to keep the edges soft and blurry on people. . . . Can't say as I blame you. Seeing nothing but the hard angles is no picnic, either, but don't worry, for this little flashback, you won't need your glasses to see clearly.

I felt the cool breeze in the hot room, the icy chill of Jack's presence whispering across my cheek. The sleepiness overcame me, and I immediately began to dream.

"Jack, what are these images I'm seeing?" I asked through a restless haze. "Are they your memories?"

Well, they're not Winston Churchill's.

CHAPTER 6

In Jack's Case

It is hard, if not impossible, to snub a beautiful woman.

—Sir Winston Churchill

New York City
July 19, 1946

HER NAME WAS Emily Stendall—the pedigreed blonde in pink polkadots who'd waltzed into his office worried about flies and swatters.

She'd gotten Jack's name from Gertrude Herbert, a fellow cliff-dweller, one of those uptown, high-rise, society dames who hired him as a bodyguard on a fairly regular basis.

"Start at the beginning, Miss Stendall," Jack suggested from across the dry, brown desktop.

"I'd rather start at the end," she said primly. "Not to

put too fine a point on it, but I'd like you to stop Joey Lubrano from murdering me. If you take my case this minute, I'll double your per diem plus expenses, and I'll give you a bonus of one thousand dollars if you're able to gather enough evidence for his conviction of a capital crime."

"The crime of?"

"I told you, killing my sister. And planning to kill me."

Jack picked up his deck of Luckies and gave them a shake. Emily Stendall nodded and he rose from his chair. He shook the pack again, watched her slip one white cylinder out of its nest, place it between her lips. He fired up a match. Soft fingers touched his, pulling the flame close. She inhaled and closed her eyes, savoring the hit.

Jack lit his own and took a long drag. "Okay—" he began, sitting on the edge of his desk.

She exhaled a long, white plume. "You'll take the job?"

"Not yet," Jack said. "You started on your end. Now do me a favor and start on mine."

Emily Stendall's brown eyes widened. "Your what?"

"From the beginning, honey," he clarified. "Tell me the story from the beginning."

"My sister's name was Sarah. Mrs. Sarah Nolan. Her husband, Melvin, secured a promotion a year ago that had him traveling on business quite a bit."

"How much is quite a bit?"

Emily shrugged her creamy shoulders. "Two weeks out of every month I'd guess."

"I'd guess that's quite a bit."

"Well, you can see how it started then. Sarah became lonely, and one night she invited him in for a drink. Joey Lubrano, I should say, our building's elevator operator—"

"*Our* building?"

"We lived in the same building on East Sixty-fifth. She lived on the ninth floor. I live directly above her on the tenth."

"Go on."

"After a while, Joey threatened her with blackmail, and—"

"How?"

"He'd taken photos . . ." Emily Stendall paused a moment, bit her lower lip. "Risqué photos. You understand?"

"I understand."

"At the time he'd said they were just for him to remember her. But obviously he'd had other things in mind."

"Mmm . . . obviously." Jack's tone had a bite. Emily Stendall noticed.

"What?" she asked. "You think she was naïve?"

"Not naïve." Jack took a long drag. "Stupid."

"Mr. Shepard, no one calls my sister stupid."

"She cheated on her husband with a man who blackmailed and then killed her. You call that smart?"

"I call that victimized. Or is that too *expensive* a word for your vocabulary?"

"Cheating on her husband with the elevator man? Her actions do suggest *other* adjectives, Miss Stendall," said Jack. "Words that aren't pretty. The kind of ugly words men use in front of their bartenders—"

Emily Stendall rose. "How dare you!" And in a blur of movement Jack grabbed her quickly approaching hand.

"Let me go!" She yanked at her trapped wrist.

Jack held. "Look, doll, I'm sincerely sorry about your sister's death, but I'm not about to start my weekend with a red-hot handprint tattooed to my cheek . . . even if it is a beautiful hand."

Emily Stendall's firm, full breasts were heaving in fury and indignation.

"Let me go," she said, her voice finally level.

Jack released her. She rubbed at the red mark circling her right wrist. Her eyes speared him as her glossy pink lips made a little-girl pout.

"A little advice, honey," said Jack, retrieving the lit

cigarette from the green linoleum floor and stabbing it out in the ashtray beside his cracked-leather davenport. "You might be able to lead your Yale men around by the leash with that indignant princess act, but when you're dealing with rough trade, you'll need another strategy."

The little-girl pout loosened to a grim frown. Jack put a second Lucky in his mouth, lit it, then transferred it to hers. She took another hit, long and needy.

"That's why I want to hire you, Mr. Shepard," she admitted. "My sister's involvement with 'rough trade,' as you put it, got her killed. Now I need someone like you to—"

"Clean up the mess."

"Precisely. So will you take the job or not?"

"I have a few more questions. Namely, why haven't the police picked up Lubrano? I assume you've gone to them?"

"Yes, of course, I went to them. They picked him up, too. They questioned him, then they released him. No evidence, they said, and, of course, he denied everything. They searched his apartment but didn't find any photos. And his alibi that night was supposedly airtight."

"What was it?"

"He'd entered a dart-throwing contest at a downtown bar. Ten cops were in the bar with him."

"That's pretty airtight, honey."

"But he slipped away to kill Sarah. I know he did. My sister's death was ruled an accident. They claim she drank martinis on top of sleeping pills then drowned in a bath. But the night she died, Sarah and Lubrano were supposed to meet. He was supposed to be exchanging the photos and their negatives for the payoff. But something obviously went wrong. Maybe my sister became angry and it went badly. Maybe he'd planned all along to murder her and tricked her into drinking a drugged martini so she could never get him into trouble. Whatever happened that night, he took the money and the photos and set her up with an accidental death. That's why Lubrano wants to kill me now."

"Because you went to the police?"

"I'm the only one who knew about the affair he had with Sarah. I'm the only one who knew about the blackmail and the photos. He didn't know it before he killed her, but now he does because I went to the police. He threatened me just the other day, told me to keep my mouth shut from now on or he'd shut it permanently—just like he did my sister's."

"When did he say this?"

"Just last night, right there in my building's elevator. That's when I knew I was in over my head. I remembered a friend had used your services some months back, so here I am . . ."

Jack nodded. The dame was right. She was in over her head.

"Mr. Shepard, I think Joey Lubrano is going to try to use those photos again, this time to extort money from Sarah's husband. If it gets out what happened—that Sarah posed for nude photos with her lover—the scandal would socially ruin and devastate not just him but his father. You know who his father is, Mr. Shepard?"

"Sorry, enlighten me."

"He's the fundraising director for St. Bernard's."

Jack nodded. St. Bernard's Episcopal Church was a Fifth Avenue institution. Its members included prominent politicians, judges, and financial scions.

"I get it, honey."

"Do you?"

Jack's interest piqued as he watched Emily close her long-lashed eyes and take another long pull on the Lucky Strike.

"And your parents . . . they don't know their little girl smokes, do they?"

Emily opened her big brown eyes and levelly met Jack's stare. "They don't know their little girl does a lot of things."

Jack's eyebrow rose. "I'll need more information from you, Miss Stendall, before I can get started."

"But you'll take the case?"

"Yeah, honey," said Jack. "You just hired yourself your own private dick."

A few minutes later, Jack was escorting Miss Emily Stendall from his warm office to the hot elevator, then to the steamy Manhattan streets.

"Seven million people in this city," said Jack Shepard, "and every last one is hailing a cab."

When the tenth hack went by, already hired, Jack muttered, "Nuts to this." He considered suggesting they each cough up a dime for the subway, but he doubted very much Miss Stendall would agree.

"Mr. Shepard, a lady of class cannot be seen taking the subway," one of his clients once had told him when they'd been stranded by her driver and no cabs were in sight. And, of course, what Jack understood was the idea of the act itself was not as repugnant as being "seen" committing it.

"Hungry?" Jack asked his client, because he was.

Emily nodded. So he rolled down his sleeves, put on his jacket and fedora, and took her into Little Roma, a cozy Italian joint near his office, ten wooden tables covered by red-and-white checkered tablecloths and wine bottles with candles stuck in the tops. Nothing pricey but no dive, either. Every table was taken. Ceiling fans moved a pleasant breeze through the room and the smell of fresh rolls and garlic stoked their appetites. They shared a bottle of chilled Chianti and ate thinly sliced veal cutlets made into a melt-on-your-tonsils dish he could never pronounce.

When they stepped back onto the street, the hot day had cooled a few degrees with a breeze off the Hudson, and the hour was well past quitting time. Not for everyone though . . .

Ten blocks north, clouds of steam continued to waft

from pressing machines in sweltering loft factories. Long into the night, the Garment District would still be making dresses like the polkadot halter number Miss Stendall wore; while ten blocks south, men without faces had forgotten what quitting time even was. Theirs was a world of shuffling feet and bottomless bottles, outstretched palms, sidewalk beds, long steady stares, and in the end, Bellevue.

Jack doubted Miss Stendall had even been down near the Bowery—he couldn't blame her. For that crowd, the Depression had never ended, and Jack didn't like to be reminded of those days, either. He'd had his bad luck like everybody. His mother dying young, his father at a loss for what to do. Putting the two girls in a convent orphanage and Jack left to fend for himself.

He'd boxed some, knocked around, then on a lucky break became a cop. And when the war broke out, and the draft began, that's the time even more bad luck had blown his way— and he thought it best to enlist his way out of it.

Maybe that's why he liked Manhattan mostly at night. He'd seen it on leave during the war, when an official dim-out had shut down the bright lights of his town, darkening its marquees and skyscrapers, shrouding even the Statue of Liberty in shadow as a precaution against marauding German subs. Wartime New York had become a somber ghost of itself.

Stepping into this postwar evening, Jack happily eye-balled the forest of buildings, all lit up like torches. This was the reason he'd never leave the city. The lights of night transformed a country boy's night into a working stiff's brand-new day, blazing the pathways to movie theaters and restaurants, gin mills and nightclubs, allowing pursuits of pleasure long past the time the suburban rube and farm boy had been forced to put up their feet.

He flagged a taxi easy now and held the door. The address was Upper East. A tree-lined street tucked between fashionable Park Avenue and utilitarian Lexington. Park was where the opulent building had been erected for tycoons past and present, and Lex was where their help shopped for groceries, took their cleaning, and bought the goods that kept them living in the style to which they'd become accustomed.

Miss Stendall's building sat exactly between the avenues. The redbrick façade matched the others on the block, with its tall set-back windows and canopied entrance.

"Good evening, miss." The doorman looked to be in his early sixties. Gray hair, gray eyes, and the flushed cheeks of a man who liked to sneak a nip or two—short jacket and cap the same color as the building's forest-green canopy; pants black with a side stripe the same shade of green.

"Good evening, Benny." Emily stepped out as Jack paid the hack. He'd paid for dinner, too. They were Miss Stendall's expenses, and she'd be charged for them eventually.

The cliff-dwellers never liked to be "nickel and dimed" as they saw it. One big bill was more their style—so they could write Jack one big check. Jack was willing to shell within reason, especially when it came to female clients. Having a dame pay his way wasn't up his alley anyway. Made him feel like a snot-nosed kid being treated to an ice cream by his mommy.

They crossed the lobby—marble floor, oak wainscoting, forest-green walls with paintings of landscapes hanging from picture rails. A high oak counter for the doorman's station, across from it armchairs upholstered in gentleman's club burgundy leather and a matching sofa.

Miss Stendall breezed in with head high, striding. Her white-gloved hand reached out to call the elevator, but Jack's fingers closed on hers before she could push the button.

For a moment, they stood there alone, holding hands. She looked up at him with surprise.

"Let me handle him," Jack advised, his voice steel.

"But—"

"Keep your lips zipped, doll," he warned. "That's what you hired me for. To handle him."

Her mouth made a little-girl *moue*, but she nodded. Jack released her hand and jammed the elevator button himself. He could hear the ringing bell all the way up the shaft.

Emily sighed. "It'll be a minute. When things are slow, Joey likes to listen to a radio he keeps on the third floor. He comes when he hears the bell."

"I see. And his boss allows it?" Jack asked gesturing to the doorman.

"Benny's not his boss. The building superintendent is. He lives in the basement, and I've never seen him emerge from his rooms unless there's a problem with the plumbing. One can only hope he'd emerge for a fire, should one occur."

"Yeah," Jack said. "One can only hope."

When the elevator finally arrived, Jack stepped to the side. Emily didn't seem to notice, but Joey would be forced to think that she was all alone. And Jack was curious to see Joey's initial reaction. This was a killer after all—a man who'd drugged and drowned his ex-lover and seemed intent on threatening Jack's client.

Keeping his body loose, Jack got ready for almost anything—from throwing punches to pulling his rod clear. With a rumbling jolt, the elevator car halted. The door noisily retracted and a white-gloved hand pulled back the gate. The glove wasn't lost on Jack—part of the uniform. No suspicion on the part of the victim. And no fingerprints.

"Emily . . ." said a deep voice, slightly urgent. "We have to talk."

Emily blinked and looked beside her, suddenly realizing Jack had stepped out of Joey's line of sight. Instantly, she searched him out, a look of panic on her face.

"Tenth floor, Joey," said Jack, stepping forward. That's when he got a good look at the young man's face—and raised an eyebrow in surprise. Because this face was one he recognized and didn't like. "Or should I call you 'Lucky Joe'?"

Lubrano's face went pale. It was a face just as handsome as it had been ten years before. Dimpled chin, Roman nose, deep brown eyes, and jet-black hair slickly combed. He'd been a strong kid at seventeen, boxed with precision in the ring—with brutality in back alleys for dirty coin, a casino bouncer with a mean streak—and now his physique looked even bigger, its muscles packed into a short green jacket and striped black pants identical to Benny the doorman's.

"What's the matter, kid?" asked Jack. "Looks like you saw a ghost."

"Who are you?" Lubrano's hands clenched into fists. "I don't know you, do I?"

"Steady, kid," said Jack. "I'm a friend of Emily's, that's all you need to know. A good friend. And I'll be taking care that she's in good health from now on and no harm comes to her. Get me?"

Jack watched Lubrano carefully. The kid's brown eyes narrowed with fury on Emily. He seemed to be waiting for her to say something. And she did.

"Tenth floor."

"You heard the lady. Let's go," said Jack.

Jack could see the moment's confusion in Lubrano's face, the consideration of what to do. Jack pushed the point; stepping forward, he put his large, strong form between the young ex-boxer and Emily.

When they were fully inside the elevator car, the inside aviator's routine took over. Lubrano's white-goved hand slid the heavy cage shut, pressed the tenth-floor button, then pushed the lever on the machine. The motor coughed to life and the car slowly ascended.

The tense silence held for three floors and then Lubrano turned, studied Jack's face—

"How do you know me?"

"I know you. That's all," said Jack.

Joey Lubrano's dark eyes narrowed. The boxer's muscles were clenching, the fists forming balls.

"Steady," said Jack. "I'm a private eye. I got a license to carry."

Joey glared at Emily again with pure fury, then he spun away, giving them his broad back until the tenth floor. When the cage opened, Jack put his body between Lubrano and Emily again, seeing that she got off without a hitch. But as they stepped down the hallway toward Emily's apartment door, Joey lunged out of the car.

"Wait just a second!" he said, reaching for Emily's arm.

She yelped as Joey grabbed her, and Jack reacted, swinging a hard right hook to the handsome kid's face. He went down holding his bloodied nose, and Jack hustled Emily forward—because he knew the kid wouldn't stay down long.

"Let's go—into your apartment *now*."

Her hands shaking, Emily fumbled for a key and opened the door.

"Pack," said Jack quietly, when she'd closed and bolted it behind them. "Take only what you need. I'm taking you out of here tonight."

CHAPTER 7

Morning News

The alarm went off with a racket that jerked me out of a wild dream and left me standing on the rug, shaking like a kitten in a dog kennel.

—Detective Mike Hammer, *My Gun Is Quick*
by Mickey Spillane, 1950

"MOM! YOU DIDN'T tell me I got *mail*," Spencer cried, dropping his spoon into his cereal bowl and leaping to his feet. He waved the letter under my nose.

It was clear that he'd been waiting to ambush me with that information the minute I crawled out of bed and stumbled into the kitchen. For a moment or two after I'd opened my eyes, I wasn't sure what decade I was in—Jack's dream had seemed that real. I shoved on my black-framed glasses, saw my son looking up at me with imploring eyes, and I was fully back to focusing on reality.

"Can I open the letter now?"

I managed a weak smile as I smoothed back my mussed auburn hair and pulled it into a ponytail. "Of course you can, honey. It's addressed to you, isn't it?"

I slipped around my son and lunged for the coffee my aunt had made before she went downstairs to open the shop. I was hoping the brew wasn't too old and bitter, though at the moment I had too desperate a need for caffeine to care one way or another.

Spencer dropped back down in his chair at the kitchen table and tore at the expensive stationery. The beige faux-parchment envelope addressed to "Calvin Spencer McClure, Esquire" had arrived yesterday, courtesy of Seymour Tarnish. The mail had arrived while my son was at Friday day camp, so he hadn't noticed the letter until this morning.

I'd seen the invitation, with the hand-stamped "M" on the back flap, and felt a shudder of dread. My in-laws, the patriarchs and matriarchs of the McClure clan, were summoning the rest of the scattered family members for their annual "gala reunion." The gathering was a massive affair—an obligatory dynastic retreat worthy of an Aaron Spelling miniseries.

Supposedly staged for the "immediate family," there were usually so many guests in attendance that it seemed like everyone in the United States with a McClure in their name and a trust fund worth a cool million was obliged to attend.

The reunion was held at Windswept, the manor house that once belonged to my late husband's parents, but which passed to Ashley McClure-Sutherland upon her mother's wishes, after Calvin's death.

As the Widow McClure—and not a particularly popular widow with the rest of the clan—I dreaded the reunion as much as my son looked forward to it.

"So what interests you in the events schedule?" I asked, feigning interest for Spence's sake. "Clowns? Pony rides?"

Spencer made a face. "Clowns and pony rides? Nuts to that, Mom. That's kiddie stuff!"

Nuts to that, I silently repeated, shaking my head. Spencer's occasional use of 1940's slang never ceased to amuse me—although, from his incessant viewing of old cop shows, it didn't surprise me.

He continued to read the glossy brochure that came with the invitation and his eyes went wide. "Wow! They're going to have a paintball game!"

"Paintball?" I shook my head. "That sounds dangerous. And I'm sure it's restricted to the older crowd."

"Mom. I'm *nine* years old," Spencer stated in a deadly serious tone over a depleted bowl of Cap'n Crunch with Crunch Berries. I did my best to keep a straight face.

"We're gonna go, aren't we?"

"Of course we are," I replied. The real invitation had actually come weeks ago, and I'd already responded in the affirmative. Spencer's missive was simply an events schedule for the younger members of the McClure clan.

Grinning, Spencer deposited his bowl and spoon in the sink. "I'm going to watch *Crime Town* on the Intrigue Channel," he announced.

"But didn't you see that same show last night?"

"I fell asleep before the end and I didn't see who the bad guy was. Lucky for me, they're repeating the same show this morning."

"All right, but you better be ready to go in an hour when your ride to day camp gets here."

"I know!"

His feet bare, he stomped through the hall to the living room. A few moments later, I heard the television.

With a sigh, I dumped the rest of the old coffee down the sink and brewed a new batch. The stress of Angel Stark's volatile author appearance, not to mention Jack's strange, unfinished case of a dream, drained me, and I didn't have enough sleep—or coffee—to function properly. Then there was the reminder of having to attend that damn McClure family soiree—not exactly a mood lifter.

If you don't like the tune, don't get on the dance floor.

"Good morning, Jack," I silently replied. "And it's not that easy. . . . Just because I have a problem with the Mc-Clure family, that doesn't mean my son should suffer. Spencer has every right to see his cousins, and participate in family events. Besides, he loves these family reunions, and he'll have a great time."

So you're just gonna put on a happy face and go? Sounds like you are *dancing—like a puppet on a string.*

"Listen, Jack. No one knows the McClures better than I do. They are master manipulators. My husband controlled me for years with his passive-aggressive assaults on my self-respect, along with his 'mood swings' and 'emotional problems.' But the days when Ashley or any of the Mc-Clure clan can manipulate yours truly ended with my husband's suicide—"

Turn down the heat, baby, your soup's boiling.

"—I have refused their considerable bribes, even if their money would make my life a whole lot easier. I removed my son from the obscenely expensive private primary school where generations of McClures traditionally matriculated into class-A snobs. And I broke out of that East Side apartment owned by my in-laws—a gilded trap if ever I saw one—whose plans for Spencer, after Calvin's suicide, suddenly included English boarding school."

Although I was wiser now, I was still angry with myself for having allowed them to push me around for longer than they should have. I slammed the coffee cup down on the counter harder than I realized. Hot coffee sloshed on my hand and drenched the counter. Inside my head, I could feel Jack recede.

"I'm sorry about my tone," I told him. "This just isn't the

best time for a conversation, any conversation, about the McClures."

But Jack was already gone, his cooling presence on this already too warm summer day dissipated into the upstairs air. "Damn," I whispered. I hadn't wanted to talk about my past again. After that dream, I'd *wanted* to talk about his.

"Fine, leave then," I muttered as I sopped up the mess with a paper towel. "But once in a while it would be nice to get a little sympathy and acknowledgment for my parental sacrifices from someone in this world—even if it's only a disembodied voice inside my head."

Of course, that voice inside my head was another reason I dreaded the coming reunion. I knew full well that the Mc-Clures blamed me for the death of their oldest male heir, and that they would love to get sole custody of my son, just so they could turn my beautiful, brilliant boy into a surrogate for my neurotic and spoiled late husband.

If Ashley McClure-Sutherland *ever* found out that I was "talking" on a regular basis to the ghost haunting my bookstore, she would surely have me committed for life—the McClures had the money and the clout to do it, too. Building an entire wing of the St. Francis Psychiatric Hospital pays for a lot of influence.

Suddenly glum, I dumped the remainder of the coffee into my cup and switched off the coffeemaker. After a quick shower, I threw on khaki pants and a white sleeveless cotton blouse, then trudged downstairs to help my aunt open the bookstore. As I descended the stairs, I saw Sadie eyeing me over her spectacles.

"Late night, dear?"

"Mina came back to the store. Johnny Napp was supposed to take her home last night but something happened. So she called her roommate and I waited up with her until her ride came."

Sadie frowned and removed the spectacles, letting them

dangle from a red beaded chain. "I think we both saw that train wreck coming. The way that Angel Stark flirted with Johnny—and right in front of Mina. Shameless . . ."

I set my coffee down next to the cash register. "I only hope Mina doesn't blame me for what happened."

"Goodness! Whatever could she blame you for?"

"I was the one who invited Angel to appear in our store."

"Oh, pooh," Sadie said with a dismissive wave. "Who in their right mind would blame you for Angel Stark's behavior?"

As she spoke, Sadie drew the key out of the pocket of her beige slacks. It was already time to open. Sadie unlocked the front door, and within minutes, the bell above it chimed, signaling the entrance of our first visitor of the day. It was Bud Napp.

"Good morning," I chirped from across the room.

Bud did not reply. I don't think he even heard me. Instead, he stared hard at Sadie, focusing entirely on her. His face was tight with worry, and his eyes were grave.

"Bud!" she cried, instantly alarmed. "What's the matter?"

"Johnny, my nephew, didn't come home last night. He's disappeared, and so has my pickup truck . . ."

"Oh, no," I murmured.

Sadie pulled Bud all the way inside the store. She checked the sidewalk in front of the shop. It was empty, so she locked the front door and flipped the Closed sign around again.

"We can open a half hour later today," she announced.

I helped her pull together a few armchairs that were scattered for customers throughout the stacks, and we sat down at the end of an aisle.

"Johnny told me he was coming over here to see Mina, and I told him he could use the truck after he finished his work at the site."

"The site" was Quindicott shorthand for the still-under-construction Finch Restaurant, the wood-framed skeleton of which is located on the shore of an inlet the locals call the Pond. Because Fiona was using local artisans, work was progressing slowly, though the pace picked up ever since Bud and Johnny began working there a few weeks ago.

"Johnny was here last night," I told Bud. "He was around for the reading, so I guess he arrived at seven thirty."

"But he did leave with Mina, right? Johnny really likes the girl, but I think both of them are too young to get serious. Then again, if they did do something crazy like elope or something . . . Well, it's bad, but not the end of the world . . . things could be worse."

Sadie looked at me. I looked at Bud.

"Actually, Johnny promised to drive Mina home, but he stood her up. Her roommate drove over and took Mina home after midnight."

Bud, usually the coolest head at the Quindicott Business Owners Association meetings, completely shocked me by exploding.

"Damn that stupid-ass knuckleheaded kid!" He rocked to his feet and started pacing the aisle. "I only hope he didn't go off and do anything stupid, like get drunk and violate his parole."

My lips moved but nothing came out. I'd never seen Bud like this. It was Sadie who calmed him down. She rose and touched Bud's shoulder. He whirled to face her.

"We want to help you, Bud," she said, "but Penelope and I don't know enough yet. Maybe you better tell us why Johnny's on probation."

Bud nodded and sank back into the plush chair. Sadie and I sat on either side of him, waiting. But just as Bud opened his mouth to speak, an urgent pounding on Buy the Book's front door interrupted him.

"Oh, damn," said Sadie. "Who could that be?"

"Don't move." I rushed to the door. "If it's a delivery, I'll take care of it. If it's a customer I'll just shoo them away."

I went to the door, drawing my own key out of the

pocket of my slacks. I peered through the glass and saw Dana Wu frantically waving at me. I unlocked the door and admitted her, locking it behind her again.

"Aren't you open yet?" Dana asked. Like me, she was casually dressed—but in tailored yellow shorts and a chartreuse tank top.

"Had to delay the opening thirty minutes. We're having a bit of a personal crisis," I whispered, gesturing toward my aunt and Bud, seated across the store.

Dana frowned. "Sorry I bothered you. I wouldn't have, except that I have a bit of a crisis, too."

"What's up?"

"I can't find Angel Stark anywhere," Dana said with a sigh. "Her car is still in the Finch Inn's parking lot, but she's not in her room or answering her cell—and Angel *always* answers her cell."

My stomach lurched, but I tried to keep my emotions off my face.

Dana brushed her hair back in a worried gesture. "God, this is embarrassing. How many publicists do you know who've lost their client?"

CHAPTER 8

Miss Placed

The next best thing to knowing something is knowing
where to find it.

—Samuel Johnson

"ARE YOU TELLING me that Angel Stark is missing?" I
asked Dana. Almost immediately, I glanced over my shoulder. Fortunately my aunt and Bud Napp were locked in
their own conversation, and not eavesdropping on me.

"Afraid so," Dana replied. "But knowing Angel, she's
probably just run off with that kid she met last night for a
wild weekend fling."

"So that's what happened?"

"I'd be willing to bet . . . heaven knows, I try not to
judge, but Angel couldn't have pulled her vanishing act at a
worse time."

"Trouble?"

Dana grinned. "Good news, actually. I just found out Charlie Rose wants to interview Angel on Wednesday. His people called me this morning! Of course, I have to let Angel know, ASAP. She needs to be prepped, too. A PBS interview is too important to wing it—and when her head isn't in the right place, our gal Angel has been known to act more like Courtney Love than Anna Quindlen."

"She throws microphone stands?"

"No, just the occasional water glass . . . or coffee cup, depending on what the production assistant hands her."

"Do you want to come to my office? Or are you going to look for Angel?"

"No time," Dana replied, glancing at her watch. "I have to get back to New York by tonight. Contrary to what some of my clients think, I actually have a life. And I have a long drive ahead of me."

"What can I do to help?" I asked, anticipating her reply.

"I need to know the name and phone number of that kid Angel was talking to last night . . . if you know him, that is. The kid looked like a local to me. I heard someone call him John or Jimmy or something . . ."

"I've . . . seen him around," I replied. "Can I get back to you on that?"

"I guess so, but ASAP, okay? FYI, I'm going to file a missing persons report on that girl the next time she pulls this stunt—just to teach her a lesson. I'd like to see how she deals with headlines like 'Little Girl Lost' and 'Angel Takes Wing.'"

I thought about the incident of the night before—the hit-and-run that wasn't.

"So this kind of thing happens often? Angel running off with some guy, I mean?"

Dana shrugged. "Usually she takes off for a couple of days of hot sex with someone she meets on the road, like she's a rock star or something. But Angel's down with the program. She knows the importance of publicity. No matter what she's doing or where she's at, the girl *always* returns my calls . . . always, until now."

Dana glanced at her watch once again. "Oh, man, I've got to go. Got tickets for the New York Philharmonic tonight—and a date."

I unlocked the front door and let Dana out. "Have a great time."

"Thanks, Pen . . ."

Then Dana paused halfway out the door. "You have my phone number. Please, do me a tremendous favor and ask around about that kid. And give me a call the moment you find out anything."

With a wave, Dana was gone. I locked the door behind her. But before I faced Bud and my aunt again, I paused. Something told me we were headed for real trouble. And that something was Jack Shepard.

There's a Chinese angle on these Houdini acts, that's for square.

"Chinese angle? You mean you think Dana Wu is some-how involved?"

Catch the lingo, babe . . . Chinese angle. There's a bend in the road . . . Something's not on the level with the Angel broad and the working square taking it on the lam.

"You suspect foul play?"

You got it. But keep things clammed until the pipes man Auntie is jawing with spits out more facts. The more people talk, the more you hear.

"What do you think is going on, Jack?"

With the dame, it could be like your Miss Wu said—our loose-limbed Angel is pitching woo in some hot-sheets love-nest even as we speak. But then why not return calls? Could be someone—maybe someone with a beef against Angel—did her in or is doing the Lindbergh snatch—

"A kidnapping!"

It happens . . . The dame's got cabbage and plenty of it. Or maybe your working-class square-john bumped this

Angel for his own reasons. Maybe the loving went sour. Or maybe he's the snatchster who put the grab on her. Otherwise this Johnny's just a rube who took a powder and Angel doesn't fit into this picture at all—but I don't truck with that since she's out of touch.

"Huh?"

I said maybe Johnny-boy killed the filly and skipped town, or he's the kidnapper . . . or he's just a patsy who took the bus for another reason that's not connected with Angel, which I don't buy and neither do you.

"You're jumping to some pretty drastic conclusions, Jack," I scolded. "No doubt due to too many years among the riffraff of the New York streets. Don't be an alarmist."

Alarmist? Me? Ha! You just turn those sweet cheeks of yours around, plant them in a chair, and ask Bud why his nephew's on parole, and we'll just see who's the alarmist.

"Well . . . I'll grant you that I didn't know Johnny had been in trouble with the law . . . and Dana does seem worried . . . so what should I do?"

Like I said, ankle over to Auntie and find out what the old geezer is bumping ivory about. You'll learn more from a peepster than you will from this graveyard gumshoe.

"Peeper? Bud's a nice old guy. He's no peeper."

PeepSTER. A witness. Someone who knows the score. Geeze, babe, you read enough of Tim Brennan's Jack Shield dime novels based on my life. The least you could do is glom on to the natural flow of my discourse.

"I guess I should tell Bud about Angel's disappearance . . . Maybe it would calm his fears a little to know that Johnny probably just ran off for a wild weekend of fun with a literary celebrity."

Nix to that.

"Why?"

Because you don't know that's what happened. Even if you don't truck with my dark scenario, I still think you ought to take my advice and keep your lips zipped and your

*wax bins open while Bud talks. Then we can both learn
something.*

Strategy set, I approached Sadie and Bud and cleared
my throat.

"Sorry for the interruption," I began. "There was
some . . . business I had to take care of."

"No, no . . . I should be apologizing," Bud replied with
something of his old demeanor. "Here I am costing you
Saturday morning business, and I have to open my hardware store, too. Folks are depending on me . . ."

Bud started to rise, but I gently pushed him back into
his seat. "Don't be silly . . . We never see any real business
on Saturdays until well past noon."

Sadie spoke up. "Bud's come over here to ask for Mina's
address and phone number. I told him we'd gladly give it
to him, but Mina will be here soon anyway, so I told him to
wait around."

"I was hoping Johnny was with her—Mina, I mean,"
said Bud.

I sat down between them and folded my arms. "Bud . . .
You mentioned something about Johnny violating his parole. But neither Sadie or I knew your nephew was in any
kind of trouble." I looked to my aunt for support. "Isn't
that right?"

Sadie nodded. "That's right, Penelope. Bud, what can
you tell us?"

"Johnny was in just about the worst trouble a kid can
get into," he began, then his voice faltered. "But it's his
business . . . maybe I better not say . . ."

Goose him, Jack advised in my head.

"What!" I silently replied. "How?"

*Keep the play innocent. Don't threaten, just throw this
out there easy: Should we call Chief Ciders?*

"Should we call Chief Ciders?" I repeated to Bud.

"Call the chief!?" cried Bud, now visibly alarmed.
"Why?"

"Jack?" I silently pleaded.

So he can file a missing persons report on Johnny Napp.

"So he can file a missing persons report on Johnny Napp," I told Bud. "If it turns out he isn't with Mina, I mean."

Bud's eyes went wide. "Oh, I wouldn't want to do that! . . . Oh, dang it . . . I better tell you the truth. The kid's name isn't Napp. Johnny's my late sister Rita's kid. I told Johnny when he came to Quindicott that it would be better for him if he just used my last name instead of his own . . . so he could fit in better, and avoid any nosy reporters snooping around."

"Why would a reporter be looking for Johnny?" I asked.

Good, doll, I heard in my head—and bit my cheek to keep from smiling, even as I lectured myself that being giddy with pride over a possible figment of my imagination was patently ridiculous.

Don't start that possible figment of your imagination stuff with me, baby. You need a reminder I'm real? I'll scare gramps into next week.

"No, don't!" I silently reversed. "Just behave, Jack . . . Please."

Bud, who of course had no idea I had been carrying on a conversation in my head about him with a ghost, rubbed his eyes. "Johnny's father—my late brother-in-law—was an Italian contractor in Providence. Johnny's real name is Napoli . . . Giovanni Napoli."

I recognized the name immediately, and nearly gasped. Bud noted my reaction. Sadie looked at me, then at Bud. She hadn't made the connection.

"Now you know why I told Johnny to use my name," said Bud. "Too many people could find him if he used his own."

"I don't think I understand," my aunt declared.

Me, either, doll. Enlighten us both.

I rose and walked to the New Releases table at the front of the store. I came back with a copy of Angel Stark's *All*

My Pretty Friends and handed it to my aunt. "Index," I whispered.

"Rita died when Johnny was six or seven," Bud continued. "I didn't have much to do with his family after that—I frankly didn't care for Johnny's old man—but I heard his grandmother worked hard to raise my nephew right. She made sure he hit the books, and after school she taught him how to cook.

"The grandmother died when Johnny was just starting high school . . . I remember going up to Providence for the funeral. After that, I didn't see much of him until his father died of a heart attack. I found out at the funeral that Johnny was accepted by the Culinary Institute of Rhode Island. Later I found out that when his old man died, the money for Johnny's schooling dried up and he couldn't go.

"But a catering company hired him full-time to work the high-society parties in the area. . . . From what I understand, things were going fine until my nephew hooked up with those rich society types—then everything went to hell."

"Oh, goodness," said Aunt Sadie, studying the pages of Angel's tome. "He's in this book!"

Bud Napp nodded. "Johnny was the one who the police arrested for the murder of Bethany Banks last year . . . but he was innocent. Probably set up by those rich folks to take the fall, but their plan backfired."

Stop the presses, Jack declared.

I silently asked my personal ghost to keep his pucker buttoned while I tried to conjure the memory of the Banks murder coverage on the news, and the arrest that followed. But the only image I could recall was the figure of a young man surrounded by policemen, a jacket pulled up to hide his features.

It's called a "perp walk," doll, said Jack. *The hammers thought they had their patsy.*

"I remember the name 'Napoli' was in the papers and on

television," I told Bud, "but of course I never connected the name to you—or to Johnny. And I don't think I ever saw Johnny's picture at the time."

"No," said Bud, "you wouldn't have. Johnny was still seventeen when he was arrested, and technically a juvenile, so the press never published his photo—thank God."

"So what finally happened?" I asked as gently as possible. "You said Johnny was on parole. But wasn't he cleared of the Banks murder?"

"Not *cleared*," Bud replied. "He was released on a *technicality*—an illegal search and seizure of his locker and car by the local police, who also violated his Miranda rights. They kept him up all night trying to get a confession out of him. He gave them some statements that were somewhat incriminating, but he'd never been apprised of his rights and no lawyer was present, so those were thrown out, too. No other physical evidence could make their case against Johnny—because he was innocent, so that's no surprise. But the Rhode Island State Police are livid that the local badges didn't call them in to handle it. I know the Staties think Johnny is their killer, and that they could have convicted based on circumstantial evidence and legally extracted statements. They did go out of their way to nail him on a lesser charge of possession of a controlled substance with intent to sell—that ecstasy stuff."

"Oh, my," murmured Sadie.

"Johnny was convicted of that drug charge, but because he was a juvenile and it was a first offense he only got six months in jail before he was paroled for good behavior—though any violation of that parole will get Johnny sent back to jail for five years."

"I can see why you don't want to involve the police," I said.

"Johnny was no saint," Bud replied. "He's had a lot of hard knocks and he didn't take them all well. When his education got sidetracked, he got mixed up with a bad crowd.

He got hooked on booze and drugs. But since his arrest and conviction, he's cleaned up his act and deserves a second chance—which is why I don't want to go to Chief Ciders. Not yet, anyway."

It's an old story, baby. The well-heeled set have the local cops in their pocket. With an obvious suspect like Johnny right in front of them, it's no surprise they'd pushed so hard for a confession.

"Do you need me to explain Miranda rights to you, Jack? They were before your time."

Don't sweat it, honey. I've picked it up from some of those TV cop shows me and your boy like to watch. Seems to me even the screwed-up handling of Johnny's rights serves the locals well—it keeps the victim's family believing Johnny did the deed and got off on a legal technicality. Which means the local badges don't have to risk angering a community of wealthy families by digging into and exposing their kids' peccadillos to find the real killer.

Though I dreaded this moment, I knew it was time to tell Bud what really happened to Johnny last night—that he'd hooked up with Angel Stark, and may have left with her after the author appearance and the ugly scene on the street.

"Damn!" Bud yelled when I delivered the bad news. "Johnny should have been smart enough to stay away!"

Just then there came a persistent knocking at the front door. My aunt hurried to answer it, leaving me with the task of calming Bud.

"How could you invite that woman to your store? How could you set up Johnny like that?"

"Bud," I said evenly. "I didn't know—you and Johnny were hiding the truth. There's no way I could have known."

Bud slumped down in his chair, the wind out of him, his demeanor sunken with defeat. "I'm sorry . . . I don't really blame you, Pen. It's just that I don't know what to do or where to turn. But it sounds to me like Johnny skipped his parole and ran off with the Stark girl."

I heard a sharp intake of breath behind me, then sobs. I whirled around to see Mina in tears. Obviously she'd heard Bud's last statement, which did nothing to improve the poor girl's day.

CHAPTER 9

And Then There Were Three

> The revelation that life simply isn't easy . . . is one of
> the most distressing aspects of the quarterlife crisis.
>
> —*Quarterlife Crisis:*
> *The Unique Challenges of Life in Your Twenties*

AFTER MORE TEARS and my aunt's comforting atten-
tions, Mina wiped her face, brushed her hair, and declared
herself fit to face the workday. Bud Napp departed soon after that, already late in opening his hardware store.

"We'll talk again tonight, at the meeting," Bud told me
at the front door. He was referring to the monthly meeting
of the Quindicott Business Owners Association, scheduled
to assemble in our store's Community Events space tonight, right after closing.

"We might actually be laughing about this situation by
then," I said hopefully. "When you find Johnny at the store

selling pipe stems, and Angel turns up sipping coffee at the Cooper Family Bakery."

Bud smiled weakly, but I could see he didn't share my optimism. With a final wave, he hurried into the bright, blue summer morning. My son soon followed as his ride to day camp pulled up. With a kiss, he was out the door, trilling how he was all ready for his next swimming lesson.

Despite the fact that it was a Saturday and the weather outside was lovely, warm and sunny, yet comfortably breezy—the reason the moneyed classes of New York and Philadelphia have made New England summers by the sea a tradition for over a century—Sadie, Mina, and I were already emotionally drained by the time we opened Buy the Book, which meant we were totally unprepared to greet the public. Fortunately, there wasn't much of a public to greet, just two women in their twenties looking for beach reading.

After selling them Janet Evanovich's entire Stephanie Plum backlist, I sought forgetfulness in other work. I booted up the computer to check the inventory, answer some e-mail queries, review publishers' catalogs, and made a note to order more James Patterson and Dan Brown books, dusted the counter, and assembled the display for the new Dennis Lehane hardcover—and after all of it, I still felt restless. Or perhaps *helpless* is a better word.

Doll, one thing you're not is helpless.

"Easy for you to say," I silently told my ghost. "What would you do if you were me?"

When waiting for the next shoe to drop, take a closer look at the shoe you've got . . . aw, hell . . . did I just make a rhyme? I hate rhymes more than nickel cigar smoke . . .

"The shoe I've got? . . . Yes, of course!"

I dialed quickly, and the call was answered on the first ring, as I knew it would be. "Professor Parker," I said, "I have urgent need for your literary expertise."

"Indeed," was Brainert's reply, and I could almost see that inscrutable, Holmes-like eyebrow of his arch.

"Did you happen to read Angel Stark's book?"

There was a pause. "Last night, I had two choices: read Ms. Stark's tome, or grade the papers from my summer school class. Now the only students more dismal than the usual bunch are those so pathetic they have to repeat classes during the summer . . ."

"So you read Angel's book."

"Actually, no. In my opinion, my summer school students are better writers."

"Come on, Brainert. It can't be *that* bad."

"Why don't you call Fiona. She swore she was going to devour the thing when I delivered the autographed copy to her last night. And knowing Fiona, she's probably already read the entire book twice and posted her copy for sale on eBay."

"I might just visit Fiona, now that you mention it," I replied. "But I still need you to read Angel's book before the meeting tonight."

Brainert moaned.

So I told Brainert about Johnny vanishing, about Angel's disappearance, and the fact that Johnny Napp was really Giovanni Napoli—a material witness and possible suspect in the Bethany Banks murder. I could tell his interest was sparked, but not stoked enough to fuel his intellectual fire, or delve into "Miss Prozac-Girl-Interrupted-in-a-Bell-Jar's" book.

"If I do read this thing, what, exactly, do you want me to look for?"

"I don't know," I replied honestly. "Connections."

Brainert agreed to do it, but still sounded skeptical about the whole project.

"Look," I said. "The only two things Angel Stark and Bud's nephew have in common are Bethany Banks's murder—and the fact that they both vanished on the same night. You have in your hand a just-released copy of a book written by Angel Stark about that very murder. Surely it's possible that you'll discover some pertinent fact if you read it. You are a genius, remember?"

"So I am."

"And please, keep everything I told you a secret for now, though I suspect the cat will be out of the bag before much longer. I'll see you tonight at the Quibblers' meeting." (Among some of its members, the Quindicott Business Owners Association has come to be referred to as the Quibble Over Anything gang—or "the Quibblers" for short.)

After I turned Brainert loose on the problem, I felt a little better. But I still didn't feel I'd done enough.

So listen to your bookworm friend, Jack said. *Pay the Bird Lady a visit, and when you get back you can let me in on what kind of pecker she's wearing on her lapel today.*

Though offensively put, Jack's—more specifically, *Brainert's*—advice to pay Fiona a visit had merit. No scandal large or small, no bit of gossip or innuendo in this town, could slip past the predatory eyes and extremely sharp hearing of Fiona Finch, let alone under her own roof. So I was fairly sure that if something fishy was going on, Fiona had probably already swooped in on it.

Enough. Your bird metaphors are killing me.

"Oh, really, and I thought you were already dead."

Can it, kid. Go get yourself some oxygen.

I cleared my throat and called to Sadie, "Hold the fort. I'm going over to Fiona's inn for an hour or so."

Aunt Sadie surprised me by stepping out from behind the counter.

"You're thinking of breaking into Angel Stark's room, aren't you?" she said. My silence was answer enough.

Sadie looked over her shoulder to make sure Mina was out of earshot. Then she faced me again. "You *are* thinking of breaking in," she whispered.

"It's hardly breaking in if you convince the innkeeper to use a pass key. Anyway, it's Fiona's property. She can come and go as she pleases."

"And bring you with her? Well, dear, you're not going without me."

Sadie scampered to retrieve her purse.

"We can't just leave Mina here without help," I protested.

"The place is empty," Sadie replied. "And besides, we're doing this to help Mina, too."

"*We're* doing this?"

"You solved a murder at this store last year, Pen," my aunt replied. "And you never even let me in on what was going on—did you think I was too old to help?"

"I never said anything of the kind!" I cried. "I was just trying to protect you."

"I don't need protection!"

Then Sadie sighed and looked at me over the tops of her wire-rimmed glasses. "Sorry, dear . . . I don't mean to snap . . . it's just that things were getting pretty dull around here until you and Spencer came back into my life. I didn't realize it right off . . . but I kinda like all the excitement."

"It's okay, Aunt Sadie. I understand. But I honestly hope things *don't* get too exciting—and by the time we reach Fiona's inn, we find Johnny and Angel are back."

I called to Mina, who was restocking the stacks at the rear of the store. "Mina, we need you up front. Sadie and I have to go out for an hour or so."

WHEN WE STEPPED into the bright sunshine, I spied one of the three Quindicott Police squad cars parked on the other side of Cranberry Street. Standing next to the vehicle, looking tall and more handsome than usual in his dark blue uniform and mirrored sunglasses, was Officer Edward Franzetti.

"What do you know? Sometimes there is a cop around when you need one," I said.

Aunt Sadie touched my arm. "Bud specifically asked us not to contact the police—not yet, anyway. It's not our place to interfere."

"I'm not going to contact the police . . . not officially. I'm just going to have a talk with my old friend Eddie. And if something about a missing person gets mentioned . . ."

My voice trailed off. Inside my head, I could hear Jack's voice, but faintly. When I let go of the door I felt him fade away completely—his spirit imprisoned inside of the brick and mortar building that housed our bookstore.

I caught Eddie's attention and waved. As I hoped he would, Eddie sauntered across the street, fingers hitched in his holster belt.

Eddie Franzetti was a longtime friend of mine, and the very best friend of my late brother Peter—who'd died drag-racing in high school. One of the sons of the man who opened Franzetti's Pizza some time in the early 1960s, Eddie decided he wanted more than a spot in the family business. So he did a tour in the military, then returned to Quindicott and joined the police force, which my late father, who'd also been part of that force, had helped him do.

"Hey, Pen. Sadie," he said, touching the brim of his cap.

"How are you, Eddie?" I asked.

He shrugged. "Working Saturday in the middle of the summer, when I should be sunning myself on the Ponsert Beach, *that's* how I am. It's not like the old days, when we were young and the living was easy, eh, Pen?"

"When we were young, we didn't have children to support," I replied.

"I'll say. Found out my oldest kid needs braces. What passes for my dental plan will pay for less than half the procedure, so I'll be working Saturdays for the rest of the summer . . . Maybe the rest of the year."

Sadie began window-shopping, tactfully moving down the street until she was out of earshot.

"Can I ask you something, Eddie . . . off the record?"

"Not if it's about the littering ticket. I'm sorry about the fine, Pen, but you weren't the only business that got hit. Lots of folks along Cranberry did . . . It wasn't my idea. I was just following orders."

I knew Eddie and his fellow "Brothers in Blue" were feeling the heat as the result of new revenue-enhancing policies instituted by Councilwoman Marjorie Binder-Smith, the most frustrating woman in local politics. Sadie and Marjorie had been feuding since before I was born, it seemed, and it was my aunt who dubbed her "The Municipal Zoning Witch." The councilwoman's newest shakedown had most of the town's business leaders buzzing, and not in a nice way. The strategy involved an insidious manipulation of perfectly reasonable trash laws.

"It's not about the ticket, which I paid in full," I replied. "Actually, it's about a missing person, who, technically, may not be a missing person—at least not officially."

Eddie reached under his cap and scratched his head. Then he put his hands on his hips. "Are you talking about the young woman who disappeared last night?" he asked.

Could it be that Dana Wu actually filed a missing report after all? I wondered. Only one way to find out.

"Do you mean Angel Stark?" I asked.

To my surprise, Eddie shook his head. "Never heard of anyone called Angel Stark. Our missing person *is* a woman, though . . . college kid who came to town for the weekend."

It was my turn to scratch my head. "I don't know who you mean."

"She's a Brown University student, over from Providence," Eddie continued. "She and her friends were staying at the new Comfy-Time Motel on the highway last night. Sometime after midnight—the roommates are not sure of the exact time—they claim the girl stepped outside to get a soda and never came back. Her car is still in the parking lot. Her purse with her ID and credit cards was still in the motel room. She was reported missing to us first thing in the morning."

"What are you doing about it?"

"Not much yet. If she'd been under eighteen and we had more information, we could issue an Amber Alert right away. But the girl's over eighteen and she hasn't even been missing for twenty-four hours, so Chief Ciders wants to wait it out before getting the Staties involved, which is more or less standard procedure. We're trying to contact her parents right now to see if she's tried to get in touch with them in any way. Once we've confirmed she hasn't called them— or shown up at any of her known addresses—then we'll ask the State Police to issue an All Points Bulletin. Till then, I've been showing the woman's picture to every gas station attendant and restaurant worker in the area to see if anyone remembers seeing her . . . No luck yet."

Eddie reached into his pocket and drew out a photograph. "Maybe you'll recognize her."

I took the picture from Eddie's hand. I recognized the girl instantly—the young woman who'd caused the disruption at Angel's reading the night before.

"The missing woman's name is Banks . . . Victoria Banks," Eddie informed me.

In a rush, some of the things the woman said came back to me . . . accusations the girl made about Angel "ruining her family." It seemed Dana's guess that she was a member of the Banks family was true.

Eddie was watching me, and I suspected that he suspected that I recognized the girl.

"Yes," I told him. "This woman was in our store last night. Attended the author reading. She and her friends left . . . early."

"Yeah," Eddie replied. "Her friends said that they attended a reading . . . I forgot they said that."

Which was, in the parlance of Jack Shepard, *raw baloney*. If anything, Eddie Franzetti was sharper than

Chief Ciders, and he never forgot anything, including the fact that I'd once led him astray in a criminal matter—at least for a little while—during my own investigation of the mysterious death of author Timothy Brennan in my own store.

Brennan's death, which started out looking accidental, turned out to be a homicide. In the end, I'd brought Eddie in. But since that time, I feared thàt Eddie hasn't quite trusted me the way he used to. I also suspected that he was wise to the fact that I was on the trail of yet more trouble right now—and his little "forgetful" act with me had been a test to see if I'd actually come clean with him.

"About *your* missing person," Eddie said. "The one who's not officially missing . . . I think you said her name was Angel Stark?"

I was suddenly at a loss for words.

"Oh, Penelope, dear," Aunt Sadie called. "Come along. We haven't got all day."

My jaws snapped shut. Saved!

"Have to bolt," I cried, silently thanking my aunt for wanting a little excitement this a.m. "Sorry, Eddie, another time. You heard my aunt. Gotta go."

As I rushed to Sadie's side, I called over my shoulder, "Drop by anytime, Eddie."

"Oh, I will, Pen," Eddie replied. "I will."

As I hurried down the sidewalk, I felt Officer Franzetti's eyes suspiciously watching my back. I fought the urge to turn around again. After walking several blocks in silence, Sadie halted and began to scold me.

"I told you not to talk to the police, Penelope," she cried. "Eddie may be an old friend, but you can't always trust the law."

Though I was too far away from the bookshop to hear Jack's voice, I was sure the ghost would have whole-heartedly agreed.

CHAPTER 10

No Clue

"I got a hot tip," said Pete mysteriously.
"Look out it don't burn your fingers."

—"Kansas City Flash" by Norbert Davis,
Black Mask magazine, 1933

AFTER SADIE AND I walked up the shady drive, lined with century-old weeping willows, I studied the cars in the Finch Inn's small paved parking lot, half expecting to see a black Jaguar with a blue and white sticker on the trunk—the same one I'd seen speeding away from the knocked-down Angel Stark the night before.

I surveyed a number of upscale vehicles—a few silver BMWs, a dark blue Mercedes, and one red Porsche—but there was no black Jag among them.

"Hard to be believe they're finally getting somewhere with that gourmet restaurant of theirs," said Sadie, eyeing the skeletal wooden structure by the Quindicott Pond, surrounded by a barricade of yellow construction rope. "Wonder how pricey she's gonna make it."

"Pricey is good," I told my aunt. "Pricey is upscale. And the perception of 'upscale' means more urban-dwelling, book-buying tourists with wads of disposable income will be trolling through town."

"Think so?"

"Sure. The elite have practically made it an axiom: The more you have to pay, the more it must be worth."

Fiona had always said the Inn's struggle for full bookings year-round was hampered by Quindicott's lack of upscale dining—Franzetti's Pizza and the Seafood Shack were as elegant as it got for twenty miles.

The Finch Inn itself was certainly charming enough to satisfy any couple looking for a romantic getaway. With brick chimneys, bay windows, shingle-topped gables, and a corner turret, the place was a classic Victorian-era mansion. The wood structure rested on a solid gray fieldstone foundation, and the exterior was characteristic of the Queen Anne style, which had made its debut in nearby Newport back in 1874. Barney and Fiona Finch even kept the place painted in its high Victorian colors—reddish-brown clapboards with a combination of olive-green and gold moldings.

Four floors held thirteen distinctly decorated guest rooms, each boasting a fireplace and views of Quindicott pond. Most unique was its proximity to the Pond, a sizeable body of salt water fed by a narrow inlet that raced in and out with the tides from the Atlantic shoreline many miles away. A nature trail, a favorite for local birders, circled the pond and stretched into the backwoods, following the inlet for about eight miles.

We climbed the six long steps and walked across the wide, wooden porch that wrapped around the entire building. I noticed several patrons lounging in wicker chairs. And one, I realized with a start, was the statuesque blonde with the Arctic eyes who'd stared at me the night of Angel's appearance. She lounged in one of the chairs, reading today's edition of the *Providence Journal*, which was delivered daily to all of Fiona's guests.

Though I was seeing the woman in profile now, and with her eyes shaded by sunglasses, I was certain it was the same person. Today she wore a bright yellow sundress with a short hemline, her long, tanned legs stretched out in front of her, manicured feet in strappy, expensive-looking sandals crossed and resting on the wooden deck.

I quickly looked away before the young woman noticed my stare. Spotting Fiona inside the foyer, behind the counter at the front desk, I moved quickly through the beveled glass doors, which stood wide open.

Fiona saw us arriving, smiled warmly, and immediately waved us over. It was ten degrees cooler inside the rich, dark wood entranceway, where two mammoth potted palm trees flanked the door in a convincing illusion of a shady oasis.

The front desk in the foyer had been created by the Finches. Walls had been broken down around a cloak room adjacent to the entranceway. Then a solid oak counter was custom made and stained to match the Inn's interior by Quindicott's resident carpenter and interior restorer, Dan DeLothian, who also taught shop class at the local high school.

Fiona Finch looked resplendent today in a light-green pantsuit accented by an off-white lapel pin in the shape of a snow falcon in flight.

"What a treat to see you both," Fiona said with a grin. "Come into the sitting room and I'll serve up some mint iced tea."

"Thanks for the offer," I replied. "But we can't stay long. Sadie and I have to get back to work soon."

"By the way, Pen, Sadie . . . That was really a delightful event yesterday at the store," Fiona gushed. "It was so thrilling to hear someone as controversial as Angel Stark read her work, and I can't wait to finish her book."

Sadie and I exchanged glances. "Actually, Angel Stark is why we're here."

"Well, then, let's all sit and you can tell me what's so urgent it can't wait until the Business Owners Association meeting this evening." Fiona directed us to a cluster of leather chairs near a front window and we all sat in a tight semicircle.

"Dana Wu dropped by my store first thing this morning," I began, tactfully leaving out the part about Bud's visit, and Johnny's disappearance. "Seems she couldn't find her client, Angel Stark . . . So, has Angel been back to the Inn since the reading last night?"

Fiona frowned. "You know I don't make it a habit to reveal the private activities of my guests," she said in a clear voice.

Then she leaned close, speaking to us in tone barely above a whisper.

"But since you ask, Ms. Stark did *not* return last night, or this morning. I turned down all the beds yesterday evening at about ten thirty. This morning when I brought the tea and coffee tray up to the second-floor sitting room, I noticed Angel was not up and about with the other lodgers.

"Then, about an hour ago, I went up to make the bed and noticed that it hadn't been slept in. The sheets were undisturbed, the wrapped seashell Godiva chocolate still resting on the pillow."

"Did you notice anything odd about the room?" I pressed. "Items missing or disturbed?"

"Oh, for heaven's sake," Fiona cried. "The room wasn't *tossed* or anything! Do you really think something suspicious is going on? Do you suspect foul play?"

"Let's just say that any clue to where Angel Stark has gone would be a blessing. Can you remember anything else that happened last night? Anything odd?"

Fiona put her finger to her chin. "Let's see . . ." She sat up straighter.

"Barney says he saw a couple heading out past the site, toward the bird trail at about ten o'clock. But that's not really odd because it's summer, the weather was nice, and lots of young couples like to walk along the trail on summer evenings for a little privacy.

"But Barney insisted that he thought the young lady was one of our lodgers. Trouble is, Barney's no good at remembering names or people, so he wasn't sure which guest it was. And we do have several young, single women staying with us. Your friend Dana Wu was one of them."

"If it was Angel Stark, then that would mean she did return to the Inn last night—even if she never made it to her room."

Aunt Sadie spoke up. "I don't suppose Barney recognized the fellow?"

"I asked him that very question, but he said he only saw the man's back, from a distance in the dark."

"When was Angel Stark scheduled to check out?" I asked.

Fiona made a face. "Technically, she had the room until noon today," she replied. "But Ms. Stark hasn't checked out or settled her bill, and her luggage is still in the room."

We sat in silence for a moment. I could hear the breeze rustling the elms on the other side of the window.

"Hmm," said Fiona. "Perhaps we do have a mystery brewing. Shall we mention it to the Quibblers? They did help out during the Timothy Brennan mess."

"I have a feeling that the Quibblers will have plenty to quibble over at tonight's meeting," Sadie predicted. "The littering fines alone have got them crazy."

"True," Fiona replied.

"But we need more information on Angel—on what may have happened to her," I pressed.

We halted our conversation long enough to allow a middle-aged couple to pass through the foyer.

"Look," Fiona whispered when we were alone again. "I can't let you into Ms. Stark's room—that just wouldn't be ethical. But what I can do is go up there myself and have a good look around. And if I do come up with something . . . anything . . . I'll let you both know. If it looks urgent, I'll phone. Otherwise, I'll bring any information I learn to the meeting tonight and we can discuss."

I nodded, pleased with myself that I'd persuaded her—and wishing Jack could have seen it. "Also, Fiona, if you haven't yet finished reading *All My Pretty Friends* . . ."

"Only two chapters left to go!"

"Oh, very good," I said. "I'd like you to bring the book tonight. It may come in handy."

Then the grandfather clock in the foyer bonged on the hour. Realizing the time, I quickly stood. "We better go," I told Fiona. "Mina is holding the fort all by herself. If there's an afternoon rush she'll be overwhelmed."

Fiona rose to show us out. At the double doors we paused under the drooping fronds of the potted palms.

"Just one last thing," I said. "I saw another one of your guests outside. A young woman, long blonde hair and longer legs. Sort of a Paris Hilton clone who has that patrician-disdain thing down pat. Brainert was thumbing through Angel's book and thought she looked like the photo of Kiki Langdon, Bethany Banks's closest friend. Could that be true?"

Fiona opened her mouth to reply but didn't. Instead, she gazed over my shoulders, eyes wide, pointing.

I whirled to find the woman in question right behind me. Even more surprising, my super-chic sister-in-law, "La Princessa" Ashley McClure-Sutherland, was standing next to her, resplendent in pristine white slacks and sleeveless shimmering pink silk blouse, her salon-highlighted blonde hair tamed into a slick yuppie ponytail and her French-manicured hand lazily fanning herself with the *Providence Journal*'s society page. It was obvious from their expressions that the two of them had overheard me. They both looked like they'd just sucked on a lemon.

"Are you gossiping about me again, Penelope?" said the Paris Hilton clone, her perfectly lined and expensively glossed lips forming the words with fashionably blasé haughtiness.

Meanwhile, my lips—coated with the current flavor of lip balm stocked by Koh's grocery—refused to form a coherent word, let alone an entire sentence. I just stood there, dumb as a post.

"I'm surprised you don't recognize me, cousin," the woman continued, her eyes level with mine.

Desperately I searched my mind for a memory hook.

I got nothing.

Fiona attempted to break the *Titanic*-worthy glacial wall. "Oh, ah, Ms. Langdon," she chirped. "How very nice to see you this afternoon. Did you enjoy your time on the sun porch?"

The freeze queen ignored Fiona's query and fixed her shark-blue expression on me.

By now I'd recovered from my initial shock. First I greeted my sister-in-law, then I met Kiki Langdon's disdainful gaze with a hard look of my own. "I'm sorry," I said evenly. "Have we met before?"

Suddenly, Ashley cut loose.

"My God, Penelope," she cried. "Don't play innocent with me. Ever since you let—" She gritted her movie star teeth, a cool $50,000 in dental, according to my late husband. "Since Calvin died, I mean, you've done nothing but hurt my family."

"What?!" I cried. The McClures cast as victims of my cruel and evil machinations was certainly a *unique* perspective. One I didn't share.

"You poison Calvin's only child against his relatives, you shun our offers of financial support. On top of that, you come back to this town—for what? To set up in some pathetic, barely break-even, small-time business!"

I was ready to protest, but Sadie leaped into the fray. "More honest than you lot of inside-traders." Her veined hands clenched into fists as she moved menacingly toward Ashley.

You, go, Sadie, I thought, seeing Ashley step back, her sneer faltering. I wasn't surprised. My elderly aunt's temper had reached the level of local legend. There was that pickpocket she'd spotted while reading on the Quindicott Commons and had beaned with a frontlist Anne Perry from two benches away. And, of course, everyone knew the story of the shoplifter whom she'd caught stuffing a Hammett first edition down his pants. She'd taken him out with a Patricia Cornwell to the head.

"I'm talking to Pen about a private family matter," Ashley told Sadie, her disdainful tone turning almost whiny. "She deliberately hurt her own *cousin* on one of the most important weeks of her life."

If this was a joke, I was waiting for the punchline. "Hurt my own cousin?" I asked. "What are you *talking* about?"

"Don't play innocent with me. It won't work. You invited that Stark *creature* to speak at your bookstore, didn't you? 'Nuf said." With that, Ashley's French-manicured fingers shoved the *Journal* into my hands, then she grabbed Kiki's arm, pushed past us, and swept up the stairs.

Aunt Sadie, Fiona, and I stood in stunned silence for a moment.

"What just happened?" I asked as Sadie took the paper from my hands.

"Oh, dear," she said, skimming the newsprint. "I understand now."

"What?"

She held it up, her finger pointing to the big, bold letters
of a society page headline:

```
Engagements Announced
EASTERBROOK-LANGDON
Donald Easterbrook, Jr. of New York
and London to Katherine "Kiki" McClure
Langdon of Greenwich. Newport wedding
planned . . .
```

"Oh, hell." For the life of me, I didn't remember Kiki
Langdon. I did vaguely recall pretty, little blonde "cousin
Katherine" from McClure family functions long past. From
Ashley's perspective, however, the sin was understand-
able—and her outrage, for once, truly justified.

Bethany Banks's murder had come and gone with the
usual glaringly intense then fading press coverage—yet
never once had the names of Bethany's prominent friends
been bandied about on a national scale.

With Angel Stark's new book, all that had changed.
Without knowing it, I'd rolled out the red carpet to a
woman whose brand-new instant best-seller had dragged
the name of my late husband's cousin—and her new fiancé—through mud higher than an L.L. Bean boot.

CHAPTER 11

Grisly Discovery

Murder is an act of infinite cruelty, even if the perpetrators sometimes look like playboys or college professors or nice motherly women with soft graying hair.

—Raymond Chandler, "The Simple Art of Murder: An Essay"

"FIONA! HEY, FIONA!"

We looked up from the paper to find Seymour Tarnish's big, heavy shoes clomping across the wooden wraparound porch. He wore his summer post office attire, a bulky mail sack slung over his rounded shoulders, his tree-trunk legs protruding from the blue uniform shorts.

"Fiona, come with me! Quick!" Seymour called, sweat glistening below his receding brown hairline. "Pen, Sadie!" he added when he saw us. "You come, too."

"Come where?" I asked. We'd all assumed he'd arrived to deliver the mail, as usual. Instead, his skin looked flush, his eyes excited. Then he was turning and moving off the porch again. "You won't believe it if I tell you. Just follow me."

Outside the Finch Inn, the wind had kicked up and the low-hanging branches of the surrounding willows hissed ominously. An errant cloud crossed the afternoon sun, casting a sudden pall over the Inn and the manicured grounds around it. On the nearby shore of the Quindicott Pond, the tide had receded and the air smelled faintly of drying seaweed and rotting flotsam.

As we stepped off the porch and onto the footpath leading to the lake, the bark of a siren sounded. Just a short burst, like the cry of a wounded animal. Then a Rhode Island State Police car raced up the drive, its roof lights flashing. But instead of pulling up to the Inn's front door, the vehicle abruptly swerved off the roadway, across a swath of Barney's carefully manicured grass, and onto the narrow birder's trail that roughly paralleled the shore of the inlet. In a cloud of dust and a cascade of willow leaves, the squad car zoomed farther, past the wood frame and masonry foundation of the restaurant's construction site.

Only then did I notice that far down the trail, just before the path was completely obscured by thick, wild greenery, a Quindicott Police cruiser was already on the trail, and its emergency lights were also flashing. Yellow tape emblazoned with the words POLICE LINE—DO NOT CROSS had already been strung across the path to keep out the public.

When the State Police car halted, the cloud it kicked up rolled over it, coating the black and white vehicle with a fine powder. Out of that same billowing dust a figure emerged. Fiona's husband, Barney Finch. Tall and gangly, his bald pate shiny under a sheen of perspiration, the older man seemed agitated, and he was stumbling as he walked up the path.

Sadie and I hurriedly followed Seymour, meeting up

with Barney just where the trail grass ended and the un-paved wilderness trail began. Fiona saw the stunned expression on her husband's face.

"Barney! My God, what happened?"

Barney's lips moved, as he gestured toward the police cars, but no words were forthcoming.

"Please tell me what's wrong," Fiona begged.

Seymour was the one who obliged. "There's a corpse floating in the Pond. Old Lyle Talbot was angling up the trail there, and he saw something fishy in the shallows . . . only it wasn't a fish."

Barney nodded weakly. "It was a dead body," he finally gasped. "Lyle pointed it out to me." Then he shook his head and fell into silence again.

The grisly discovery had turned Fiona's husband so ghostly pale that the sparse patches of red hair on either side of his bald head were the only hint of color on the man's waxy features.

I tugged at Seymour's mailbag. "How did you find out?"

"I was walking up the drive to deliver the mail when I saw Chief Ciders fly past in his Chief-mobile. He wasn't using his sirens, but he was in an awful hurry—which got me interested."

"Did either of you see . . . the corpse?" I asked.

Seymour shook his head. "Apparently only Lyle and Barn actually saw it. Lyle called nine-one-one on his cell phone, and Ciders responded himself and roped off the scene first thing."

"I wonder if the dead person is anyone we know?" I asked.

Seymour shrugged. "I tried to get a peep at the stiff, but Ciders shooed me away. All I saw was a blanket."

Barney shook his head. "I didn't look close enough to see the face."

I stared down the trail, at the twin police cars. I was tempted to walk down there and find out the identity of the corpse for myself. Then I noticed one of the State Troopers, standing at the door of his cruiser. The man was talking on the radio, no doubt summoning reinforcements. I knew then that nobody without official clearance was going to get close to that scene for a long time.

"Come on, Barney," Fiona said as she tugged on her husband's arm. "You look like you have sunstroke. Let's get you home and I'll pour you a nice glass of iced tea."

I watched as Fiona and Barney hobbled off, Barney leaning on his wife for support.

"I'd better go with them," Sadie declared. She immediately hurried off to catch up to Mr. and Mrs. Finch. Seymour and I remained behind, watching the police secure the scene.

"Sunstroke my tired butt," said Seymour. "Old Barney took this dead body thing a little too hard. Usually the guy's a lot of laughs, but the floater really threw him. You'd think he'd have picked up one of his old lady's true crime books once in a while. Most of those things have photo inserts."

"You can't blame Barney for being upset," I replied. "A photo is one thing. A real corpse is another. And the thing turned up in his own backyard. I'm surprised you're not at least a *little* disturbed."

Seymour waved his hand. "You forget. My route takes me along Pendleton Street—Quindicott's very own Mold Coast. Hell, I found three stiffs in two years trying to deliver Social Security checks to retirement row. It got so bad my supervisor offered to send me to grief counseling. Maybe I should have taken him up on the offer, I could've claimed a disability."

"Yeah, but then you wouldn't be able to afford the mint-condition issues of *G-8 and His Battle Aces* that just came into the store," I pointed out.

"You're joking. When?"

"Don't drool, Seymour. Sadie set them aside for you

already." Seymour's only discernable passions—besides trivia, which had helped win him $25,000 on *Jeopardy!*— were old pulp magazines.

"Fan-tastic!"

A siren, distant at first, then suddenly blaring, heralded the arrival of another official Rhode Island State Police vehicle, this one a Mobile Crime Investigation Unit. Seymour and I moved clear of the trail to let it pass.

"Geeze, Louise . . . Who's in those woods? Hannibal Lecter?"

"It sure didn't take Ciders long to call in the Staties," I said sourly. My own experience with them hadn't been pretty, considering last fall one Detective-Lieutenant Marsh had planned to arrest me on suspicion of murder. (Thank goodnesss, with the help of Jack, the friendly ghost, I delivered them the true perpetrator.)

"The Staties were a foregone conclusion, Pen, and you know it," said Seymour. "Ciders is in over his head when it comes to anything beyond handing out speeding tickets, littering fines, and keeping the peace at high school football games. Besides, this town can't afford more than three police cars. So how's it supposed to pay for a murder investigation?"

"So you think it's murder, too?"

His mouth snapped shut for a moment. "Well . . . when you put it that way. You're right. It *could* be something else. I mean . . ." he hesitated. "What do you think?"

Suicide was my first thought—most likely because of my own experiences with my late husband. But it could have been a tragic accident, too.

"I don't know" is what I finally told Seymour as I watched the forensics team emerge from the State vehicle and begin to speak to Ciders. "But for now I'm keeping my distance."

Displaying too much curiosity might once again land me on a State Trooper's suspect list.

* * *

ON MY WAY back to the Inn with Seymour, I spotted Ashley McClure-Sutherland and Kiki Langdon in the parking lot. They had just piled some luggage into Ashley's silver BMW and were about to depart. I hung back a minute until they had rolled down the drive and out of sight.

From Fiona's front desk I phoned the bookstore to let Mina know she hadn't been forgotten. The girl didn't answer until the sixth ring, so I figured the store was busy. When she finally did pick up, I could hear customers' voices in the background.

I explained to Mina that we were delayed, but would be getting back to the store within the next hour. She gamely reassured us that things were under control. I could hear a strain in her voice, as if she suspected—or feared—that something was amiss with Johnny. I kept my mouth shut, figuring that this wasn't the time or place to tell Mina that a corpse was found floating in the inlet, especially since I hadn't a clue as to the identity yet. Not even if the body was male or female.

I'd no sooner hung up the Finch's phone than in strode Chief Ciders, his big black boots clomping officiously along the Victorian inn's polished hardwood floor. Typically, a large, commanding presence, Ciders was meaty but not fat, his dark blue uniform fitting snugly around a barrel chest. He was in his fifties, and he'd been on the Liliputian Quindicott police force for thirty years now. He had a broad nose and small eyes, and his graying hair had receded, leaving a round visage tugged down at the jowls by time, gravity, and a repeated disinterest in lifting his expression into anything remotely resembling a happy face.

Why his manner was seldom pleasant, nobody could say. He was, by all accounts, in a long-standing, happy marriage with three children and a number of grandchildren. My own theory was that he'd spent too many years devoted to the kind of petty law enforcement that trained him to constantly suspect somebody of being up to something. To put it bluntly, after so many years on the job, his immediate response to any violation of the law, small or large, appeared to be not a gleam in the eye for the thrill of a crime-solving challenge, but a weary scowl as he calculated how much time the confounded case would end up taking away from his poker nights and fishing trips.

"Mahnin'," said the chief, removing his battered hat.

"Hey, Chief, what brings you here?" said Seymour. "Let me guess . . . you saw all those leaves blowing around outside and decided to slap Fiona with a littering citation?"

The chief narrowed his pale blue gaze at Seymour as if he'd just watched a dog owner stroll away from a public sidewalk without pooper scooping. Then he saw me and his expression changed. Now he looked like he'd accidentally swallowed a wad of chewing tobacco.

"Is Mrs. Finch around?"

"Oh, Chief, let *me* get her for you," Seymour declared.

On the carved wooden counter Fiona had placed a decorative antique brass bell. Seymour bounced his hand up and down on it several times. With each strike the bell clanged loudly.

"Innkeeper! Innkeeper!"

Fiona hurried through the doorway that led to the kitchen. "What is all that noise about?" she demanded.

Then Fiona saw Chief Ciders and her spine stiffened.

"Can I help you, Chief?" she asked as she tactfully moved the bell away from Seymour's reach.

"You can tell me if you have any guests missing," the chief replied, almost accusatorily.

"Hmm. . . . what sort of guest?" Seymour asked, as if he were back at his contestant's podium on *Jeopardy!* and trying to clarify a question from Alex Trebek. "A man? A woman?"

"Not talking to you, Tarnish," said Ciders tersely.

"Besides which: I do questions, you do answers." He speared Fiona with his gaze.

"Well, ah, that depends on what you mean by 'missing,' " Fiona replied.

"Come on, Fiona," Seymour goaded, "this isn't an impeachment hearing. Do you have a missing guest or what?"

"Well . . ."

"One guest is missing," I interrupted. "Her name is Angel Stark. She didn't sleep in her room last night, and she was supposed to check out an hour ago but she hasn't turned up to do that as yet."

Chief Ciders slapped his hat against his knee. "Doggone it, Pen, that is not the answer I wanted to hear."

"Of course not," I replied, deciding to take a leap. "You were hoping the young woman you just pulled out of the Pond was Victoria Banks, the Brown University student who vanished from the Comfy-Time Motel last night around midnight."

Suddenly the foyer got so quiet you could hear the buzzing of a fly tapping the window, and the sound of the wind rustling the willows outside.

"How in hellfire did you know that?" Chief Ciders said.

My shrug obviously didn't satisfy Quindicott's top cop.

"This Angel Stark," he said, continuing to eye me. "Was she in town for a particular reason?"

"She's an author. She gave a reading of her new book with us last night. Her publicist, Dana Wu, dropped by this morning when I opened up and reported Ms. Stark missing."

"Yet this Dana Wu didn't drop by *my* office and file a missing person report. Now *why* is that?"

"Dana thought maybe Angel had run off with . . . some guy she met at the reading."

Ciders gave me a sidelong glance. "Local guy?"

"Er . . . Not really."

Again, Chief Cider's hat slapped against his trousers.

"I should have known you'd be involved," he barked.

"So who's the stiff you just fished out of the lake?" Seymour asked.

"Don't you have mail to misdeliver, Tarnish?"

"All finished for the day, just like you . . . Now that the Staties are here to do your job you can go back to issuing littering tickets."

Chief Ciders shot Seymour a withering look that was formidable enough to intimidate Seymour into silence, at least temporarily. Unfortunately for Ciders, that look did not work on me.

"So who is it?" I asked. "Do you have any clue? Do you want me to try to identify the body?"

"It might come to that," Ciders conceded. "But right now I need the phone number of that woman you mentioned. This Dana Wu."

Keep pushing. I could almost hear Jack's voice back at the store. "Do you think you've found Angel Stark's body?" I pressed. "The author I told you about? You can't tell me there's nothing to go on."

"The corpse was missing any ID." Chief Ciders admitted with a frustrated sight, "but we did find something in her pocket."

So it's a *her*, I thought, relieved for Bud and Mina's sake that it wasn't Johnny Napp.

Ciders reached into his jacket and drew out a small clear plastic evidence bag. Inside was an old-fashioned long-stem brass key attached to a small wooden placard. Burned into the wooden tab were the words "Finch Inn" and the number nine.

"Can you identify this, Mrs. Finch?" said the chief, almost mechanically, since it was obvious that anyone who lived within twenty miles of Quindicott could.

"That's one of our keys," Fiona cried. "Room nine . . . The room where Angel Stark was staying."

CHAPTER 12

Fall Guy or Felon?

Thanks to you and yore meddlin', we finally got us a
clue.

—Merle Constiner, "The Turkey Buzzard Blues,"
Black Mask magazine, 1943

I'D BARELY DIGESTED the surprise of seeing the key
before I was rocked by another shock. Bud Napp rushed
through the Inn's open doors, looking nearly as pale as
Barney Finch.

Chief Ciders hitched his fingers in his belt and faced
him. "Thanks for coming in, Bud."

"You said it was urgent," Bud replied. Then he noticed
the rest of us standing around with funereal faces. "What
the hell is going on here, Chief?"

"Bud . . . are you still selling that bright yellow lawn
rope?"

"You hustled me over here for an inventory report?"

"Just answer the question."

"No," Bud replied. "I told you last week when you came to buy some to tie up your tomatoes, the company stopped making it. Some issue with the dye. They're switching to neon orange."

"Have you sold any yellow rope in the past week?"

Bud shook his head. "I have a few bolts in my truck, that's all. And I'm using them for my building business."

"Let's go on out into the parking lot, Bud. I need to get a look inside of your truck."

"Are you looking for something in particular?" Bud asked suspiciously. "Maybe I should ask to see some kind of warrant?"

"You can give me permission to search your truck now, or wait until the State Police get a warrant issued," Ciders replied wearily. "Getting that warrant should take all of about five minutes—and then the Staties might want to do more than search your truck. If they have to go to all that trouble for the paper, they'll probably include your garage, your business, your home."

Bud swallowed. "I didn't bring the truck. I drove over in my Explorer."

Now it was Ciders who was suddenly suspicious. "Where is your truck, then?"

"Johnny has it," Bud replied uneasily. "He had a date last night, I told him he could borrow my truck."

"And where is Johnny right now?"

When I saw the look in Ciders's eye, I knew this was the question he'd been itching to ask all along. I still didn't figure out how a yellow rope was involved, though I'd seen some of it strung around the restaurant's construction site—no surprise since Budd was supplying the crew.

"Johnny . . . He hasn't come home yet."

"What about his date? Who was she? Was she staying at this inn?"

"Hell, no. Johnny was dating a local girl. Mina Griffith. Works at Pen's bookstore."

Now Ciders turned to me. "And is Mina at work today?"

I nodded. "But she doesn't know where Johnny is either."

"And why is that?"

I snapped my mouth shut and kept it that way. Ciders was grilling me, and I didn't like it. He studied me—and obviously didn't care for my attempt to remain uncooperative. "Okay, don't answer," he told me. "I'll just have to track down Mina and ask *her*."

My eyes narrowed on the Chief. Mina was in an emotional state as it was. I couldn't let him upset her even more.

"Mina doesn't know anything because he never kept his date with her last night," I reluctantly admitted. "I know because she came back to the store late. They were supposed to meet for pizza, but he never showed up, so I waited with her while her roommate drove over to pick her up and take her home. I've already spoken to her about it."

"Was Johnny at your bookstore at *any time* last night?"

"Johnny came to the store, stayed awhile. But he left before we closed and, as I said, never came back to pick up Mina."

"He left *alone*?"

I felt cornered. But I couldn't lie about something that had been witnessed by people other than just me. "No," I said in a soft voice. "He was on the sidewalk outside the store . . ." I looked down, hating Ciders for making me admit it. "He was talking to Angel Stark the last time I saw him."

I heard Bud release a disgusted breath. I couldn't meet his eyes.

Ciders cleared his throat. "Bud, maybe you and I should finish this conversation somewhere in private."

Bud exhaled again, but this time in defeat. He shook his head. "There are no secrets in this town, and Pen and Sadie already know some of what's going on, as you just figured out."

Then some of the old fire rekindled behind Bud's eyes. "We've leveled with you, Ciders. Now it's time for you to level with us. What is going on? Why did you want to search my truck?"

"Bud, we just found a body floating in the pond. The body of a young woman. From the condition of the corpse, the State forensics people say she hasn't been in the water more than ten or twelve hours, maximum, which means she died late last night or, more likely, very early this morning."

"What does this have to do with me? With Johnny?"

"We found a length of yellow rope around the dead woman's neck. The same stuff you sold at your hardware store," Ciders replied. "It appears the killer used that rope to strangle her."

Bud pointed in the direction of the pond. "That construction site out there has a length of that same damn rope. Anyone could have gotten it from there."

"I checked the rope at the site," the Chief said evenly. "There's only one bolt securing the area. Both ends of that bolt of rope still have the plastic tabs attached—which means that length of rope has never been cut. So the killer probably got that yellow rope from somewhere else."

"Okay, so maybe it wasn't that rope. But anyone could have bought yellow rope like that," insisted Bud. "Maybe the killer bought it last season when yellow rope was everywhere, or in another town that still sold it . . ."

"Bud," Ciders began. "I know *all* about your nephew—the conviction, the parole, and about the suspicion of murder charges that were leveled at Johnny in that big Newport heiress death last year. The Bethany Banks case."

I was surprised. So was Bud Napp.

"We're not all Keystone Kops," said the Chief, "despite what our local letter carrying *Jeopardy!* genius here thinks."

Seymour harrumphed, and Chief Ciders continued,

"Bud, when your nephew moved here, his parole officer notified me of Johnny's criminal record and his place of lodging and employment. I never bothered the kid out of respect for you . . ."

"You and I both know that those murder charges were dismissed," Bud pointed out.

"That's right, Bud," Ciders replied. "But they were dismissed on a legal technicality, not for lack of evidence."

Bud's face reddened. "There was no *real* evidence or they would have tried Johnny anyway!"

Chief Ciders nodded. "I know, and I understand how you feel. But the woman in the pond . . . she was strangled. Just like Bethany Banks. And until we locate Johnny, and have a long talk with him, he's the main suspect now, which means I have no choice but to issue an All Points Bulletin for the arrest of your nephew on suspicion of murder."

"Wait a minute!" Bud cried. "Murder of who?"

Angel Stark, of course, I thought to myself. She had to be the lady in the lake—unless, of course, some other woman had been carrying around Angel's room key, which was technically within the realm of possibility. So I wasn't surprised when the Chief said . . .

"Angel Stark, of course. Technically she's not yet identified. But since Mrs. McClure volunteered to help ID the body, we can settle the matter of the woman's name right here and now."

Then Chief Ciders faced me. "Penelope, you and I are going to take a little walk . . ."

CHAPTER 13

Lady in the Lake

"I still ain't heard who killed Muriel . . ."

"Somebody who thought she needed killing, somebody who had loved her and hated her . . ."

—Raymond Chandler, *The Lady in the Lake*, 1943

THE LESS SAID about the next half hour, the better. Suffice it to say that a corpse that has been strangled in summer and submerged in water for "only about ten or twelve hours" has pretty much lost all resemblance to anything human.

Black swollen tongue, blue-gray skin mottled with angry red-black patches, stringy, mud-soaked clothes and hair, and the incongruity of a bright sunflower-yellow rope embedded deep into the puffy flesh at the throat—the victim was not a pretty sight. And I'm not even bringing up the insects.

Through features like hair (long and copper), eye color

(brown), and items like clothes the woman was wearing (that one-of-a-kind Betsy Johnson pink and green sundress with the lace-up corset and gauzy skirt), I became convinced the corpse belonged to Angel Stark, and told Chief Ciders and two officers from the Rhode Island State Police crime scene unit exactly that.

"From her fingerprints and dental records, the crime lab people should be able to positively confirm her identity within a few hours," Ciders told me as we walked back to the Inn together.

"Sadie and I really have to get back to the bookstore," I told the Chief. "We left poor Mina on her own for the last two and a half hours."

A few minutes later, Ciders released us all, saying he'd be over to the bookstore soon to get a corroborating statement from Mina. Bud offered Sadie and me a lift back to the store. Seymour decided to tag along as far as the post office. Fiona returned to nurse her stricken husband, whom she'd "put to bed for a long nap." It was a solemn, quiet group who trudged out to the Inn's parking lot and piled into Bud's Ford Explorer.

After we dropped Seymour at the local post office, Bud pulled up in front of Buy the Book. I was surprised when he cut the engine and followed Sadie and me into the store.

For a summertime Saturday afternoon, the place was fairly busy, and I breathed a sigh of relief when I spied a familiar face at the register alongside Mina. After bagging a bundle of paperbacks and passing them to the customer, Linda Cooper-Logan gave us one of her big, open smiles. In her late thirties, Linda still wore her short platinum hair in the spiky, punkish style she'd first worn in the eighties. These days, she usually favored long flowered skirts and a copious amount of silver bracelets, but on this warm afternoon she wore cut-off denim shorts and a chocolate-brown "Bakers Do It Early" T-shirt, which was dusted with flour.

"Boy am I glad to see you," I gushed.

"Not half as glad as I was," said Mina.

Linda dismissed my thanks with a wave of her hand. "I brought the pastry over for tonight's meeting and saw a line of customers, so I volunteered to fill in until you guys got back."

Linda and her husband, Milner Logan, operated the Cooper Family Bakery, a small but profitable bread and sweet shop down the street from Buy the Book. Linda handled the comfort foods, and Milner the fancy French stuff. (He and Linda had met when Milner was teaching a cooking school class in Boston on the art of French pastry.)

"Honestly, I can't thank you enough," I told her.

"So what's going on? I've got to know," Linda asked.

Yeah, said Jack Shepard. *I'm with the blonde porcupine— What in hell happened at Bird-Woman's lace-doily nest?*

I was about to reply when I looked beyond Linda's shoulder, to see the look of worry and apprehension on Mina Griffith's face. Mina, in turn, was watching Bud Napp and Sadie head toward a set of comfortable chairs near the back of the store, speaking in hushed tones as they went.

I took a deep breath and broke the news to Linda and Mina about the discovery of Angel Stark's body along the wildlife trail near Finch Inn. I also told them that Victoria Banks, Bethany's sister, was also missing. Linda was intrigued, but as I expected, Mina took the news hard. Harder still was the next bombshell I dropped on the poor girl.

"Chief Ciders believes Angel was strangled, murdered— and he thinks Bud's nephew Johnny had something to do with it."

"My God," Mina choked. The shock was too much and she broke down. Linda took over the register, and I brought Mina upstairs to privately comfort her with a cup of tea and a shoulder to cry on. I hated having to tell Mina the truth, but I knew it would be better for her to hear it from me than Chief Ciders, when he sought her statement.

Mina didn't say much, just sipped her tea and said that she couldn't believe this was happening—that Angel was dead and Johnny was being sought as a likely suspect.

"I admit he was really stupid to go off with Angel like that," said Mina after blowing her nose, "and I was really angry with him . . . but, Mrs. McClure, I really like Johnny. Up until last night, he's been the kindest, sweetest guy I've ever gone out with."

I nodded. "I'm glad," I said, "but I really don't know Johnny."

"He spent hours last weekend helping my little brother and his friends build a treehouse, which he knows how to do because for years he's volunteered his time to Habitat for Humanity to help build low-income houses. He loves his uncle, and I know he cares about me . . . he told me so . . . he's a good guy, Mrs. McClure, he . . ."

Mina began to cry again. Then she shook her head. "One minute with that *stupid* Stark girl would tell anyone she's trouble," murmured Mina, wiping her nose. "I don't know why he went off with her like that."

As I poured the last of the tea for Mina, I felt the slightest whisper of a cool breeze on my cheek. *You know this is a frame job, don't you?* said Jack in my head.

"I want it to be," I silently told the ghost. "But is it really? How can you be so sure Johnny isn't guilty? Jack, I'm afraid Johnny just isn't as 'nice' a guy as he wants Mina and his uncle to believe."

You could be right. But there are an awful lot of notes in play here . . . and it's a kind of tune I've heard before.

After Mina dried her eyes and insisted on continuing her shift—she said it would help keep her mind off her worries for Johnny—we went back downstairs to the store.

Bud and Sadie were still deep in conversation, and things seemed fairly quiet. I thanked Linda for her help. She went on her way, and Mina took over the register.

"I think we need fresh stock on the new release table," I told her. "If you cover the counter, I'll take care of it."

"No problem," said Mina, blowing her nose one last time as I headed toward the archway leading to the Community Events space. I crossed the empty room, then strode quickly down the short corridor, past the restrooms. When I got to the storage area, I called to Jack, hoping to continue my communication with the gumshoe from beyond.

"You were saying that someone might be trying to frame Johnny . . . ?"

Like an original van Gogh, doll.

The storage room was nothing fancy: a plain white box with stacked cartons of books waiting their turn to be placed on the selling floor and an old wooden desk from the store's early days against one wall—which we now used to hold office supplies. The room felt warm and a little bit stuffy when I'd walked into it, but Jack's presence had dropped the temperature and the air around me felt comfortably cool. Too bad his ghostly presence couldn't be constant and in every room, I mused to myself; the store would save a fortune in air-conditioning.

Very funny, said Jack, overhearing.

"Come on, Jack, don't get testy."

The cool air suddenly got decidedly colder. I shivered as a mini whirlwind swirled around my thin sleeveless cotton blouse and bare shoulders, seemed to whisper at my ear. *You remember that dream I gave you last night? There's a case file in those boxes that'll finish the story. Look for the file marked "Stendall."*

I shook my head. "I don't have the time for that right now."

Make the time, baby. The files are five feet away.

Jack was right, of course. After his still-unsolved murder here in 1949, one of Jack's acquaintances, a young reporter named Timothy Brennan, took possession of his files—and created an internationally best-selling series of books featuring the hard-boiled private detective Jack Shield. On every dust jacket, Brennan boasted that the Shield stories were based on Jack Shepard's case files (a boast Jack wasn't exactly keen to learn about).

After Brennan was also murdered here a year ago, his son-in-law, who subsequently took over the writing of the still-popular series—and owed me the favor of a lifetime—agreed to let me keep the original files here for him in storage. His only condition was that he first review them himself so he could Xerox "selected files" that interested him. I assumed the ones selected would be precisely the ones his late father-in-law hadn't yet gotten around to exploiting for his fictional Jack Shield book series.

A week ago, the promised boxes finally arrived, and I had been hoping for the time to go through them—a part of me even fancying the idea that I myself might be able to puzzle out some theories about who might have killed Jack and why. But finalizing the Angel Stark appearance had left me with very little free time to peruse the files. And now that she was dead and Bud's nephew the prime suspect, I *really* didn't have the time.

"Couldn't you just give me the shorthand on that case?" I asked Jack as I gathered and stacked on a handcart an array of hardcovers and paperbacks that made up the most recent releases by various publishers.

The shorthand is that this Johnny was obviously framed for the Bethany Banks murder. Legal technicalities can throw out confessions and incriminating statements, but if he'd really done the deed, there would have been enough physical evidence on the body for the DA to put him on trial. What seems more likely here is the frame didn't stick—the locals didn't have the stomach to look hard at the sons and daughters of any powerful, well-heeled families and the deb's real killer got off. Except now your authoress was trying to keep the case alive in the public eye—so she gets bumped and once more Johnny gets blamed.

"You're saying the person who killed Angel also killed Bethany?"

That's the bet, honey. Not a sure thing, but if it were a horse, I'd give it pretty decent odds.

"Who then?" I asked.

Who were the people around Angel last night, who were also around Bethany the night she was murdered? Besides the old man's nephew, of course.

"Kiki . . . she was at the reading. And she was staying at Fiona's inn last night, too, which is where Angel was staying."

Who else?

"Let's see . . ." I grabbed a box cutter from the desk near the door and slit open a carton of *All My Pretty Friends*. I piled five books on the handcart and flipped through the sixth until I got to the color photo insert.

"Angel claims there were plenty of people at the party but only a small circle who had strong motives to kill Bethany. Bethany's fiancé, Donald Easterbrook, was one . . ."

I studied the photo, which looked like the typical candid shot found in any photo album of a young man hanging out on an athletic field. Sporting jeans, a rugby shirt, and effortless posture, Easterbrook was tall and muscular with short, dark hair, blue eyes, a strong, square jaw, and a broad, easygoing smile. According to the caption, Easterbrook was the offspring of an aristocratic, polo-playing father and a wealthy Brazilian mother. The combination had produced a strikingly handsome young man.

"He's described in the caption as a 'young prince of Newport,' " I murmured. "Hmm . . . very JFK, Jr."

Who?

"John Kennedy, Jr.?" I replied impatiently.

Baby, I need more.

I winced, realizing to whom I was talking. "Sorry, Jack—before your time. JFK, Jr. was the famously good-looking son of a famously charismatic president who was assassinated in 1963, an event that gave their family legendary status in America ever since. The son died in a tragic small-plane accident—"

Collision?

"No, he wasn't instrument rated, but he tried to fly through overcast skies at night anyway. Refused to change plans even though he got a late start and the weather warned of visibility problems. Apparently, he lost his bearings and flew right into the ocean."

Got it. He's what we'd call a victim of the carefree, careless class. They like to roll the dice, take their risks, for an entirely different reason than the street punk, but fate often gives them the same outcome.

I sighed. "Well it was a national tragedy, I can tell you. JFK, Jr. was a charismatic young man, and the country loved him almost as much as his father . . . It looks to me like Easterbrook has the same features as the late president's late son, who was very popular with the ladies, too, by the way. Easterbrook's also engaged to Kiki now," I noted. "And Kiki is apparently also my cousin, through marriage, but let's not go there—"

You may not want to go there, doll, because it's another motive for Kiki to have killed Bethany—if she was in love with this super stud Easterbrook and wanted him for herself. Did you see Easterbrook at the reading?

"No. But it doesn't mean he couldn't have been around Quindicott." I flipped another page. "Another of the circle Angel mentions is a young woman, Georgette LaPomeret, but she committed suicide after this book was published."

Next.

"There's a young man named Hal McConnell." The photo of Hal depicted a typically preppie young man in a polo shirt and khakis. Brown hair brushed neatly back, good-looking face with regular features, and hazel-green eyes. He was shown laughing with Bethany on the deck of a yacht, an almost tender expression of affection on his face. "I didn't see him around either."

What's his motive?

"I do believe he was in love with Bethany. Unrequited." I looked down at the book again to find I'd reached the end of the photo section. "That's it."

What about the little girl who blew a gasket at the big show?

"You mean Victoria Banks? Bethany's little sister."

Hold the phone. That little girl was Bethany's little sister?

"Yes . . . Oh! And I forgot to tell you, I learned from Officer Eddie Franzetti, on the way to Fiona's, that Victoria Banks's friends reported her missing around midnight. She'd left their motel room for a soda and never came back."

Is Banks, the younger, in that book?

I flipped through the book some more, went to the index. "No. Nothing on Victoria Banks. What makes you think she might have killed Angel?"

You're kidding, right? Angel smeared her late sister's name in that book you're holding, revealed all kinds of trash. And Victoria threatened Angel in public. You heard her yourself, sweetcheeks.

"Don't call me that."

Why not? You've got nothing to be ashamed of, baby—they're a luscious pair. Aces.

Despite my having been exposed to Jack for some time, my face flamed. "Stop it, Jack."

Male laughter filled my head and I felt the room's cool air grow icy for a moment, enough to raise goosebumps. The ghost was playing with me again. "Jack. Stop it."

He laughed once more, but the chill receded.

Okay, Miss Priss, he finally said. *Set me straight, then. What's your big theory on the Banks girl?*

"Just that Victoria's public threat is exactly why I wouldn't put her at the top of the suspect list. Too many

witnesses to her threats. How stupid would she have to be
to carry out a murder right on the heels of it?"

*Maybe she didn't care. You're forgetting about someone
trying to run Angel down right on the street out front. It
could have been Victoria and her friends. Don't you see?
She could have killed Angel and fled. That's why she's
missing.*

"But you said that the person who killed Angel also
killed Bethany, and Victoria didn't kill her own sister."

*First of all, you don't know Victoria Banks well enough
to say that. Second of all, Victoria's murder of Angel also
set up Johnny as the fall guy. If Johnny did kill Bethany,
then wouldn't that be the perfect revenge—to set him up
with a second chance to be convicted of a second murder
while getting rid of the dame that's dragging your late sister's rep through the mud?*

"I'll grant you that the theory holds water . . . but Victoria looked too small and frail to have strangled Angel by
herself."

*Listen and learn, doll. One thing this business teaches
you is, don't rule out anyone based on size or appearance
or the perception that they're ever too smart or too dumb to
inflict the big chill. Everybody who's sucked in a breath
and let it out again is capable of murder, given the right set
of circumstances, and rage has been known to send every
rational thought out of people's heads—that's what a
crime of passion is. Victoria Banks might be young and
delicate looking, but there wasn't much to Angel, either.
Little Vicky may have had her friends help her, too. On the
other hand, she may have done the deed alone. She had a
loud mouth and a hot temper last night. And, in my experience, mousy exteriors can hide a lot of rat.*

For some reason, I thought of Mina, but I didn't like the
thought—

Of course you don't. She's been a good employee and

*never gave you a second to doubt her . . . but you wouldn't
be a decent dick if you didn't consider she had a motive.*

I sighed, remembering the look of hurt and anger on her
face the night before when Angel had thrown herself at
Johnny, the way she'd violently tossed around those event
room chairs after they'd gone off together. Could she have
confronted Angel after Johnny had stood her up?

Her roommate picked her up, Jack pointed out. *So if she
confronted Angel, then her roomie probably drove her to
the scene to do it. Easy enough to check out. Unless roomie
is sworn to secrecy.*

"Speaking of secrets," I said, continuing to fill the handcart with books. "I wish I knew what Bud and Sadie were
talking about. They've been at it since we got back."

*I got an earful, baby. It's personal stuff. The old man's
telling your auntie about his wife's death from cancer a
couple of years back, and how he was glad to help out
Johnny. He was telling how much he liked the kid and how
he can't believe Johnny's guilty. Mostly, I think the old guy
is feeling lost and betrayed and alone. Little Sadie's helping him through it just fine . . . I suspect the old girl's got
the eye for Bud, by the way.*

"Bud's a good man . . . but I think you're mistaken.
They're just friends. So what's my next move?"

That's easy. Let the cops handle it.

"I can't do that, Jack. I'm worried about too many peo-
ple here. If Johnny's guilty, I want to know it—as much for
Mina's safety as every other young woman in this town.
And if he's not guilty then I want to help the kid—for
Bud's sake."

*Baby, listen to me. You want to fit yourself with my fe-
dora, but you haven't learned the angles, not by a long shot.*

"Okay, fine. I haven't learned the angles. So you can
teach me along the way. You can help me prove Johnny did
it—or find the real killer."

There was a long silence. The room, which had been comfortably cool, was slowly becoming warm and stuffy again. I felt Jack's presence receding.

"Jack? Don't leave me. Come on! You can consider it a pastime. Helping me solve another murder has *got* to be more interesting than watching a sluggish parade of over-heated customers make their beach reading selections."

The silence was interminable.

"Jack? *Listen.* I'm going to do it anyway—with or without you."

Finally, the room cooled again. I felt a whisper of a breeze against my cheek.

One condition, he growled in my head.

"Name it."

Read my files. Starting with the one marked "Stendall."

"Fine. Okay, after I . . ."

NOW.

I jumped. "Okay, okay, calm down . . ." I swallowed nervously, hating that Jack's haunting temper could still rattle me and walked over to the files—eight boxes of them. I lifted the top off the first, hoping to find some part of the alphabet, the M's through the O's or the T's through the W's. But the files weren't alphabetical.

"Talbot, Lionetti, Hague, Zika, Walters, Karpinsky," I recited, reading the typewritten labels on the dusty beige folders. "You've got to be kidding me. Jack, what was your filing system?"

Alphabetical, sweetheart. Two things I prided myself on when I was alive—an organized mind and an organized office.

"But these *aren't* alphabetical. They're a big mess is what they are."

And they're not the way I left them. What did you expect after fifty years of the biggest a-hole in the world pawing through them, stealing my life to create his best-sellers. And from what I remember about the louse, Timothy Bren-

nan was cheap as a dime store kazoo and orderly as a ty-
phoon. This proves the latter.

With a sigh, I pawed through the first box, then placed
the lid back on it and went to the second. I finally found it
in the fourth box I opened.

"Stendall! Found it!"

Bravo, baby.

As I pulled the folder free of its dusty confines, a tremendous sneeze shook me, and I nearly dropped the file. In the
process, I felt something slip out and fall to the floor with a
ding.

"What fell?" I muttered, looking around my feet. The
wink of silver caught my eye and I bent down to pick up
the coin. "It's a nickel . . ."

A buffalo nickel, to be precise—a coin minted only from
1913 to 1938, after which it was replaced with the Jeffer-
son nickel. Seymour Tarnish had excitedly brought one in a
few months back after one of his ice cream truck customers had passed it to him without noticing.

The profile of a rugged, dignified American Indian's
head was engraved on one side with the word *Liberty* and
the year 1937. I remembered Seymour saying that the artist
based his image on a composite of three models: Iron Tail,
Two Moons, and Chief John Big Tree. The reverse side displayed an American bison in the center of the coin, *United
States of America* arced over the bison's head, and *Five
Cents* stretched beneath its hooves.

"Jack?" I whispered, running my fingers over the old
coin. "Was this yours?"

"Yeah, baby."

With my eyes still fixed on the engraved buffalo, I slowly
realized that Jack's answer hadn't been in my head. The
ghost's voice, for the first time since I'd initially heard it almost a year ago, sounded as if it had been projected from
two feet in front of me. Perplexed, I lifted my eyes—and
gasped.

"Jack . . . ," I rasped, "I can . . . see you . . ."

"You've seen me before," he pointed out.

"But not . . . like this . . ."

Over the past year, I'd seen Jack Shepard in my dreams mostly, or in the black-and-white photo on the flap of Timothy Brennan's Jack Shield books. On very rare occasions, I thought I'd glimpsed him in other ways—as a silhouette or shadow, but nothing more than a flickering blink. This time, Jack appeared before me as real and solid as the stacked brown boxes around me in this storage room.

He was tall, over six feet, and his powerful form was draped in a gunmetal-gray double-breasted suit that rose in a V from his narrow waist to his acre of shoulders. Beneath his fedora, his forehead was broad with brows the color of wet sand; his nose like a boxer's—slightly crooked with a broken-a-few-times bump. His jaw was iron, his chin flat and square—with a one-inch scar in the shape of a dagger slashing across it. And his eyes were the most intensely piercing gray I'd ever seen.

He blinked at me, then pushed up the brim of his hat with one finger. A tiny smile touched his lips. "Take it easy, baby. You look like you're ready to kiss concrete."

I swallowed. My mouth was suddenly filled with cotton balls. "Yes . . . I do feel a bit . . . shaky . . ." I turned away, went to the old wooden desk, and sat down, placing the nickel carefully on the desktop to wipe off my suddenly sweaty palms. I spun the chair to face Jack again—but he was gone.

"Jack?"

"Pen! . . . Penelope?"

The voice was male, but it wasn't Jack's. And it was coming from down the hall.

"Bud?" I croaked, seeing Bud Napp pop his head into the storage room. The space had become warm and stuffy again. My throat was still dry, my heart still pounding like a carpenter working overtime.

"I'm about to head out, but Chief Ciders is pulling up. Sadie wanted me to let you know. He's probably here for Mina's statement."

I nodded. "Thanks. I'll be right there."

Bud left, and I rose on unsteady legs. I crossed the room to pick up the Stendall file, placed it on the handcart, and rolled it into the hallway. Before I snapped off the light, I remembered the buffalo nickel. I went to the desk, picked it up, and shoved it into the front pocket of my khaki pants.

"Jack?" I called again. But he was gone.

CHAPTER 14

The Little Sister

"Mind your own business about my sister Leila," she spit at me. "You leave my sister Leila out of your dirty remarks."

"Which dirty remarks?" I asked. "Or should I try to guess?"

—Raymond Chandler, *The Long Goodbye*, 1949

WHEN I ARRIVED on the selling floor, I saw Sadie had taken over the register. Mina stood by the new-release table, wringing her hands as she peered at Chief Ciders speaking to Bud on the sidewalk.

I rolled the handcart up to Mina and asked her to help me arrange the titles—a task I'd hoped would get her mind off what was to come. Within five minutes, however, the bell over the front door tinkled and Chief Ciders came swaggering in.

"Mina Griffiths," he called.

The pale, freckle-faced girl seemed to go even paler.

"Take it easy, Mina," I said softly. "He's just going to ask you a few questions."

"You know why I'm here?" asked Ciders, striding up to her.

"Yes," said Mina.

"You want to come to the station to talk to me about Johnny or answer my questions here?" asked Ciders.

"There's no need for Mina to have to go to the station, Chief," I interjected.

"That's right," agreed Sadie, rushing up like a mother hen. "There's plenty of privacy in the Community Events room. You can talk to Mina in there."

"I'll take care of it," I told Sadie. "You cover the register." Sadie nodded and I led the way into the adjoining room, set up two folding chairs, and gestured for Mina and the Chief to sit down.

I took my place, standing behind Mina, and the Chief looked at me the same way he had back at the Finch Inn— like a wad of chewing tobacco had just gotten stuck in his esophagus.

"You can go now, Mrs. McClure."

"Oh . . . um . . . but couldn't I stick around?" I threw a worried glance at Mina.

"No," barked Ciders. "Please give us some privacy."

"Oh, okay . . ." I sighed. At least he'd said *please*, I thought, feeling my spine stiffen. I spun on my heel, but then slowed my movements and drifted ever so languidly toward the archway that led to the main store. I lingered there, trying to eavesdrop. Unfortunately, there was nothing to hear. When I turned around again, I found the Chief squinting at me with open hostility.

"Mrs. McClure, you've already given me your statement. If you don't leave the *premises*, I *will* have to take Mina to the station—"

"No, don't do that," I said. "I'll go. I just have to get my purse and car keys upstairs, okay? It'll take a few minutes."

"Fine, you do that."

Cursing silently, I snagged the Stendall file before ascending the stairs. Then I dropped the file on my bed and grabbed my purse and car keys. I told Sadie I'd be back in an hour and, in the words of Chief Ciders, left the premises.

A brand-new All Things Bed & Beautiful superstore had opened recently on the highway and I had yet to check it out. I decided to spend an hour away from "the premises" there. We needed a new shower curtain, Spencer would love a set of Spider-Man sheets, and I hadn't been able to find imported English lavender shampoo since I'd left Manhattan. If the superstore carried it, I'd probably indulge myself with one bottle of the obscenely expensive product—if only to use as a once-a-week treat for the next six months.

Behind the wheel of my used blue Saturn, I powered down the windows to enjoy the warm summer day. I drove along Cranberry, past the outlying suburbs, and through the thick Quindicott woods where an occasional clearing would reveal a small farm. The radio, which would normally be blaring Radio Disney's hip-hop "light" for Spencer's amusement, stayed off as I tried to consider Johnny Napp and whether or not he was capable of murder.

I came to the highway on-ramp and joined the relatively sparse traffic pattern. The thick Quindicott woods flanked the four-lane road. Oaks, pines, and maples flew by as I sped along. After a few miles, I noticed the sunset-orange Comfy-Time Motel sign looming up ahead and got to thinking about what Eddie Franzetti had said—that Victoria Banks and her friends had been staying there last night when Victoria disappeared.

"Jack thinks Victoria had a strong motive to kill Angel," I muttered. "Which I suppose she does . . . especially if she thinks Johnny killed her sister and got away with it. She could have killed Angel out of spite and revenge and simultaneously set up Johnny as the killer . . . the perfect crime . . . *if* she gets away with it . . ."

As I considered that maybe Victoria's two friends were still at the motel, my heart beat a little faster, and my foot pressed a little harder on the gas pedal. "I'm sure if Jack were here, he'd have me stop," I continued to mutter. "I mean, what harm could it do to check out the parking lot for a black Jag with a blue and white bumper sticker?"

Good idea, baby.

I jammed on the brakes and swerved to the shoulder. A surprised driver laid on the horn behind me.

"God in heaven! Jack?! Is that you?"

It ain't the Easter Bunny.

I exhaled, my hands shaking as if I'd just been spooked. Then I realized—I *had.*

"I don't understand!" I cried, automatically searching the empty confines of my Saturn. "I'm not in the bookstore, I never heard you outside the bookstore—you said you couldn't leave the bookstore!?"

Ya got me, doll. All I know is I was back there, bored to tears with Ciders's less than ingenious questioning of freckle-face, thinking about what you'd have to say about it, and suddenly I'm in your head again . . . but this isn't exactly like the store . . . something's different . . . I can't explain it worth a plugged nickel.

"Nickel . . . Jack . . . the buffalo nickel from your files." I reached into my pants pocket and pulled out the dull silver coin, running my thumb along the grooves of the engraved bison. "You must be attached to it somehow . . . either that or you're still trapped in the store and you're . . . I don't know, *transmitting* through it, like some kind of cosmic cell phone."

Your chatter sounds crazy to my ears, doll: but then I used to think this whole life-after-death thing was a coffee-and-doughnuts grift. I'd always trucked with Harry Houdini on

that score: ghosts were just a carnival racket. I'd say this
whole spirit thing was a buffalo, too . . . if it weren't me
who ended up the spirit . . .

I gathered my wits and pulled back on the highway, then
quickly turned off again into the paved parking area of the
newly built Comfy-Time Motel. The place was part of a
national chain of budget lodgings that provided clean, af-
fordable rooms for travelers—just the sort of place you'd
find on a highway outside of Anytown, U.S.A., its design
and décor exactly the same whether you were standing under the blistering sun of Albuquerque, New Mexico, or the
threatening snow clouds of Erie, Pennsylvania.

The white-and-orange-trimmed structure was basically
U-shaped with an office at the bottom of the U, breaking the
wings in half. There was parking on the outsides of the U,
and a large swimming pool tucked between the wings. The
model of stark, modern efficiency, the Comfy-Time was the
antithesis of the charming and eccentric Queen Anne Victorian that was the Finch Inn, which is why I hoped its exis-
tence wouldn't hurt Fiona and Barney's business.

I coasted slowly around the lot, squinting at the parked
cars in the bright afternoon sun. I counted only seven. That
was good news for Fiona and Barney—not many guests—
but bad news for me. Most of the cars were American
made: a red Buick; two Ford pickups, one green and one
blue; a beige Chevy van; and two SUVs, both white. No
black Jaguar. The only black car in the lot was an Audi.

"Dead end," I muttered.

Hey, baby, watch your language.

"No offense. I'm just disappointed there's no black Jag."

Doesn't matter. You're not done here. That postal worker
character, Seymour, said he'd seen Victoria Banks and her
friends drive away in a black sedan after last night's read-
ing. You've got a black sedan right in front of you, and now
that I'm here, I'm curious. Victoria's friends might still be
checked in.

"But that black Audi might not be their car," I pointed out.

Only one way to find out, said Jack. *Park and ask.*

I was a little nervous about doing just that, but I found myself cutting the engine nonetheless. As I swung open the door and stepped onto the hot, gray pavement, I tried to reassure myself that with Jack in my head advising me, I could handle a little snooping.

Don't worry, baby, cooed Jack. *Bracing a couple of co-eds will be a piece o' cake.*

"Are you crazy? I'm just going to the office to ask if Victoria Banks and her friends are still checked in. I'm not about to *brace* anybody."

We'll see.

The motel had two stories, with second-floor access via a second-floor walkway that ran completely around the entire structure. The rooms lined both the top and ground floor, and each had an outside door, painted orange, and a tiny window with a white shade. Rooms on the outside of the U faced the paved parking lot and the thick woods beyond. Inside, guests looked out at the pool.

I was about to head for the office when I recognized one of the young women who'd escorted Victoria out of my store last night. The pale woman was obviously coming back from the pool, her flip-flops clip-clapping along the concrete sidewalk under the eaves on the ground floor of the motel. Her curly red hair was wet and slicked back, and a big white motel bath towel modestly circled her hips—though the powder-blue string-bikini top she was wearing left little to the imagination.

You can say that again!

"Be quiet, Jack."

That legal, what she's wearing?

"Yes. And I hope she keeps that towel around her hips because I'm betting that bikini has a thong bottom."

And a thong is?

"Uh . . . let's just say you'd think it was indecent."

You don't say? Well, it looks like I've finally come across something I like about your century.

"Excuse me," I called, hurrying to catch up to the young woman. "Aren't you a friend of Victoria Banks?"

The girl stopped, key in one hand, the other one grasping a doorknob to room 18. At the sound of my voice, she turned and squinted in my direction.

"Are you . . . calling me?" she asked, eyes unfocused. "I'm not wearing my glasses."

By then I was at her side. "Yes," I replied. "I'd like to ask you some questions . . . about Victoria."

"Oh, I don't know if I can answer them," was her suddenly guarded reply.

Just then the door to the motel room opened from the inside, and I saw angry dark eyes peering out from the gloomy interior. It was the raven-haired woman with the pierced lip, the one who practically threw me against the wall and called both me and Angel Stark a bitch last night at Buy the Book.

"Who are you and what do you want?" the young woman demanded.

I was glad she didn't recognize me. But I wasn't surprised. She'd only glimpsed me for a second the day before, and I had looked much different in my businesslike pantsuit and contact lenses and with my hair in a tight French twist. Today my green eyes were behind black-framed glasses, my shoulder-length auburn hair was down, and my attire of khaki pants and white cotton blouse was much more casual.

"The police were already here, and we told them everything we know," continued the raven-haired girl.

Come down fast and hard, Jack barked in my head. *She's pushing. You push back. Wedge your body into the room so she can't shut you out—*

"No." I silently told Jack. "I've got an angle. Let's try it my way." Then, in a gentle voice, I told the two coeds, "I'm not from the police. I just want to ask a few questions—"

The raven-haired girl cut me off. "Then you must be a reporter. Go away!" She grabbed her friend's arm, dragged the girl into the motel room, and slammed the door in my face.

I stood there, dumbfounded.

Say, baby . . . your way didn't exactly work like a charm, did it?

I sighed.

Want some pointers?

I sighed again.

Make like you're leaving. Get in your car and drive toward the exit.

I did. The end of the motel drive and entrance to the highway was just ahead. "Now what? Forget the interrogation and go for the Spider-Man sheets?"

No. Turn around and drive all the way around the motel, pull up close enough to spy on their door but not so close that they can spot your car.

I followed Jack's directions. *Now what?*

Now wait.

"For what?"

For the door to open . . .

I waited five minutes. Ten. Fifteen. It wasn't all that bad actually. Jack kept me entertained with a long story about a bookie and a call girl. After about twenty minutes of suppressing blushes, I noticed the girls' motel room door open. The raven-haired coed with the pierced lip strode out in denim shorts and a black tank top. She walked toward the office.

Go, now, baby. Knock on that door and try your little spiel again. Curly's inside and she's the softer touch . . .

I knocked, expecting the girl inside to ignore me, but to my surprise, she slowly cracked the door.

"I'm here to help, please give me a chance to explain," I quickly said. "I'm a member of the Quindicott Business

Owners Association, and I'm here to express our community's concern over the news that your friend is missing and to see if there's anything at all we can do to help you find her."

Through her small, frameless, rectangular glasses—which looked exactly like the two-thousand-dollar pair I saw in a Newport boutique window two months ago but could in no way afford—the redhead looked at me with wide eyes. "Oh . . . so, you're not a reporter or anything?"

"No. I'm not. See no notebook, no recorder"—I spread my empty hands—"and I'm all alone."

If you don't count me.

"Jack," I silently warned. "Stop cracking wise."

The door slowly opened all the way, and I stepped through. Because of the strong sunlight, it took me a few seconds to adjust to the darkness of the room.

"My name is Penelope Thornton-McClure," I said, reaching out.

Hearing my name, the young woman's expression seemed to relax a bit. It made sense. The McClure name was well enough known among the well-heeled set. Likely as not, this girl had gone to boarding school with one of Calvin's cousins.

She shook my proffered hand. "Courtney Peyton Taylor," she said. She'd changed from her bikini into a small white T-shirt and paisley pink capri pants.

I smiled and she offered me a chair. The room was gloomy and untidy, one of the beds still unmade, as if someone had just gotten up. Courtney walked to the window and opened the blinds, dispelling some of the darkness. I was about to begin asking some questions when I heard the sound of approaching steps. Angry Girl had returned with a bucket of ice—and a vengeance.

"What the hell is this!" screeched the young woman, barreling toward me.

"Stephanie, will you take it easy!" cried Courtney.

"No!" She turned on her friend. "Why did you let her in?!"

"She's *not* a reporter," said Courtney.

Stephanie narrowed her black eyes. "What is she then? And why is she here?"

"The Quindicott Business Owners Association wants to help locate your missing friend," I told her. "We feel terrible that this happened in our town, but we have all sorts of resources at our disposal."

"Oh," said Stephanie. A few seconds later, she seemed to physically deflate. With a sigh, she set the bucket of ice on a nightstand and fished into her pocked for an elastic hair band from her denim shorts. "What sort of resources?"

"Well, we can distribute flyers with Victoria's picture, for instance," I explained as Stephanie violently pulled her short black hair into a tight ponytail. "We can canvass the surrounding areas, contact other businesses in nearby communities. We can even mount a search party if necessary."

I wasn't lying to these women. Members of our Business Owners Association had done these very things last year, when Milner Logan's rottweiler broke free of his leash and wandered off. Bruno was eventually located by sunbathers while chasing sea gulls along Ponsert Beach five miles away, and the happy couple was eventually reunited.

"I'm sure we can help, Ms . . . ?"

"Usher. Stephanie Usher."

Courtney looked at me with hopeful eyes, while Stephanie sunk down on the unmade bed.

You got 'em, doll, good work. Now start the real questions. Just get 'em to spill whatever they've got—exactly when and how Victoria vanished. What her thinking was when she came to your store yesterday . . . anything and everything . . .

"What I need to know is when Victoria vanished, and under what circumstances—"

"We already told the police everything," said Stephanie.

"I understand that," I replied evenly. "But we can't help you if we don't know all the facts. Why were you in town, for instance?"

Stephanie flopped backward until she sprawled across the bed. "It wasn't my idea," she grunted.

I faced Courtney.

"We came to attend Angel Stark's reading at the local bookstore," Courtney explained, one eye on her friend.

"Oh," I replied, feigning surprise. "So you're fans of the author?"

"Ha!" Stephanie cried. "Not hardly. I'd like to kill that bitch."

I silently queried Jack. "Did you hear that?!"

Cool your heels, doll. There's a big difference between an expression and a confession.

"Angel Stark's book . . . mentions Victoria's family," Courtney added. "Victoria was very upset by some of the things written in that book."

"So Victoria came here to confront Ms. Stark?" I pressed.

"Oh, no," Courtney replied.

"Hell, yeah!" said Stephanie, sitting up again. "You wouldn't believe the things that money-grubbing hack bitch said about Victoria's family, her dead sister. Hateful things. Libelous things. Vicky loved her big sister. That stuff made her sick."

"But why confront the author in public like that?" I asked. "Aren't there other ways—attorneys, lawsuits? The Banks are an influential family. Surely they have resources."

Stephanie sneered again. "Her parents didn't want to get involved. They're in denial, like it's just a bad dream. They think if they sue it will just give Angel more publicity. So they're hiding in Europe for the summer, and probably the fall, too, assuming it will all just go away—blow over by Christmas."

"Tell-all books like this usually do," I pointed out.

"That's what I said," Courtney cried, looking not at me but at her friend. "But Victoria couldn't sit still for it—"

"I don't blame her," Stephanie said. "Her parents might be too caught up in 'how things look' to fight Angel, but she isn't."

"Was Victoria upset enough to . . . try something . . . I don't know . . . desperate?" I asked carefully.

"Like what?" asked Courtney.

I shrugged. "Like maybe *hurt* Angel in some way . . . physically."

Keep your eyes open, baby, advised Jack.

Stephanie and Courtney exchanged a look.

"They know something," I silently told Jack.

Or suspect something. You notice they haven't denied the possibility.

"She's been pretty upset since Angel's book came out two weeks ago," Courtney finally replied. "She got real secretive, too. Kept getting late-night phone calls on her cell—wouldn't tell us who it was that was calling her though, and we usually shared everything. I also think she was e-mailing Angel . . . threatening her."

Stephanie was frowning at Courtney, like she wasn't too happy the girl was continuing to talk.

"Did Victoria receive any calls last night, before she vanished?" I asked, returning to the missing persons line of questioning.

"She got a few while we were at the bookstore," said Courtney, "but she didn't check her messages until we got back here. I don't know who called her and she didn't tell us."

"Is her cell phone here in the room?" I asked hopefully, even though I was sure the police would have impounded it.

"It's not," said Stephanie. "Victoria took it with her when she went out last night. Said she wanted to get a soda from the vending machine and make a call."

Courtney gave Stephanie a sidelong glance and added, "She probably wanted some privacy . . ."

"This was what time?" I asked.

"A little after midnight," said Courtney.

"I think it was closer to one a.m.," said Stephanie.

"So she stepped out for a soda and you think to place a private call and then you never saw her again?"

Both women silently nodded their heads.

"Have the police searched the area?" I asked.

"Oh, yes," Courtney replied. "That one policeman—the cute one, Officer Falconetti—"

Franzetti, I thought, but didn't correct her.

"—he searched the whole place, the swimming pool, the laundry room, looked around the parking lot and the woods, talked to the people in the motel office and all the guests. He even had the motel people let him search every empty room, but he didn't find anything he said looked out of the ordinary."

"The cop also said that because she was an adult, they still had to follow up on all known addresses and confirm she was really a missing person," added Stephanie.

"Officer Falconetti did say he'd take a photo of her and send it to the State Police," noted Courtney, "so they could put out a bulletin . . . I gave him one I took of Victoria last week . . . I'm sorry I don't have another to give you for the flyers."

"Oh, that's okay," I said. "We can talk to the police and work something out." Then I rose. "Well, thank you for all of your help . . . Will you be staying in town much longer?"

Stephanie's face was set. "I'm not leaving without Victoria."

I walked to the door, then paused. "One more thing. Is it possible Victoria simply went back home to Newport or somewhere else without telling either of you?"

"Not unless she hitchhiked," Stephanie said. "She left

her purse here, along with her wallet—the police took them, though."

Courtney nodded in agreement. "Victoria can't drive, and Stephanie's license is suspended. I'm the only one with a valid driver's license. We came up together, in my Audi. It's still parked outside."

I peered through the window. "The black one?"

Courtney nodded.

"Well, thank you for your time . . . We'll be in touch," I said as I slipped out the door. I left Stephanie with her perpetual sneer in place, and Courtney's doe-eyes imploring me to use all of my resources to find her friend.

And I would. Not just for their sakes, or Victoria's, but for Johnny's, Bud's, and Mina's.

Where you going, doll? said Jack as I began walking toward my car.

"I'm leaving," I replied.

Oh, no you're not. You haven't given the place the up-and-down.

"The what?"

You haven't cased the joint, baby.

"Cased the joint? You've got to be kidding. The police already searched the area."

Jack laughed.

"Why are you laughing? What do you expect me to find?"

That's easy, doll. You'll find what they didn't.

CHAPTER 15

Guesswork

.

Some time ago I read in a New York paper that fifty or sixty college graduates had been appointed to the metropolitan police force. . . . The news astonished me, for in my reportorial days, there was simply no such thing in America as a book-learned cop. . . .

—H. L. Mencken, 1942

I FOUND THE vending area easily enough. A short stroll past a dozen motel room doors took me to a recessed area under a wide orange-and-white striped awning that reminded me of the sherbet swirl bars Seymour sold out of his ice cream truck. I heard a humming before I turned the corner—but I rounded it so quickly, I walked right into seven feet of metal.

"Dammit!"

Whoa, baby, are you all right? What is that thing you just head-butted? asked Jack in my head.

"An ice machine."

Excuse me?

"You've never heard of an ice machine? You just press the handle and freshly made ice comes tumbling out of a chute."

The hell you say? I know a few bartenders would have loved that in their joints.

Next to the ice machine was a soft drink dispenser. "Five varieties," I murmured, "Coke, diet Coke, iced tea, apple juice, and bottled water."

Jack made a sigh of disgust. *Bottled water,* he muttered.

"Not again, Jack." We'd had this discussion more times than I could count.

Really, baby, how much are they charging this time to resell you what's free at every public drinking fountain?

"Let's see . . . a dollar twenty-five."

The biggest grift of your time yet.

Ignoring Jack, I continued to glance around. No food dispenser, no change machine, just a sign warning that the vending area was only for use by guests of the Comfy-Time Motel.

There wasn't much to see beyond that. Smooth concrete floor mostly covered by a thick rubber mat so the customers didn't call any slip-and-fall lawyers. There were also blobs of half-melted ice on the ground.

"The ice must come tumbling out so fast it sometimes misses the bucket," I guessed.

Well, don't you miss the bucket. You've got plenty of swift, so start casing the area.

"There's nothing to case, but whatever you say," I muttered, then bent low, trying to avoid contact with the melting ice on the rubber matting as I searched under the equipment for . . . what? I didn't know.

A grill blocked any object larger than a dust mote from tumbling under the ice machine, but the soda dispenser was jacked up on three-inch legs. I saw dirt, gum wrappers, and bottle caps underneath. Far, far in the back, almost to the wall, a quarter twinkled. From its silvery gleam amid the filth, I deduced it had rolled there recently.

I rose and crossed the sidewalk. There was a three-inch drop from the paved concrete to a narrow swath of earth. On the ground I saw an outline of what looked to me like Eddie Franzetti's size-twelve boot .

"If there was anything to be found here, Officer Franzetti found it," I told Jack.

Don't count on it. Buttons like him are aces when it comes to getting cats out of trees or grifting speeders, but as a rule, small-town copper's don't get enough action to stay sharp where the detection racket goes.

"But there's nothing here, Jack. Absolutely nothing."

After a long silence, Jack spoke.

Have you forgotten my advice, back when you needed a wise head?

I was hot, and not a little exasperated when I snapped back. "You make a lot of suggestions, Jack. Which one are you talking about?"

The one that netted you that goose who was wrecking your inventory list.

"I remember."

A few months before, I was convinced our bookstore was being ripped off by a persistent and selective shoplifter. At that time, titles I should have had on hand kept disappearing, even though their ISBNs never turned up on daily sales summaries. Once in a while a missing book would magically reappear.

Think like a derrick, doll-face, Jack had advised. *Ask yourself what kind of mug would snatch-and-grab, and why. Then put yourself into the grifter's head.*

As things turned out, Jack's advice was sound. By

thinking like the "grifter" I tried to figure out what logic there was behind stealing a book, then returning it—thereby risking getting caught twice. Finally it occurred to me that I might not be getting robbed at all. Instead, I began to suspect that some financially strapped reader was hiding a particular title among the stacks until he or she could return to the store and finish reading it. When they were done, they replaced the title right where it belonged—which explained why the title would reappear as mysteriously as it had vanished.

A close review of the shelves one evening revealed the guilty party's hiding place: I'd discovered a new John Grisham hardcover tucked between the Yankee cookbooks, of which I kept a small collection, right next to the regional travel books I stocked for tourists passing through the area. Inside the book, the page was marked with a folded scrap of paper.

I placed the book back—with a small note written on the paper, telling the reader that he or she was causing me to worry about inventory and I would consider a solution to his or her book-buying difficulties if he or she would just step forward and identify him or herself.

A few days later, a widow from Pendleton Street approached me with red cheeks. "I got your note, dear. I'm terribly sorry if I caused you any difficulties."

Eighty-two-year-old Ellie Brewster quietly admitted she was reading our hot new bestsellers a little at a time, in our Shaker rockers, without buying them or removing them from the premises.

I quickly assured her that she had every right in the world to do that, considering the way we'd set up the store. But I'd much rather give her a chance to take the book home with her. Since she was on a fixed income, and our public library always had an endless waiting list for only two or three copies, we struck a bargain. She would buy the book, take it home with her, and bring it back whenever she liked, and I would buy it back from her when she was finished with it. If it was in good enough condition, I would pay her almost the entire cover price—if not, I'd pay her at least half. Then I'd resell the book as gently used.

We shook, and our problem—mine and hers—was solved that afternoon. Not only that, she came the following week with a proposal on setting up a revolving lending library at the Peddleton Street Assisted Community Living Home, where she now lived. After speaking with the management there, we came up with a financial plan that wouldn't break their budget, but would still allow the elderly, especially those who couldn't easily leave the premises, a chance to read the hot new books.

Adopting Jack's technique now, I tried to put myself into the mind of Victoria Banks—a young college coed, sheltered most of her life, who was forced to face the harshest of realities when her beloved older sister was murdered, the perpetrator still unknown, or, if it was Johnny, set free on legal technicalities. As if that weren't enough misery, along comes a Kitty Kelly clone in Betsy Johnson chic, revealing her sister's skeletons.

Under the stress of grief and anger, a person could easily make many missteps and bad decisions—like confronting Angel Stark in a very public setting. As the bad incidents mount up, petty annoyances take on global significance. A hangnail can reduce the person to tears, focus becomes difficult, the person gets clumsy—maybe drops a quarter under the machine instead of in the slot, or even . . .

I dipped my hand into my right-hand pocket (my left-hand pocket held the buffalo nickel, and I wasn't parting with that for anything). After drawing out the proper amount of change, I began dropping coins into the vending machine slot.

Now you're thinking like a shamus, babe, said Jack.

"Thanks . . ." I smiled and pressed the button for a bottled water CHOOSE ANOTHER SELECTION appeared in red letters on the digital display. I pressed another button, then *all* the buttons—with the same result. The machine was empty. I punched the coin return and my change spilled with such force that a quarter popped out of the return chute, bounced onto the rubber mat, and rolled under the machine—taking its place right next to the gleaming quarter I'd spied a minute earlier.

"This vending machine is empty," I told Jack. "Victoria Banks had to find another!"

I hurried up the stairs to the second level, then followed the signs along the second-floor walkway until I found another ice machine and soda dispenser. A hand-scrawled OUT OF ORDER sign was taped to the beverage machine, the coin slot sealed with a strip of duct tape.

Any more machines?

"Let's see . . ."

I went back down the steps to the ground floor and found a third vending area all the way around the facility, on the opposite wing of the motel. The motel was mostly empty and just one car was parked on this side of the building. I dropped coins into the slot of the soda machine and out tumbled an ice-cold bottle of Moose Hill Spring Water.

Okay, so we know the vanished vixen likely ended up here, said Jack.

"I think you're right."

I bent low and stared under the machine. In the far corner I spied a silver oval the size of a makeup compact.

"Jack, I see something!"

Beautiful, doll.

"I can't get it . . ." I searched for something to extend my reach. In the end, I had to cross the narrow strip of parking lot and head along a dirt path that led into a wooded area beyond.

Under the canopy of trees, it was shady, quiet, and at least ten degrees cooler. Bugs buzzed in front of my face as I glanced around. The single path I was on stopped at the juncture of a tall oak where a metal "Private Property" sign, white with rusted edges, hung lopsided on one nail. The path split into a Y at that point, and the two trails veered off among the trees and brush. None seemed well-trodden, but then vegetation and rocks were strewn across the dirt paths. I found a long, sturdy twig and picked it up.

Stick in hand, I emerged from the woods into the sunlight. I crossed the parking lot and, without much trouble, snagged the oval-shaped silver object under the soda machine and dragged it into the daylight. The letters *VB* were engraved on the top of the oval.

"This must be Victoria Banks's."

What is that thing—a girly compact?

"It's a cell, Jack."

A what?

"You must have seen them advertised on TV by now. It's a wireless transmitter, kind of a non-cosmic version of your buffalo nickel."

You mean a two-way radio? We used them in Germany during the war, only that one's a helluvalot smaller. Is it military equipment?

"No, no, it's not military. It's a mobile private phone. Everyone has a cell now."

You don't.

I shrugged. "I'll get around to it, when Spencer is older and I want to keep track of him. I'll get him one, too."

So . . . Victoria Banks dropped her, uh, 'cell' without realizing it, and it somehow got innocently kicked under the soda machine. Or she struggled with someone and in the tussle it was knocked under there.

I shook my head. "I find it hard to believe she dropped it by accident when the very reason she came outside was to get a soda and place a call. I'd say it's starting to look like Angel Stark wasn't the only one who met with foul play last night."

I think you're right about that, but it doesn't necessarily follow that Victoria is an innocent. Who's to say her call wasn't to somebody who helped her do the dirty deed of offing Angel? She could have made the call as a signal to be picked up here and the cell got lost in a speedy departure. Or maybe she hired someone to give Angel that tight necktie and things went south after that—like maybe the hired gun snatched Victoria, hoping to bargain for a higher payday.

I nodded. Jack had laid out some interesting theories.

Okay, baby, he purred. *You know the next question to ask?*

"Who did she call?"

You got it. Whoever she called will have some answers.

I considered that there might be fingerprints on the phone besides Victoria's. If there were, I'd probably just smeared them while adding my own. And since the damage was done, I decided I might as well press on. I didn't own a cell and I wasn't sure how they operated. I opened the compact. A green glow illuminated the display screen, and a melodic warble told me there were messages waiting.

I attempted to check those first. The display panel told me that the last five calls all came from the same telephone number. I didn't recognize the area code—and suspected it was a cell number. I wasn't sure how to retrieve the voicemail messages. Fearing I might erase them if I did something wrong, I highlighted the phone number of the last message instead and pressed the GO option. Then I placed the cell to my ear. An answer came on the first ring.

"Jesus . . . Hello? . . . Who is this? . . . *Victoria?*—" The voice was male and ceased to speak when I did not reply.

"It's not Victoria," I said. "Ms. Banks has been reported missing by her college friends. What do you know about her disappearance?"

A long silence followed. I spoke again, softening my tone. "Since you didn't hang up, I assume you are as anxious as I am to find her."

"Who is this?" the man said again.

"I could very well ask you the same question."

"Don't get cute or I'll hang up," he threatened.

Hanging up won't get you anywhere, Jack whispered in my head.

"Hanging up won't get you anywhere," I repeated to the stranger.

"Jack, why?" I frantically asked the ghost.

You have his number. He doesn't have yours.

"I . . . I have your phone number and I can easily find out who you are. Whereas you don't have a clue who I am, only that I'm using Victoria's phone . . ."

Good, said Jack.

"What do you want? I don't have all day here." His pronunciations were perfect, not a Rhode Island dropped "r" in sight—and beneath it all, the sort of everyday, casual disdain that reminded me of my in-laws. Another member of the sheltered class, I deduced.

"I'm not the police, if that's what you're asking. The authorities are involved, however, though right now they think she might have run off for some reason, and they want more time to pass before they'll initiate a major search. But I think Victoria may be in danger."

"Just get to the point. What do you want from me?" demanded the voice on the phone.

Set up a meeting, Jack advised. *The bookstore.*

"But I don't even know *where* this person is," I told Jack. "He could be halfway around the world for all I know."

Don't start hand-wringing now, baby. Take a chance.

I swallowed my nervousness, forced my voice to sound commanding. "Listen carefully. I want you to meet me in Quindicott. I'll give you two hours. We'll meet in a public place . . ."

"Where?"

"A place called Buy the Book. A specialty bookstore on Cranberry Street, in the middle of town."

"I know the place." An unhappy sigh followed. "All right. I'll be there in two hours."

I closed my eyes in relief.

"How will I know you?" asked the man on the cell.

"You'll find me in the nonfiction section," I told him quickly. "I'll be reading a copy of Angel Stark's *All My Pretty Friends*."

I waited for a response, but the voice on the other end of the phone simply grunted in disgust, then the line went dead. With trembling hands I folded the cell phone and tucked it into my pocket.

You did good, kid. I do believe you're getting the drift of it.

But I didn't feel good. I hadn't realized how tense I felt until the phone call ended. Now my mouth was as parched as the Sahara. Mechanically, I drew the Moose Hill Spring Water I'd bought out of the soda machine dispenser and broke the seal. Then I took a long gulp, my gaze automatically wandering across the parking lot to the shadowy woods beyond.

Hmm, said Jack. *I guess bottled water's not a complete sham if you're five miles from a hospitable tap.*

"Why, Jack . . . I do believe you're getting the drift of it."

CHAPTER 16

Mystery Man

If it's going to be a long story, let's have a drink.

—Raymond Chandler, "Goldfish,"
Black Mask magazine, 1936

"IT'S SO DIFFICULT, all this waiting," I silently griped, pacing the nonfiction aisle of my bookstore.

Welcome to my world, sweetheart. When I was alive, waiting was the name of the P.I. game. Now that I'm dead, time is all I've got.

"I never thought of it like that," I said, suppressing a yawn.

Well, it was easier when I was breathing. If I were, I'd be easing my pain with a belt about now.

The door opened and a young man entered.

"Look . . . here comes a likely candidate."

When my aunt Sadie heard the sound of the bell over

the door, she instinctively looked up at the new customer from behind the counter, caught herself, then abruptly looked away.

Not *too* obvious.

The newcomer was in his twenties, wore summer khakis and a loose shirt, and seemed like a suitable match for the voice I'd heard over the cell phone. Before I spoke again, I raised the hardcover of *All My Pretty Friends* to my face and turned my back on Bud Napp, who lingered at the new release section trying hard to look like a customer. I didn't want Bud to think I was talking to myself—which I suppose some would say I was.

"Do you think that's him?"

Don't be a bunny, doll. That guy ain't Jasper and you know it, Jack replied, a tad impatiently I thought.

"But he's the right age."

You can't be sure of the guy's age—

"He sounded young—"

The tenor of his pipes mean nothing, sister. A voice funneled through the Ameche doesn't reveal as much as you think it does. Anyway, the square john who just walked in doesn't have enough berries to live in a swanky burb like Newport. His shoes are from hunger, and the cuffs of his pants are showing threads.

As the man passed by, my eyes lingered on his footwear. Jack was right, his shoes were worn, the heels rounded. And the cuffs of his pants were frayed, too. "Good eyes," I marveled.

I don't have eyes anymore, baby, just . . . shall we say . . . awareness?

I sighed. Whatever the identity of my mysterious stranger, he was certainly not punctual. Almost thirty minutes had passed since the scheduled rendezvous time and there was no sign of him. I made good use of the extra minutes by skimming Angel Stark's book, skipping the self-obsessed, self-indulgent passages about her feelings and her anguish in an effort to get to the meat-and-potatoes facts about the Bethany Banks murder and its aftermath.

The doorbell tinkled again and a tall, preppie young man entered, conspicuously overdressed for the weather. I knew at once he was our man.

"Jack, that's the one!"

Calm down, sister. Your heart's beating like a bangtail's hoofs. You're giving me a gin mill concussion, and I haven't even got a brain anymore.

"I recognize him, Jack, he's—"

Stop ventilating your gums. Just read your book and act nonchalant. Let him make the first move.

I didn't have to wait long. The young man glanced in my direction, caught the title of the book I had open in my hands, and our eyes met. Dropping all pretense, Henry 'Hal' McConnell—the man-boy with the lifelong unrequited crush on Bethany Banks—walked right up to me.

"You are the woman who phoned," he said in his now-familiar voice. It was not a question.

I nervously adjusted my black-framed glasses and set the book aside. I felt Bud Napp's eyes on me, saw Sadie trying hard not to stare. "Let's find a secluded spot to talk," I murmured.

His lanky frame followed me to the rear of the store, where an overstuffed armchair was mercifully vacant. I gestured for him to take the chair, but he shook his head. "You take it."

I sat down myself and Hal McConnell sat across from me in a straight-backed wooden seat he dragged from under a lamp in the corner. After plunking down and arranging himself, he offered me a withering gaze.

"You're Hal McConnell," I began.

"As you no doubt know from that piece of tripe you were reading." There was venom in his voice, a cold anger. The kind that didn't climb out of his heart to reach his eyes, which were still as flat as a wall.

"Angel Stark's book, you mean?"

He nodded. I estimated Hal McConnell to be in his early twenties. He was well-dressed for a summer Saturday, which suggested to me that I'd snagged him on his way to or from a formal appointment. His blue blazer was impeccably tailored and his buttoned-down shirt crisp and white, his silver-and-blue striped tie perfectly knotted in a snug Windsor.

His features were regular, his teeth white, his brown, wavy hair worn longish. He'd changed its style since the published photo, in which he'd brushed it away from his face. It fell forward now, which was a more attractive and trendy style, making him look more appealingly rakish. His chin was a bit weak, but his hazel-green eyes were penetrating, and the intelligence behind them was palpable. Something about him reminded me of my late husband, Calvin, and the reminder made me more than a little uncomfortable.

"Who are you and what do you want?" he asked.

I saw no point in playing it coy. "My name is Penelope Thornton-McClure. This is my store. Angel Stark spoke here last night. Then she left with a friend of mine. And now they're both . . . missing."

Angel's dental records were probably confirming her identity as I spoke those words, and the news of her death would likely hit the broadcast world any minute, but right now I thought the less said the better.

"I can imagine the kind of 'friend' you're referring to," replied Hal. "Young. Male. Buff and working-class. Not at all sophisticated—certainly not enough to see through Angel's games, her manipulations. Angel always did like to slum—for a fling."

My blood pressure rose with his insult to Johnny, or any kid like him—which is to say any kid who didn't have a trust fund and a private school blazer. It wasn't as though I hadn't encountered this attitude before—among my in-laws it was practically genetic. Maybe that's why my anger flared as abruptly as it did.

Take it easy, kid, Jack's voice soothed. *Stay in control. Don't let him play with your reflexes. You play with his.*

I cleared my throat. "That's very interesting . . . that Angel liked to slum. I can only assume from what I've heard about her murder that Bethany Banks did, too."

Hal McConnell winced at the remark—the first sign of vulnerability he'd exhibited since we'd met. But his reaction wasn't anger as much as pained defeat. "What happened to Victoria?" he said, his concern sounding genuine. "You said she's missing, too?"

"Victoria Banks came to this bookstore last night, with two of her friends. She confronted Ms. Stark in the middle of her lecture, caused a bit of a scene."

He cursed—another crack in the shell. "I told Vicky to steer clear of Angel Stark. That Angel was a dangerous, unstable person—and no friend of her sister Bethany."

I was surprised at his blunt admission.

Don't be, baby, you're cracking him like antique china, said Jack. *Keep the heat under him.*

"What do you mean by that?" I asked pointedly.

"I mean Angel was sleeping with Bethany's fiancé behind her back, that's what I mean. Donald Easterbrook was playing Angel right up to Bethany's murder and beyond, as far as I know."

I'd skimmed enough of Angel's book to know she'd never revealed such a relationship, never even hinted at it, either past or present. Interesting what Angel chose *not* to tell in that tell-all book of hers.

Hal McConnell cleared his throat impatiently. "You were saying that Vicky is missing?"

I nodded. "Apparently, sometime last night, after Angel's appearance here at the bookstore, Victoria stepped out of her motel room for a soda and a little privacy, in order to make a phone call. She hasn't been seen since. Her purse, her clothes were left behind. Her friends reported her missing this morning."

"By 'friends,' do you mean Stephanie Usher and Court-ney Peyton Taylor?"

I nodded. Hal sat back, scowling. "The dyke and the ditz."

I frowned at his insults, and made a note he was no friend of Victoria's friends. "Victoria was calling *you*," I reminded him. "I believe she spoke with you last night."

"No, she spoke with my voicemail," Hal replied. "I was on the West Coast all week, interviewing for graduate school, and I took the red eye, so I was out of range for cell communication all night. When the plane landed, I checked my voicemail. She'd left a lot of long, rambling messages, asking me to call her. I tried to return her call, but she never picked up."

"You called her 'Vicky'? Just how well did you know Bethany's sister?"

Hal placed his hands on his knees, leaned forward in his chair. "How is this any of your business Miss McClure—"

"*Mrs*. McClure"

"You haven't answered my question, Ms. McClure."

"I'm not asking about your relationship for the sake of gossip, Mr. McConnell. I co-own this bookstore. Victoria Banks caused a scene here and now she's missing along with the author she threatened. The police aren't yet taking Victoria's disappearance seriously. She's over eighteen and hasn't been missing twenty-four hours yet. You might say I'm an 'unofficial' investigator."

"I can't help you." The wall behind his eyes was up again. He lifted his chin.

He's clamming up. Tenderize him. Just keep bumping gums till he yammers.

"Can you at least give me a sense of how much of Angel's book is true? For instance, what she said about you and Bethany—was it all lies what she claimed? Didn't you feel anything for Bethany?"

I expected my question to hit a wall and drop away. But Hal McConnell's shoulders sagged. His tight scowl loosened into a sad frown. The expression, combined with the long hair falling forward around his face, made him look every bit the sensitive, intelligent man-boy Angel had described.

"I loved Bethany . . ." He swallowed. "But Bethany and I were never lovers . . . does that answer your question?"

So Angel was right about that one, noted Jack.

I nodded. "And *why* did Bethany's sister call you last night?"

"Vicky and I were friends. I tried to help her through the worst of it." He sat up straighter, met my eyes. "We both took her death very hard. After the funeral, we began to talk. E-mails, phone calls at first. Soon we became closer."

"But you were never lovers?"

Hal's eyes narrowed. "Whether or not we were lovers is not your business, and I refuse to discuss the issue. Especially since Victoria is missing and, as you obviously presume, foul play was involved."

"You sound as though you know something you're not telling me."

"I know nothing. *You're* the one informing me. I just know that Vicky hasn't been 'all right' since her sister's murder—and things became much worse after the publication of Angel Stark's book, which dragged the whole tawdry affair into the limelight once again. I knew it was possible that Vicky would confront Angel. I'm only sorry I wasn't here to prevent it. But at least . . ."

Hal paused. I waited for that wall to come up again. But, once again, the sad boy seemed to overwhelm the cautious man. He leaned forward in his chair. So did I.

"Look, a few weeks ago, around the time Angel's book was first being hyped, Vicky called me from her parents' home in Newport. I was surprised to hear she was back at the family's place because she had been excited about immersing herself in a special film studies program she'd signed up for during the university's summer session. Then she told me she'd come home for only one reason—to steal a gun from her father's trophy room. She claimed she'd read excerpts from *All My Pretty Friends* and was going to get even with Angel at one of her book signings."

"What did she mean by 'get even'? Did she want to kill her?"

"Vicky *wanted* to kill Angel; we all did. But I think she just wanted to scare Angel witless by pointing the weapon at her. I told Vicky she was crazy, of course. I tried to make light of her plan, and I also offered to conspire with her to make a better one. She told me to come over, and I went."

Hal tightened his already tight tie, looked around.

"It was pathetic, really. She'd hauled down some antique from World War One, probably didn't even have the proper ammunition—as if either of us would know. Vicky begged me to help get even with Angel. After hours of letting her cry on my shoulder, I returned the Mauser to its display case." Hal shook his head. "The next morning, I drove her back to Providence. I left for California not long after that. I hadn't spoken with Vicky for over a week, hadn't even heard from her until last night . . . and that's really all I know, all right?"

Hal McConnell rose. "Now, Ms. McClure, you have to excuse me. I have to get back to Newport."

I stood. "What's the hurry? Don't you want to stick around? Maybe talk to the local police? Aren't you worried about Victoria Banks?"

"Of course I'm concerned," he snapped. "That's why I'm leaving. You said yourself that the local police aren't taking the missing persons report all that seriously yet. That situation will change once Cambridge Upton Banks enters the picture."

"Victoria's father?"

"Of course. Mr. Cambridge Banks is a punctual man. He should be finishing his afternoon golf game right about now. If I hurry, I might just catch him at the country club."

Then Hal McConnell's eyes hardened. "I certainly wouldn't want old man Banks to hear such disturbing news from anyone else *but* me. So I thank you for your concern, Ms. McClure, but I can assure you that this matter will be well taken care of and you can drop your 'unofficial!' interest from this moment on."

With that, Hal McConnell turned his back on me and strode to the front door. The bell tinkled as he went through it, into the sun-splashed afternoon. I hurried to the window, watched him climb into a silver BMW.

Needless to say, I was disappointed it was not the black Jaguar with the blue and white bumper sticker on the trunk that had nearly run Angel down the night before. Things might have gotten simpler.

It's okay, kid, said Jack. *You got some good info.*

"I'll say," I whispered in reply. "Angel lied in her book. She herself was cheating on Donald Easterbrook while he was engaged to Bethany. And, according to Hal, it sure does sound like Victoria was planning to kill Angel herself—as we've suspected all along.

One more thing, sweetie. According to Stephanie Usher, Victoria's parents are on the grand tour of Europe. So who was lying to you? Hal or Stephanie?

I sighed in frustration. And confusion. "This thing is getting complicated. We need some help to sort it out."

The coppers?

"No, the Quibblers."

Oh, my God, not that yammering band of cracker-barrel philosophers and coffee-klatsch raconteurs you call a business association?

"The very same," I replied. "A half dozen heads—"

You mean head cases.

"—are better than one, so I'm taking this case to the Quindicott Business Owners Association."

Doll, please. Spare me an evening with those fruitcakes.

"No."

CHAPTER 17

Kangaroo Court

You got a tender spot in your heart for the palooka but it's not going to do him any good.

—Frederick Nebel, "Take It and Like It,"
Black Mask magazine, 1934

AFTER CLOSING THE bookstore at seven, I set up the folding chairs in the Community Events room, placed a table against the wall, and prepped the coffee urn. Then I locked up and went upstairs to the somewhat rundown yet cozy three bedroom apartment above the store to have dinner with my son. My aunt had stepped out already to have quahog cakes with Bud at the Seafood Shack. (And before you ask, quahogs—which comes from the Narragansett Indian name "poquauhock"—are usually referred to as "hardshell clams" outside of Rhode Island.)

By nine, I was pulling the plug on Spencer's *Shield*

of Justice marathon, which was playing on the Intrigue Channel.

"But Mom!"

"No buts, Spencer. I agreed to let you watch TV until nine. Now it's time for bed."

"But I'm gonna miss the next episode. My favorite one's the next one . . . The one where Jack Shields goes undercover at a racetrack and at the end he has to chase the bad guy down on the back of a horse!"

A soft male chuckle rolled through my head.

I silently asked Jack if that particular episode was based on his case files.

Only the racetrack part, baby. Those horseback antics are pure Hollywood

I smiled. "You won't miss a thing," I promised my son. "I've got a tape in the machine. You can watch it in the morning."

"Thanks, Mom."

While I was less than thrilled that my nine-year-old was enamored of crime melodramas, I was relieved he'd taken an interest in anything after the suicide of his father. Sometimes I still worried that moving him away from the life he'd known in New York City, away from the private school and luxurious Manhattan apartment, might have been a mistake. But one look at the smiling face of my seemingly normal and healthy boy told me I did the right thing.

After tucking Spencer into his narrow bed with a recent children's Edgar winner, one of the many young adult mystery books we carried, I was ready to implement my plan, beginning with presenting the facts in the case of Johnny Napp to the rest of the Quibblers. I headed back downstairs to turn on the lights and start the coffeemaker. But as I proceeded to the Community Events room, I was startled by a noise—something had bumped against one of the metal folding chairs in the darkened room.

For a split second I wondered if it was the ghost of Jack causing some sort of poltergeist mischief, as he had been prone to do when I first opened the new wing of the store over a year ago. I moved to snap on the lights. But before I could feel the switch in the darkness, a callused hand clapped over my mouth and a strong arm encircled my waist. A man's voice hissed in my ear.

"Don't scream."

I didn't. I stomped down with all my might on the intruder's toe instead. He howled and released me. Stepping backward, he threw his hands up in surrender.

"Mrs. McClure! . . . It's me . . . Johnny Napp!"

I flattened myself against the wall next to the light switch, flicked on the lights. It was Johnny all right, blinking against the sudden glare. Beneath an open grease-stained denim workshirt, he appeared to be wearing the same baggy blue jeans and black T-shirt he'd worn to Angel's reading the night before.

"How did you get in here?" I cried, unable to suppress the hysteria in my tone.

"I jimmied the lock on the back door. I thought nobody would come back until morning."

"Your uncle is looking for you."

I realized Johnny was at least as rattled as I was. "My uncle Bud isn't the only one. I tried to get home, but spotted a State Police car staked out around the corner, another in the alley behind my uncle's hardware store. They're out to get me again!"

"Yes, they're looking for you. But they only want to ask you some questions—"

Johnny violently shook his head. "The last time cops 'asked me questions,' they grilled me all night and roughed me up in the process. They want to pin Angel Stark's death on me, Mrs. McClure, just like they tried to frame me for Bethany's murder!"

"You heard about Angel?"

He nodded. "On the pickup truck's radio. They talked about Angel's books and said her death appeared to be a homicide. When I heard the news, I turned around and came right back. I knew Uncle Bud would help me figure out what to do. But then I saw the police, and I was scared they'd grab me before I even got a chance to talk to my uncle."

The kid's in a panic. Tell him to take a breath.

"Calm down, Johnny. Okay? If you're innocent, you have nothing to fear."

Johnny's look made me feel naïve, and I realized that if I were arrested for a murder I didn't commit, I probably wouldn't have much faith in the system either.

"My uncle's the only guy who believed in me. He's the only person who ever stood up for me."

"It's up to a jury to decide who's guilty or innocent. That's why we have a justice system," I replied, even though I knew it probably sounded like a platitude to Johnny.

I closed my eyes and took a deep breath. "Jack?" I silently asked. "What do I do here?"

You said it yourself. It's up to a jury . . .

"What are you saying?" I silently asked. "Turn him over to the cops?"

No. Your little gang of cornball yahoos. Have him tell his story to them. See if he's believable. Get a whiff of how his case'll play out on the witness stand.

I met Johnny's scared, brown eyes. "Listen," I told him, "you have your side of these events, right?"

"Yeah . . . ," he replied warily.

"Then I want you to tell it."

"But the cops—"

"Not to the police—not yet, anyway. You uncle is on his way over here. I want you to tell your side of events to him, Sadie, me, and a few other people whom he trusts."

Johnny looked doubtful.

"Just think of us as a jury of your peers . . ."

"I OBJECT!" BELLOWED Seymour Tarnish, jumping to his feet.

Fiona's eyes narrowed. "You object to what? I haven't said a word."

"I object to getting the wobbly folding chair. You got another one stashed around here, Pen?"

"Sure, Seymour."

"That's what you get for showing up last," said Milner, who was busy with wife Linda, setting out Cooper Family pastries around the coffee urn.

I dragged out several more chairs—deciding we needed one or two near the wooden podium, as well. Earlier, I had set up more chairs than a typical meeting would require, but this was certainly not going to be a typical gathering of the Quindicott Business Owners Association. Usually the subject of our merry band of bold commercial entrepreneurs was the town's parking woes. Lately a popular topic has been the draconian sanitation rules imposed by the city council, along with the tickets that go with them—the newest ploy by the municipal zoning witch (don't ask) to squeeze Quindicott's small business owners just a little bit drier. But no matter what issue was on the table, within an hour the conversation usually veered into a spirited discussion of the pastry of the evening, politics, books, or just local gossip shared over coffee.

But not tonight. Tonight, by mutual consent, we would decide whether or not to turn a young man over to the authorities who would undoubtedly pin a murder rap or two on him—maybe even three. To my relief, everyone had agreed with my plan to hold a mock trial and decide if Johnny Napp should go to the police and turn himself in, or if we had enough evidence to believe Johnny innocent, and hide him away until—hopefully—the real culprit's identity would be revealed.

Before the meeting even started, I'd been on pins and needles waiting for the Quibblers to arrive. A few minutes after my aunt came downstairs, Fiona and Brainert appeared, followed by Milner Logan and his wife, Linda Cooper-Logan.

Like his wife and her shades-of-Annie-Lennox spiky hair, Milner had held on to some fashion trends of his own youth—albeit a decade before Linda's. He wore a small gold hoop in his left ear and his hair in a long ponytail, now more wiry salt-and-pepper than midnight black. Milner was quarter-blood Narragansett Native American, and he frequented our store for crime novels, noir thrillers, and the occasional front-list Tony Hillerman. Linda preferred her big best-selling authors like James Patterson and Stuart Woods, but she was also game for reading anything Sadie or I might recommend.

Mr. Koh and the newest addition to our club—his eighteen-year-old daughter, Joyce, who had graduated high school in May and was helping him run his store for one last summer before college—showed up with a ten-pack of soft drinks. Bud Napp showed his face just as the meeting was scheduled to start, and Seymour, typically, arrived fifteen minutes late.

As soon as Bud called the meeting to order, I moved we postpone all outstanding business. Brainert seconded the motion. Then I told them everything I knew about Angel Stark's death, Victoria Banks's possible abduction, and the disappearance of Johnny Napp. Despite protestations from Bud, I also revealed Johnny's identity, his felony conviction, and his connection—rightly or wrongly—with the Bethany Banks murder.

While the Quibblers were digesting that vast array of facts, I went to the office where I'd stashed Johnny until I could make my case. I knew that the true test of how things would go would be the Quibblers' reaction when I sprang Johnny on them—and told them my plan. The look of relief on Bud Napp's grizzled face when he saw Johnny made it all worthwhile. The shock, surprise, and consternation on everyone else's face when they saw Johnny was not as comforting, however.

Then I told them my plan to hold a mock judicial hearing to determine Johnny's immediate fate. "Bud and I are both heavily involved, so we'll be witnesses. Brainert will take to the podium as presiding judge. Johnny can present his case and we can weigh the evidence."

"Let me defend the kid," said Bud. "I know he's done nothing."

"But you're too close to the case, Bud," Milner pointed out. "You'd do better as a character witness."

"How about a prosecutor?" said Linda Cooper. "We need a prosecutor."

I scanned the room, focused in on Fiona Finch and the predatory peregrine falcon pin she wore on her blouse. "How about Fiona? She's read enough true crime novels to channel Vincent Bugliosi. And she's read Angel Stark's book—"

"Cover to cover," Fiona said with the Cheshire cat grin of a motivated attorney.

"Great idea, Pen," said Brainert. "Fiona, no doubt, will be dogged. However, I must correct you before the jury."

"Correct me?" I asked. "For what?"

"Evoking the name Charles Manson, as you did when you mentioned Los Angeles prosecutor Vincent Bugliosi, can be construed as prejudicial."

For a moment I thought perhaps I'd made a mistake in my choice of judge.

Nah, doll, said Jack in my head. *He's as pompous an ass as most judges I've dealt with. Maybe the attitude comes with the robes.*

"Brainert's not wearing any robes," I silently noted.

Judge Parker cleared his throat. "Since we have a prosecutor, we need a defense attorney as well," he declared. "Someone who can press Johnny's case, and *stand up* to the prosecution."

Not even her husband could stand up to Fiona Finch. But one of our number did go toe-to-toe with her on a regular basis. Brainert sent his glance across the room. "Someone like . . ." His gaze stopped on Seymour.

"Why me?" whined Seymour.

"Brainert ignored the plea and pounded on the podium with his hand. "Order! Order!" he cried. "Consider yourself appointed, Tarnish. Now take you seat next to the defendant and we'll get this procedure underway."

"Goodness," said Sadie. "Brainert is certainly taking his judge role seriously."

As Seymour unfolded his new chair, I took a seat among the jurists. Though I still had doubts about how the rest of the evening would go, I felt a little better now that Jack was looking on over my shoulder—or wherever the heck he was looking on from. Suddenly, I was shaken from my thoughts by Brainert pounding on the podium with a hammer he'd dug out of the desk in the storage room.

"This court is now in session," he cried. "Judge J. Brainert Parker—that's me—presiding."

CHAPTER 18

And the Verdict Is . . .

No, Charlotte, I'm the jury now, and the judge, and I
have a promise to keep. Beautiful as you are, as much
as I almost loved you, I sentence you to death.

—Detective Mike Hammer in *I, the Jury* by Mickey Spillane, 1947

"THE NIGHT BEFORE Angel Stark was found dead, you
approached her right after the hit-and-run incident. Describe what happened in your own words . . ."

Fiona Finch paced back and forth in front of the accused. Clearly, she'd missed her calling as a hard-line
prosecutor.

Seated in a metal chair on the right side of the podium,
Johnny Napoli squirmed under the scorching gaze of the
assembly. His haunted eyes shot a look at Seymour, who
nodded silently, signaling that Johnny should answer the
question.

"Well, I was standing in this store, near the front door, when I heard Angel scream," Johnny began in a halting voice. "I ran outside. Then I saw the car—a black Jag—practically drag her down the street. Angel hit the pavement and I rushed over to see if she was all right."

"You called her Angel just now. How well did you two know one another prior to that evening?"

Waiting for an answer, Fiona paced back and forth in front of Johnny, who followed her with nervous eyes.

"I knew Angel. From that time I worked for a catering company in Newport."

"The same time that Bethany Banks was murdered?"

Johnny nodded.

"So at your reunion the other night, what did you talk about?"

"Well, at first Angel was pretty rattled about the accident and all. She kept cursing, calling the driver a bitch and stuff—"

"Not *son* of a bitch?" Seymour asked.

"I object," Fiona cried. "We're pursuing *my* line of questioning. Mr. Tarnish will have an opportunity to cross-examine."

"The defendant may answer the question. It may be pertinent to the case," Judge J. Brainert Parker declared.

Johnny shrugged. "She could have said son of a bitch, I guess. But I thought it was just bitch . . . but guys are called bitches just as much as girls, it doesn't matter . . ."

"That's right," eighteen-year-old Joyce Koh blurted out. "It's like calling a guy a girlie-man."

Mr. Koh shifted in his seat, glanced uncomfortably at his daughter. Joyce hardly noticed. The teenager's full attention was on the drama unfolding on the podium—and on Johnny. Because of the summer heat, the strapping youth had left his denim workshirt in my office. His black T-shirt outlined a muscular chest and bulging biceps. A barb-wire tattoo circled one of his sculpted arms.

"Let's move past the profanity. Get back to Fiona's subject," I suggested.

"Prosecution, please continue with your original line of questioning."

"After Angel Stark settled down, when you and she were finally alone, what did you discuss?"

"Well, she thanked me for coming to her aid, retrieving her shoe, which she'd lost in the scuffle. Then Angel told me she didn't know I was out of jail or she would have looked me up. I thanked her for saying the things she said in the reading, about me being innocent of Bethany's murder and all . . ."

Fiona swooped in on Johnny's admission like the bird of prey on her lapel. "If you were an innocent victim as you claim, why did you serve time in prison, Mr. Napoli?"

"I don't like her tone," huffed Bud.

I leaned toward Bud. "It's not personal," I reminded him softly. "Fiona's just trying to get to the truth."

Johnny shifted nervously on the folding chair, trying to find the words. "I . . . I went to jail for possession of drugs. *Possession.* But . . ." His voice faded.

"*But*, Mr. Napoli?"

"But I was selling them, too. To that rich crowd in Newport. I was catering this party, one of my first ones, and I'd taken a break out back to smoke a joint. One of the rich kids came out to smoke a cigarette and he bought one of my joints off me for ten times what I'd paid. He said I could make a mint supplying his friends."

"So you started selling drugs for profit?"

"I really needed the money to go to culinary school. And I knew the streets, so I could buy the stuff cheap in Providence or Massachusetts, then turn it around at these parties for ten times what I paid because these kids had tons of cash and really didn't care how much it cost."

Johnny hung his head. "I'm not proud of it, but yeah. It wasn't just the money, though. Having drugs on hand . . . it made me popular with that crowd . . . important, you know? They liked having me around. Pretty soon, after the formal party I catered ended, the real partying began, and I was partying just as hard as they were. In the end I used all the cash I made selling to take care of my own habit."

I watched Bud's face completely fall. I knew he believed his nephew had been railroaded from the start, that the drug conviction was just part of an elaborate frame-up. But it was obviously hard for him to hear the truth, right out of Johnny's own mouth.

"Listen, Bud," I whispered, leaning close once more. "You said yourself that Johnny got mixed up with the wrong crowd. Being around money can lead you to rationalize all sorts of behavior—believe me, I know. But at least he's telling the truth now. And it can't be easy to do that, so hang in there."

Bud nodded, but he still looked stricken. Then my aunt put her hand on his shoulder and whispered, "I'm here for you, Bud." He patted it gently and looked at her with something like gratefulness.

"Tell me, Mr. Napoli," Fiona continued, "was Angel Stark one of your customers?"

He shook his head. "Nah. Angel was already off drugs. She wrote that book of hers and everyone pretty much knew she was clean."

"How about Bethany Banks? Was she one of your customers?"

Johnny nodded. "Everyone else in that clique was a customer at one time or another—Bethany, Georgette LaPomeret, Donald Easterbrook, Kiki Langdon, they were all regulars. But even if Bethany hadn't been a customer, I would have noticed her. She was something special. She and Donald Easterbrook were the leaders of that pack, so I guess it made sense that they would hook up."

Fiona began to pace again. "Let's get back to that night," she said, still in prosecutor mode. "You remained outside with Angel Stark while everyone else went back into the bookstore, is that correct?"

"That was because Angel—she just wouldn't let go of me. Hung on like I was her lifeline or something. I thought maybe she was just scared, later on I found out differently."

"We'll get to 'later on' in a moment," Fiona said quickly. "Just tell us what happened next."

"Well, Angel asked me if I'd give her a ride to your inn. I wasn't keen on the idea, seeing as I was supposed to meet Mina after she finished work. We were going to have some pizza, go for a drive."

"But Angel convinced you to accompany her to my inn?"

"I felt sorry for her after what happened and all. And she kinda limped, so I thought she was hurt."

Fiona's eyes narrowed suspiciously. "You swore to tell the whole truth and nothing but, Mr. Napoli. Sounds like you're holding back . . ."

Brainert slapped his own forehead. "Damn, I knew I forgot to do something. We didn't swear him in."

"We need a Bible for that," said Linda.

"Where are we gonna find a Bible in a mystery bookstore?"

Aunt Sadie rose. "I'll just go fetch mine . . ."

"Relax, Sadie, it doesn't matter," Seymour offered. "My client is here to tell the whole truth and nothing but, right Johnny?"

The frowning youth shifted in his chair, then nodded. "There was another reason I went with Angel," Johnny continued. "Angel told me something . . . something that forced me to go with her."

Fiona pulled a doubtful expression. "*Forced*, Mr. Napoli?"

"Angel told me she knew something about that night . . . the night Bethany was murdered. She claimed she found out stuff while researching the book, stuff that could clear me of the crime forever by pointing a finger at the guilty party."

"So you drove Angel to my inn. But you never got there, did you?"

"We did," Johnny insisted. "Angel didn't go to her room though. She said it was a 'resplendent' night, said we should go for a walk around the pond. So we followed the path to the construction site."

"You're telling us that you went walking with Angel at the very spot where her corpse was later found?"

Seymour jumped to his feet. "I object!" he yelled.

"Too late, mailman. He's already admitted he was the last to see Angel alive," Fiona shot back.

"I said I went walking with her," Johnny cried. "I never said I was the last to see her alive. The *killer* saw her last, and I *didn't* kill Angel."

"The kid's right!" roared Seymour. "My client merely stated he was with Angel that night. He never said he was the last person to see her alive. You're leading the witness, or the jury, or—I guess *both*."

Fiona crossed her arms. "Johnny admitted that he was with Angel where her corpse was later discovered. I merely pointed that fact out."

"Yeah, okay," said Seymour. "But I didn't like the *way* you pointed it out."

Brainert rocked the podium with his hammer. "Order, order," he cried.

Where's the kangaroo in this courtroom?

"Easy, Jack. They're doing their best."

"To restate," said Fiona, facing Johnny again, "Angel claimed she had information on Bethany Banks's murder. Did Angel tell you what that information consisted of?"

"No. When we got to the construction site, she totally changed on me, got real nasty. Said she knew all about my drug pushing to her friends—how I always had something special behind the bar at the parties I catered. Angel said she knew I'd done the time for possession, but also knew I'd never been brought up for dealing—something she could prove to the cops, who were still looking for an excuse to lock me up forever. She even blamed me for Georgette's cocaine addiction—but I knew Georgie was copping coke from everyone. She made two or three trips to Boston a month to buy powder."

Johnny gulped from a bottled water Seymour handed him. He wiped his lips with the back of his hand. "Then Angel brought up why Bethany came down the service stairs that night . . . that Bethany came there to meet me, which was true, but old news since the cops knocked it out of me the night of her murder."

"Which is why they couldn't use that statement against him," Bud pointed out from his seat. "They violated Johnny's rights a dozen times over that night."

"Yes," Fiona told Bud, "Angel discussed all that in her book. But she never actually said *why* Johnny was meeting Bethany." Turning back to Johnny, she pointedly asked. "Was it a drug buy?"

"Bethany wanted to have sex—at least that's what she told me," Johnny replied.

This time it was Mr. Koh who moaned. "Time to leave, daughter," he said, getting to his feet.

"I'm not leaving," Joyce replied. "I want to find out what happens—"

"But—"

"Oh, come on, Dad. You only want to go because of the dirty talk. But it's no worse than my soaps!" She tugged on his sleeve and he reseated himself with a huff.

"Go on," said Fiona. Johnny shrugged.

Mr. Koh shook his head, muttering something in Korean while Joyce leaned forward, waiting to hear more.

"I didn't think Bethany slept around," said Johnny. "I mean, she was engaged to Donald Easterbrook. And she never came on to me. Not before that night, anyway. I should have known it was too good to be true. That something else was going on inside her head."

"Please elaborate."

"At the lake last night, Angel gave me the 411 on what had been going on the night of the New Year's Eve ball—that Bethany had found out her fiancé was cheating on her with one of her best friends—"

"Who?" asked Fiona.

"Angel claimed it was Kiki, and I believe her because there was gossip to that effect. Then Angel told me that Bethany had asked Donald to meet her in the utility room at midnight. Bethany wanted him to catch us both in the act—as revenge on him for cheating on her."

An old story, said Jack.

"Wow! This is better than my soaps!" declared Joyce.

Mr. Koh grunted.

"Did you make the rendezvous?" asked Fiona.

"I got there, all right. But Bethany was already dead." Johnny's expression darkened. "When I found her, Bethany was just lying there. I almost didn't recognize her. Her tongue was sticking out, her face was purple . . . a belt was wrapped around her neck—*my own* belt as the police told me later—"

"That's right! Your own belt!" Fiona cried, jumping to her feet.

"I object," barked Seymour, jumping to his feet. "It's my turn to—"

"Let Johnny . . . er, the defendant, answer the question," Brainert said, with a pound of his hammer.

Seymour frowned and sat down.

"She was killed in the utility room, a big storage area really. We—that is, the catering staff—we used it as a changing area. There were lockers to put your street clothes in. We all wore white-jacket uniforms for formal parties. My clothes were there inside the locker."

"How did it get unlocked?" asked Fiona.

"Those lockers didn't have locks."

"Ah-ha!" cried Seymour "So anyone at that party could have grabbed your belt?"

"Yeah, that's right," said Johnny.

Seymour began to pace, "After you found the corpse, what did you do?"

Johnny sighed. "I panicked. I had drugs on me, and in my car, too, so I didn't want to have anything to do with the police that night. I went to my boss, the catering manager, and I told him there was a girl in really bad shape in the utility room and he should call an ambulance. Then I was going to just motor out of there, but he grabbed me and made me take him to the room. He called a security guard over on the way to come with us and I was stuck after that. They wouldn't let me leave till the local police got there. Man, I was freaking."

"Because of the drugs?" Seymour asked.

"Yeah, and the Bankses and Easterbrooks. They're really connected—judges and lawyers and bankers and stuff. The kind of folks who'd cleaned up their kids' messes by making a few phone calls. And now it looked like I had messed with them. I was sure the fix would be in, that the police would try to blame me for the murder . . . and that's exactly what they did."

Fiona folded her arms and tapped her chin. "Why do you think Angel brought up all this with you last night?"

"She said she found the evidence that would incriminate me," said Johnny. "Bethany's missing gloves."

"Ah, yes, the gloves," said Fiona. "Please elaborate."

"Well . . . Bethany was wearing these long white gloves that matched her white dress the night of the New Year's Eve party. You can see her wearing them in the party photos. But the gloves were gone from her body after she was . . . you know . . . murdered. The local cops never found them. That's why they were so eager to find them that night in my locker or car. They had my belt, but they could see the lockers weren't locked—"

"Which meant anyone could have grabbed it," Seymour reminded the jury.

"Right," said Johnny. "And they figured her gloves would have my DNA on them, so they were sure if they found them, that would slam-dunk my conviction, you know, totally link me to the murder. But they didn't find them. They *never* found them. Now Angel claimed she had recovered the gloves and that my DNA was on them—"

"Did you believe her?" asked Fiona.

Johnny shifted. He rubbed the back of his neck. "I don't know what happened to those gloves . . . nobody did. But . . . Bethany did touch me with them that night at the party . . . while she was inviting me to meet her in the utility room at midnight."

"Touched you how?"

"She brushed my bangs back . . . she was being flirty, you know . . . and I'd been running back and forth with a lot of heavy trays all night . . . so some of my sweat could have ended up on her gloves . . . And now Angel was saying she was going to take them to the police, unless I did her a favor."

"What kind of a favor?" asked Fiona.

"She wanted me to kill someone," said Johnny.

The room gasped.

"Forget your soaps, Joyce," said Milner. "Now it sounds like one of my noir crime novels."

Joyce waved her hand. "Sorry, Mr. Logan. You obviously haven't been watching daytime television lately."

"And just who was it that you killed for Angel Stark?" Fiona cried, ignoring the peanut gallery.

This time Seymour pounced. "I object. The prosecution is making baseless accusations and is openly hostile to the witness—"

"I'm *supposed* to be hostile," said Fiona, hand on her hip. "That's my job."

"Enough already. I want to pursue a new line of questioning, just so I can get a word in edgewise," said Seymour.

Fiona stomped her foot. "I object!"

"Overruled," said Brainert. "I think it's time we heard from the defense."

"Johnny, tell us: Who was it that Angel wanted you to harm?"

"I didn't stick around to find out, because I told Angel flat out I wasn't going to do it, no matter what she claimed about having Bethany's gloves."

Seymour whirled on Johnny so suddenly he flinched. "Did you believe Angel was serious about wanting someone killed?"

"Word," replied Johnny.

"What?" asked Sadie.

Huh? said Jack.

"He meant *yes*," interrupted Joyce, "as in, you can take his word for it."

Brainert turned to Johnny. "The witness will refrain from using hip-hop slang."

Johnny shrugged.

"What did you do next, Johnny?" asked Seymour.

"I refused to take care of her problem. Then I told Angel that she could go to the cops if she really wanted to because I wasn't some hit man. I'd take my chances with the authorities because I wanted to set my life straight."

"Then what happened?"

"Angel freaked. Started calling me names. Started screaming about everyone in Newport conspiring against her. Then she opened that handbag of hers and yanked out a handgun, a .38-caliber police special. I thought she was gonna shoot me, so I ran off, back to the parking lot."

"Hmm," said Fiona, pacing, "That's rather interesting . . ."

"What?"

Fiona spun around and pointed her finger. "You knew what caliber of gun she was holding? How?"

Again, Johnny shrugged. "I knew because my drug supplier had a gun just like it."

"Are you sure it wasn't because you have one, too—and you were the one who pulled the gun, not Angel?"

"No! No way! It's like I said, I swear!"

"I object!" cried Seymour. "Fiona is a pest!"

Brainert raised an eyebrow. "You mean she's pestering your witness?"

"That too."

"All right," said Brainert. "Sustained. Fiona, get on with your next question."

"Fine," said Fiona. "Now where was I? Oh, yes . . ." She began pacing again. "You say you ran away. Did Ms. Stark follow you?"

Johnny nodded. "Angel caught up with me at my uncle's truck while I fumbled with the lock. I got behind the wheel, but she grabbed the door, tried to shove the gun into my hand. I threw it on the pavement and the next thing I know I got a face full of bullets—"

"What?" Bud leaped to his feet. "She shot at you!"

"No, no, Uncle Bud, chill," said Johnny. "Angel had bullets for the gun—I guess it wasn't loaded. When I tried to leave she threw them in my face. I just brushed them off the seat, the dashboard, and slammed the door. I was buggin' and I accidentally flooded the engine. The pickup stalled, so I had to wait a few minutes, but I tried again and it finally started. Then I drove off, and that's the last time I saw her, I swear."

"So where were you for the last twenty-four hours?"

"I got scared. Figured Angel was going to the police," Johnny said. "I was almost at the Canadian border when I came to my senses and decided to come back, face the music—tell the authorities my side of things. But when I got close to Quindicott, I heard about Angel's murder on the radio and I panicked. I ditched my uncle Bud's pickup and hoofed it back to town through the woods. I tried to get home, but I saw cops staked out at my uncle's house and the hardware store so I came here and hid."

"Where did you ditch the truck?" Bud asked. "I should go get it."

"If you do that, the police will know you've seen Johnny," I said. "The truck was reported missing with him, remember?"

"Yeah, I forgot," said Bud. "I hope it's safe."

"Don't worry, Bud," said Johnny. "I drove it up the old service road near the highway."

"Hmm," grunted Bud. "I thought that road was blocked by a couple of concrete posts and a steel cable."

"It is," Joyce Koh said. "But the cable is loose and you can unhook it yourself."

Johnny nodded. "The kids around here use it for a lovers' lane sometimes."

Mr. Koh glared at his daughter. "How do you know of this place, Joyce?"

"Everybody knows." Joyce shrugged.

Her comment was followed by a string of Korean words.

"I never did," Joyce insisted. "I just know about it. But it's no big deal."

Mr. Koh countered with more Korean.

"Order! Order!" Brainert cried, pounding his hammer.

Johnny stood up. "Stop arguing all of you!" he cried. "I've made up my mind. I'm going to turn myself in to Chief Ciders."

All at once the Community Events room was plunged into silence.

"He's right," said Bud, rising. "Innocent men don't run. And if we try to hide him, we'll all get in trouble with the law." His gaze found his nephew's eyes. "We'll go to Chief Ciders together."

CHAPTER 19

Dark Discovery

I haven't got the heart to see a nice-looking young man
like you go to jail.

—Erle Stanley Gardner, "Leg Man,"
Black Mask magazine, 1938

THE QUIBBLERS' FAREWELL to Johnny was a sad
sight. Linda and Milner wore grim faces as they wished
him good luck. Joyce Koh tearfully hugged the young man
with her scowling father looking on. Even my aunt Sadie,
who usually maintained a flinty exterior, appeared a bit
misty, and I realized she was not watching Johnny but Bud.

"Good luck, kid," said Seymour, shaking Johnny's hand.
"If you ever need a good lawyer, look one up in the phone
book, because you can do way better than me."

"I second that assessment," said Fiona.

After a final respectful nod from Judge Brainert, I

escorted Johnny and Bud out of the Community Events
room and through the dimly lit store. I unlocked the front
door to let them out, and Johnny turned to face me. "Thanks
for everything, Mrs. McClure. I left a note in your storage
room. On that old desk. It's for Mina. Could you make
sure she gets it?"

I nodded. I had sequestered Johnny in that room until
the meeting began. "I promise she'll get your message first
thing in the morning."

"I told her everything." He shook his head. "She's been
the best thing in my life since all the bad stuff happened.
She made me start to feel good about myself and . . . I
don't know . . . to *want* to be a better person, you know?"
He shrugged. "I decided she deserves to know the truth . . .
everything . . . and then she can dump me if she wants to. I
won't blame her."

"Mina cares about you, Johnny," I assured him. "I
haven't known her long, but I don't think she's the kind of
young woman who gives up on people. You'll see."

As they exited the store, Bud Napp put his arm on
Johnny's shoulder, gave his nephew a reassuring pat—a
paternal gesture that just about tore my heart out.

"What's your verdict, Jack?" I silently asked.

*Poor dumb Johnny wanted to be a player. And the smart
set ended up playing him. But the evidence is stacked, baby,
and the cops are likely to be leaning in the same direction.*

"But Johnny's innocent," I replied. "And Bud believes
the court will clear him."

*The old guy's sucking hope through an air hose, kiddo.
Bud's happy thoughts and square-john rectitude ain't
gonna keep that kid from wearing a fresh fish special—*

"Huh?"

*A prison haircut. You're fresh fish when everyone knows
you're the new guy because you've just been clipped. My
point being that these are high-altitude crimes, with crème-
de-la-crème stiffs pushing up daisies, so the heat's on the*

suits in the system to throw a neck-tie party—even if the guest of honor's just a patsy.

"But—"

No buts. There's yards of circumstantial evidence to make the charges stick like a floozy's chewing gum.

I returned to the Community Events room, where a funeral pall had descended over the assembly. Seymour and Brainert were silently munching cinnamon rolls. Fiona clutched a cup of tea, and was leafing through a copy of *All My Pretty Friends*. Joyce Koh was dramatically blowing her nose into a tissue.

"Poor Johnny." She sighed. "He's so young and cute. It's like, how could anyone so buff be a criminal? Bummer."

"You think he's innocent, then?" I asked.

Joyce blinked. "Don't you?"

"I'd like to know what everyone else thinks."

"Well, I think he's been framed," said Seymour. "And not because I represented the guy. I know those rich bums up in Newport. I'm sure one of them did it. They're all pond scum."

"That's a blanket generalization," said Brainert. "Overruled."

"Listen, Judge, the trial's over, and I speak of what I know."

"What has the Newport set ever done to you, Seymour?" Linda asked.

"That's easy. Remember last year, after I had to have my ice cream truck repainted after some dude's guts got splattered all over it?"

I shuddered, recalling the murder of a young Salient House publicity assistant that occurred right in front of this store.

"That paint job set me back a few dollars, let me tell you. Plus I lost a week of selling while the work was getting done. My ice cream business struggled for the rest of the summer, until I feared I'd have to sell a few pulps to swell my bank account. I decided to extend the ice cream season, instead."

Brainert adjusted his bow tie and huffed impatiently. "What's your point, Tarnish?"

"Well, then came autumn and I was still working to make up for lost revenue. I was parked down at the Inn during Fiona's Oktoberfest celebration when a few rich snots from Newport asked for sundaes. I whipped them up, served them up with a smile, and the a-hole who ordered them just walked away with his friends without paying— like it was free or something. I tried to collar them, but the guy just laughed. 'It's only ten bucks,' he said, like it was too little of an amount to bother fishing out of his wallet. When I got more adamant, I was muscled by some bodyguard-type, and those a-holes just strolled away."

Brainert frowned "That's no reason to brand an entire class."

"Why the hell not?" Seymour replied. "I'm like an elephant that way. Do me wrong, I never forget."

The room fell silent for a moment, everyone lost in thought. Suddenly Aunt Sadie spoke. "What if Johnny *is* innocent? He's no Klaus von Bülow. He can't afford proper legal representation. I feel like we've condemned the poor boy to the gallows."

For once these cornpone yahoos are talking sense, said Jack.

"Quiet, Jack," I silently replied. "And my friends are not yahoos."

"I think he's guilty," said Milner. "It doesn't make sense, otherwise. If Johnny didn't do the crimes, who did?"

Fiona slapped her book closed loud enough to get everyone's attention. "I know I'm supposed to be the prosecutor here, but to be frank, I can finger a few other suspects just by perusing Angel Stark's book."

"I read that book, too," said Brainert. "And despite what she claimed at her reading here, I thought Angel dropped the ball when it came to blame, wrapping it all up with the old 'unanswered questions' summation."

"She didn't *name* anybody," Fiona replied. "But a close reading reveals some tantalizing clues."

Brainert huffed. "If you say so. I yield to your true crime expertise."

We faced Fiona. Some of us were hopeful. Others—like me—were dubious.

"Well, it says on page two nineteen that Donald Easter-brook, Bethany's fiancé, disappeared from the party about an hour before Bethany's body was found. Angel also writes that Bethany cheated on Donald many times. That's certainly a good motive for him to murder her in a fit of rage."

"I don't know," said Brainert. "Maybe Donald Easter-brook didn't care."

"He cared," said Milner. "What man wouldn't?"

This time I spoke up. "Okay, maybe Donald had a motive for killing Bethany, but that doesn't explain Angel's murder *or* Victoria Banks's disappearance."

"Okay," said Fiona. "What about Hal McConnell? Un-reasoning rage caused by unrequited love . . . Maybe he followed her to the utility room, tried to force his affections on her, she had choice words for him and he kills her?"

Joyce nodded with enthusiasm. "Sounds like it could happen."

"Only on one of your soaps," said Seymour.

"It did," said Joyce. "Last month on *Destiny*."

"*Destiny*?" asked Linda. "I don't know that soap."

"Korean channel. Out of Boston," said Joyce. "Chin loved Bo-bae with all his heart, but she was cruel to him and one day when he declared himself, she humiliated him, and in a fit of rage, he smothered her with a silk pillow."

The Quibblers stared at Joyce.

Linda Cooper-Logan leaned forward, wide-eyed. "What channel?"

"Seventy-two."

I cleared my throat. "Getting back to Johnny's case . . . Hal McConnell might have killed Bethany, true, and he might have even killed Angel. But he never would have hurt Victoria, because, in my opinion, he's transferred all the affection he felt for Bethany to her younger sister."

"Hey!" Seymour cried. "Then maybe Victoria isn't dead or kidnapped. Nobody's found a corpse or a ransom note. Maybe Angel killed Bethany then Victoria and Hal killed Angel and then ran off."

"Sounds good, except I spoke to Hal today," I informed him. "He hasn't run off. And he said he was on the West Coast interviewing at a grad school. He took the red eye last night and just got in this morning."

Seymour's face dropped. "Oh."

"You just read too many of those damn pulp novels," said Fiona. "That, or you're an incurable romantic."

Seymour snorted. "Forty-five years of bachelorhood has cured me of any residual romanticism, I assure you."

"Anyway," said Brainert, "according to Angel's book, Bethany slept with dozens of men. Any one of them could have been the killer."

"Yeah," said Milner, nodding. "I couldn't tell you the number of crime stories I've read that had the victim dying during rough or kinky sex. And Angel wasn't exactly pure as the driven snow. Maybe she ran afoul of the same pervert."

Mr. Koh groaned again.

"Take it easy, Dad," said his daughter. "It's nothing I haven't heard on Court TV." But Joyce's words did not reassure her father. Once again, he said something in Korean, and she came back at him in the same language. Then they continued arguing back and forth.

"Well, the meeting has finally degenerated, so I move we call it a night," Brainert declared.

"I second the motion," said Linda. "Mil and I have to get up early and start baking."

Brainert slammed the hammer down. "This meeting is adjourned . . . and I'm getting me a real gavel for the next get-together. The damn thing is quite useful."

"Good God," I groaned. "I've created a monster."

After everyone left and my aunt climbed the stairs to bed, I turned off the coffeemaker and the lights in the community room. Then I headed to the storage room to fetch the note Johnny left for Mina. I wanted to make sure she found it as soon as she got to work on Sunday, as I wouldn't be here to give it to her. Tomorrow I was scheduled to take Spencer to the McClure family reunion at Windswept, an outing I would have gladly traded for a more pleasant experience—like a root canal sans novocain.

I found the note in the center of the old desk—a letter, really, sealed in an envelope culled from boxes of stationery, Mina's name in ink, printed in neat script on the front.

As I picked it up to take it into the store, I spied Johnny's denim work shirt draped over the back of the metal chair he'd been sitting on. He'd shed the garment earlier in the evening and had apparently forgotten it when he left. I picked up the shirt, and a bundle of keys dropped out of the breast pocket with a loud clatter. The keys to Bud's store, his home—and the Napp's Hardware truck concealed in the woods near the highway.

"Jack, are you there?"

Lay it on me, doll.

"Johnny forgot his keys . . . do you think there's something inside that truck that might back up his story and help to clear him?"

Or incriminate him. Sure. Or there could be nothing but fresh air . . . We'll find out when we get there.

"What?"

Come on, doll, humor me. Except for this afternoon I've been penned in this den since 1949. Let's broaden my horizon.

IT WAS MIDNIGHT before we got on the road. I'd checked on the sleeping Spencer and told Aunt Sadie I was ducking out to the all-night convenience store for a few things. She raised an eyebrow but didn't ask any questions.

The heat of the day had given way to a breezy night. With my car windows rolled down, the pungent scent of Quindicott's saltwater inlet permeated the air. The cloudless sky was jammed with stars, and the roads were virtually deserted as I moved through tow and out into the countryside. I didn't see another pair of headlights until we approached the main highway. Along a wooded stretch without streetlights, I slowed the car.

"The lovers' lane is along this stretch of road somewhere, if I remember correctly."

And you know this how?

"Jack, even I was young once . . ."

Hmm. Makes me wonder, babe . . . Just how many smooching parties did you attend?

"None. I was a wallflower. My husband was my first and only real boyfriend. But my late brother Pete was a heartbreaker. He used to talk about this place to his friends, and I eavesdropped."

I see, baby . . . practicing your surveillance techniques even then.

"Funny, Jack."

I swerved off the highway, onto the shoulder, then slowly edged my car onto a narrow, unpaved service road consisting of two worn wheel paths with vegetation growing in the middle. As we bumped along, I could hear the tall grasses scraping along the bottom of my car. After rolling

along for about a hundred yards, the road was blocked by
two concrete posts with a steel cable strung between them.

End of the line, doll.

"Not according to Joyce Koh."

I stopped the car, threw it into neutral, and popped the
door. The interior alarm beeped, informing me I'd left the
keys in the ignition. The door only opened about halfway
before it hit a wall of scrub weeds and gnarled trees. I had
to squeeze my way around it.

Over the purring engine I could hear night sounds—
crickets, the buzz of cicadas, and the roar of traffic on the
highway, still almost a mile away. In the glare of the headlights, I examined the barrier. Despite Joyce's assurances,
it didn't seem possible to detach the steel cable and pro-
ceed, except on foot. Then I noticed that the ring bolt on
one post lacked a nut to hold it in place. I grabbed the cable
with both hands and tugged. The ring nut popped out of its
hole and the thick steel cable dropped to the ground.

Neat trick, noted Jack. *Put the cable back and it looks
like a dead end. The patrolling prowl car jockeys who come
along think the place is jalopy free, meanwhile half the
bobby-soxers in town are using the strip like a hot-sheets
motel. How did Johnny-boy find this spot, I wonder?*

I smiled. "My guess is that Mina showed it to him."

*Hmm. Still waters run hot, I guess. Wouldn't be the first
time.*

Back behind the wheel again, I drove between the concrete poles and onto the road beyond. As we crawled along,
the headlights cast bizarre shadows all around us. The
brush was so close on either side that it seemed like we
were moving through a narrow tunnel. Trees leaned into
the roadway like giant hooded sentinels, their branches re-
sembled curling claws that seemed to reach out like hands
ready to strangle. I tried to forget the memory of Angel's
corpse, the yellow rope wrapped around her throat; the de-
scription of Bethany's murder, the belt around *her* throat.

A branch bumped the windshield, startling me.

"Talk to me, Jack, so I don't feel all alone."

How far back does this rabbit trail you call a road go, sister?

"Couldn't say."

Just when I feared I would have to back all the way out of a dead end, I came to a wide, circular clearing large enough to accommodate a half-dozen vehicles. Though the area seemed remote, I saw twinkling lights through the thick, old tree trunks—a faraway building probably—but I could not make out any details. I circled the area until I spied a gleam of metal in the headlights' glare. Half-smothered in branches, sat a big red pickup truck with *Napp Hardware* in black letters on the side. I stopped the car and cut the engine.

Inside the trees the night sounds were more pronounced, the traffic roar muted. I heard an owl hoot as I moved carefully to the truck, the flashlight from my glove compartment in hand. I tried three keys in the door before I found the right one. Finally the lock clicked. I reached for the handle when a voice in my head stopped me.

The bulls and the lab boys will get around to finding the truck sooner or later. They'll be dusting for prints, so you don't want to leave any behind.

"How—"

Use the material from your blouse like a glove—

You want me to take it off?"

I didn't say that, but now that you mention it . . .

"Don't worry, Jack. I'll manage."

I stuck my hand into the tail of my shirt. The door opened with a metallic groan. In the dim glow of the roof light I could see the messy interior of the cab, which smelled of oil, turpentine, and fresh paint. There were tools and boxes of nails between the two bucket seats, sheets of sandpaper scattered on the floor, and several old copies of the weekly penny-saver newspaper.

"Jack, what are we looking for?"

Won't know until we find it, cupcake.

I crawled inside the cab, careful not to touch anything with my hands. I used the flashlight to check the back of the pickup, which was filled with building materials, a toolbox, some electrical drills and saws, a portable lathe, cans of paint, and bundles of rags. I also spied coils of yellow rope—probably the same type found wrapped around Angel Stark's throat. Since it was nearly impossible to squeeze into the open bed of the pickup from the cab, I focused my attention on searching the driver's area. As I rifled through the glove compartment, I moved my leg and several tiny metallic objects clattered to the floor. I played my flashlight along the floor mat until I saw them—two bullets, with brass casings and silver tips.

Bingo, dollface. Those are .38 caliber slugs. Didn't Johnny-boy say that trampy Emily Dickinson threw bullets in his face?

"That's right! What do we do? Call the police?"

Nix to that. Best that we were never here, officially anyway. Johnny will tell his side of the story. When the coppers come up here, they'll find a bullet and know that part of his story is true, anyway.

"There are two bullets, Jack."

We're going to take one slug and leave the other. That way, if the fix is already in on Johnny-boy, you can go to Chief Ciders and admit you were here first and show him what you found.

"The chief would only say I made a story up to protect Johnny."

Possible—unless you find Angel's gun, and they can lift prints off one of the bullets. So let's hope we never have to go that route. Now, grab one of those slugs with your blouse, wrap it up real gentle like, so if there is a print on it you don't smear it.

There was no way I was going to reach one of the bullets

with the shirt still on my back. I sighed and stripped it off, then wound the material around my hand. Dressed only in my khaki pants and white cotton bra, my skin prickled in the night's slight breeze and I felt Jack's eyes on me—which was, of course, patently ridiculous.

Now that's what I call broadening my horizons, baby.

My cheeks flamed. "Cut it out, Jack."

My fingers closed around the slug and I grabbed it, wrapped it, then I climbed out of the cab, closed the door, and made sure it was locked. I felt naked and vulnerable and I nearly screamed when headlights flashed through the trees—not from the direction of the service road, but from whatever that building was beyond the trees.

Then the headlights went out and I swore I heard voices, faintly and far away. That got me curious. I moved away from my own car, toward the light peeking through the trees. I found a path and followed it, my flashlight beam stabbing through the darkness.

Another pair of headlights shone through the woods, and I soon realized I was approaching the parking lot of the Comfy-Time Motel. Lit up beyond the trees was the very vending area where I'd found the cell phone earlier in the day.

"Jack . . ."

I know. This doesn't look good for Johnny-boy. Victoria Banks was snatched less than a hundred yards from where he stashed his wheels—too close to be a coincidence, the coppers will insist.

I sighed. It was after midnight, and I was lurking in the woods near a motel parking lot in my bra with my blouse wrapped around a bullet.

"I think I've seen enough, Jack."

I turned and panned the trees with my flashlight—the light caught the edge of a dingy white rectangle, and I saw it was that old rusting Private Property sign hanging from one nail on the giant oak tree that split the single trail in two.

I retraced my steps down the trail where I had come from but more paths branched off and I realized that it was easier to find a building in the darkness than a car parked in the woods.

"Oh, God, Jack . . . I think I took the wrong path . . . I think I'm lost . . ."

Don't panic, kid.

But I did. I turned around and retraced my steps once more and started again. I began moving so quickly I almost outpaced my own flashlight beam. The column of light danced with my every step, throwing crazy shadows. My heart raced as I stumbled along. Suddenly my foot caught something and I went down onto my hands and knees. I still clutched the bundled blouse with the bullet, but the flashlight flew from my hand.

It landed off the path, rolled and stopped. The beam of light fell on what looked like a squirming black mass. I blinked as a cloud of flittering night bugs rose from the heap on the ground. I looked closer, saw a length of yellow rope encircling puffy black flesh, straw-blonde hair pulled into a tight ponytail, and pale, mottled skin still crawling with insects.

Then I screamed.

CHAPTER 20

The Getaway

I'm the sucker in this deal. *You're* the smart guy.

—Raymond Chandler, "Blackmailer's Don't Shoot,"
Black Mask magazine, 1933
(featuring Philip Mallory, the precursor to Philip Marlowe)

I WAS SICKENED, horrified, panicked. I picked up the flashlight and blindly ran. Branches clawed my head and arms, scrub brush tore my slacks, stones invaded my sandals.

Baby, wait! Slow down!

Jack tried to stop me, but I wasn't a hardened ex-cop turned P.I. with a hundred crime scenes in my past and a gun strapped under my shoulder for protection. I was a widowed single mother completely lost—and in over my head.

Penelope!

The sound of my own name finally broke through. I couldn't remember the last time Jack had called me anything but doll or baby. My steps slowed.

"Jack . . . it was . . . Victoria Banks . . . ," I rasped, trying to catch my breath. "She was strangled, just like Angel . . . with yellow rope . . ."

I want you to calm down, go back to that body, and take a closer look.

"No, Jack. I have to get out of here. I have to call the police."

But . . .

Jack kept talking, but I wasn't listening. I continued moving along the path, not sure where I was going, just as long as it was *away* from those grotesque remains. My heart was beating faster than moth wings against a porch light, and my palms were so slick with sweat I almost dropped the flashlight.

When it felt to me as if I'd run far enough, I began sweeping the milky beam in wide arcs to either side of the trail, looking hard into the woods until, thankfully, I caught a glimpse of Bud's red pickup about twenty feet away. I jogged through the trees toward it. From there, I made my way back to my Saturn.

I opened the trunk, ripped a section of paper towel off the roll I kept there, carefully transferred the bullet into it, put it in my pocket, and threw my blouse back on. Inside the car, I pulled out the small silver cell phone I had thrown into my purse earlier.

Baby, what are you doing?

I opened the phone. The display screen's neon green lit the pitch dark interior of the Saturn with an eerie glow. "What do you think I'm doing?" I snapped aloud. "I'm calling the police. Then I'm waiting right here until they arrive and I'm going to tell them everything."

I understand why you want to do that, but take my advice. Don't.

"Why?"

You hid Johnny in your back room when you knew the police were looking for him, that's why. You withheld evidence to protect him, you're in the middle of the woods after having tampered with more evidence and you don't have a get out of jail free ticket—

"What are you talking about? This is murder, not Monopoly!"

Listen up, doll. A 'get out of jail free ticket' is a private investigator's license. Something you don't possess, the last time I checked, and if you're not careful, they'll start looking at you with accessory and obstruction charges.

"But you were the one who suggested we come out here!"

Don't go soft on me now, sister. You were the one who asked for my help on this case—even employed a little emotional blackmail as I recall. I was the one said you better take a few swimming lessons before you jumped into the deep water. Well, it's too late to turn back. You're not just involved, you're in over your head, and there's only one thing to do when you get on a ferry like this . . . ride it all the way to the other side of the river.

"What river would that be, Jack, the river Styx?"

Don't get cute.

I collapsed backward against the car seat and closed the cell phone. "I'm not going back out there. I mean it."

A long silence followed.

"Jack?"

Start the engine.

I did.

Now drive.

AT A DESERTED rest stop along the highway, I pulled up to a pay phone and called the State Police. Doing my best to disguise my voice, I told them I saw a dead body in the woods behind the Comfy-Time Motel, gave them a good idea of where to look, added that I didn't want to get involved, and hung up.

Then I drove home, checked on my sleeping Spencer, and went to bed. It would be many hours, however, before I could calm down enough to go to sleep.

"Jack? I don't know what to do with this . . . Victoria was strangled so close to Johnny's truck . . . and with that same yellow rope he's been carrying in his pickup . . . but Johnny's not some sort of a sick killer who strangled Bethany, Angel, *and* Victoria. He just can't be!"

My head was pounding. In my sleeveless cotton nightgown, I rose from the bed and went to the bathroom. In the mirror, my shoulder-length reddish-brown hair looked a tangled mess. My arms were covered with unsightly scratches, and the expression in my bloodshot green eyes appeared crazed. I took two aspirin, knocked it back with tap water, and groaned.

Take it easy, kid . . . you're making yourself sick.

"I'll be fine." I doused the cuts on my arms with antibacterial spray.

You see why my racket ain't for the faint of heart? You see why I didn't want you involved?

I ignored that and went back to the bedroom. "All three of these young women had been strangled," I continued reasoning as I sat down on the mattress, "and what Milner said earlier was right . . . I've also read enough thrillers to know that light strangulation during sex is a kinky turn-on for some individuals, which can lead to a form of autoerotic death."

That's right.

"There was a case in New York City some years ago involving a wealthy East Side debutante and a prep school classmate—the sexual experimentation had gotten out of hand and the girl had ended up dead. I want to believe Johnny's innocent . . . he has to be for Bud's and Mina's sake . . . but, Jack, how do I prove it?"

The room went quiet. Too quiet. Then the ghost said, *Maybe you don't.*

"I can't accept that."

I know.

"So who killed Victoria, Jack? Who killed Angel? Who killed Bethany?"

You aren't going to figure that one out tonight. And that's an angle you've got to master in this game, baby. It's like a trick knot. The harder you pull, the tighter it gets. Listen up now, are you listening . . . ?

"Yes, Jack."

You've got to learn to relax. Let your troubles make a getaway for a night.

"I can't."

You can.

"I don't think I can . . ."

Try.

I clicked off the lamp, lay back on the mattress, hugged a pillow, and sighed. "When you were alive, what did you do to relax?"

Me? Jack laughed. *Two ways, baby . . . You want to hear them?*

"Sure."

First way: a bottle of good Scotch—

"I'd prefer white wine."

Vino works, too . . .

"And the second way?"

Jack laughed again, but this time the sound was deep and low and very male. *Close your eyes,* he whispered, *I'll show you . . .*

The cool kiss of his presence breezed up the length of my thin nightgown, making me shiver in the warm room.

"No, Jack."

Come on, baby, I can give you a dream you'll never forget.

I blushed. "Jack, please don't."

More male laughter.

All right, Miss Priss. Then why don't you just get your mind off your friend Johnny's case by putting it on another.

"Another what?"

Another case. When a homicide stumped me, I'd read up on other cases. Where's that Stendall file you carried up here?

I sat up, clicked on the lamp, shoved on my black-framed glasses, and fished the file out of the nightstand drawer. Inside the dusty beige folder, I found a surprisingly neat and orderly collection of documents. The first was a typewritten list of expenses—dinners, taxis, pay phone calls. Clipped to the back were receipts, yellowed with age but still readable. I rifled through them.

"Little Roma," I read aloud. "O'Donnell's Pub, Club Creole, Chop Suey, Pirate's Cave, The Bar Car, McSorley's Old Ale House, Le Parisian . . . Looks like you had an awful lot of night's out with this case."

Most were the client's idea, not mine. But you can skip all that, baby. Find my report.

Beneath the log, I found a neatly typed document. I pulled it out and skimmed the first page . . .


```
            Jack Shepard
        Private Investigations

          August 7, 1946

          Emily Stendall
```

Protection and Investigation into Threats
July 19, 1946 - August 5, 1946

On the afternoon of Friday, July 19, 1946,
the Client, Miss Emily Stendall of 67 East 65th
Street, entered my office and retained me to
provide her with protection. According to Miss
Stendall, the Subject, Joey Lubrano, an
elevator operator in her building, and residing
at 16 East 7th Street, had made threats to her
regarding her safety.

Also according to Miss Stendall, Mr. Lubrano
had carried on an affair with her sister, Mrs.
Sarah Nolan, also a resident of 67 East 65th
Street. During this affair, Mr. Lubrano took
photos of Mrs. Nolan in various states of
undress and in lewd poses. Mr. Lubrano had
promised these photos would remain private but
later used them to blackmail her.

Mrs. Nolan also confided in Miss Stendall
that she had arranged an exchange with Mr.
Lubrano but the night it was to take place,
Mrs. Nolan was found drowned in her bathtub,
under the influence of a combination of alcohol
and sleeping pills. Mr. Lubrano having had a
solid alibi was not held by the police. The
death was ruled accidental.

Miss Stendall believed that Mr. Lubrano took
the money, kept the photos and negatives,
drugged Mrs. Nolan, and drowned her. The police
agreed to search Mr. Lubrano's residence but
recovered no evidence and, with no evidence
from the medical examiner's office that her
death was a homicide, the case was dropped.

Mr. Lubrano, now in the clear, approached

and threatened Miss Stendall. In her words: "He
threatened me just the other day, told me to
keep my mouth shut from now on or he'd shut it
permanently—just like he did my sister's."

The Client speculated that Mr. Lubrano still
had the incriminating photos and would begin a
second blackmailing scheme, this one perpetrated
on the deceased's husband.

After my initial interview of the Client, I
dined with her at Little Roma. Afterwards, we
took a cab to her 65th Street apartment. There,
I observed Mr. Lubrano operating the elevator,
as she had claimed, and I found him to be
hostile to her, as she had claimed.

After I physically discouraged the Subject
from advancing on my Client, I instructed Miss
Stendall, for her own safety, to pack her
belongings and leave the premises with me. She
agreed to check into the Plaza Hotel and
invited me to stay with her. I declined. . . .

I raised an eyebrow at those last lines. "What does it
mean that your client invited you to 'stay with her' at the
Plaza? Did she have a suite with a second bedroom?"

No, baby.

"Then she wanted you to . . ."

*Heat up her sheets, do the horizontal tango, go to bed
with her, what do you think?*

"But you declined, right? It says right here you did."

That night.

"Excuse me?"

*I had work to do that night—putting a tail on Lubrano.
But the invitation from Miss Stendall to share her bed became a standing one, and I took her up on it the next night.*

"You slept with your client?"

Yeah, baby. And more than twice.

I shook my head. "I just can't believe you did that."

Why not?

"Because in the Jack Shield books, Jack never slept with a client, even when tempted. He said it would compromise the investigations and—"

These aren't Jack Shield's files you're reading, baby, these are Jack Shepard's—the files of a real man, who lived a real life, and made real mistakes.

"So you admit it was a mistake to sleep with Miss Stendall? That it was unethical?"

Technically.

"Then why did you do it?"

She was a knockout and she was hot for me, and I went to bed with her . . . and, boy, but if I didn't call that one on the money.

"What?"

You've been avoiding my files because you were afraid of what you'd find.

"No—"

Yes. You don't like the look of the truth, so you just don't want to see it—especially when it's about people you care about and it's not pretty. But you better be ready to believe the worst about people, because that's the name of this game you're in now.

I frowned as I considered Jack's charge. It was true that during my disastrous marriage I'd refused to see my husband for what he was . . . and, during the marriage, I'd blinded myself to my in-laws manipulations and insults, taking in silence whatever they'd dish out by telling myself they were simply trying to "help" or that they meant well and really didn't mean to come off as disparaging. But I'd woken up to all of it eventually (after they began to blame me for Calvin's suicide and began "advising" me—during my vulnerable period of mourning—that the "best thing" for Spencer was to send him away to English boarding school). Still . . . Jack wasn't wrong that I did prefer to focus on the good in people.

"I'll admit I don't want to see the worst in people I care about," I confessed, "or even strangers for that matter. I mean, I hate to think any person is capable of stealing a book from our store, let alone a triple murder. But this isn't *just* about me. It's also about you."

Why do you think I'm stuck here in limbo, sweetheart? If I were a saint, don't you think I'd be playing a harp about now?

"There you go again, implying your life trapped in an independent bookstore is akin to eternal damnation. Well, I'm not buying it. You may not be playing a harp at the moment, but you can't have been all bad, or else you'd have gone a lot farther south than Rhode Island—and I'm not talking Cartegña, Mr. Shepard . . ."

Jack snorted. *We're getting off the subject. Keep reading.*

I did and found the report impressive. Despite the copious use of outdated slang in his thoughts to me, Jack knew how to write well—or at least put two ideas together on paper. It was also clear he had a highly organized mind.

"I can see why Timothy Brennan found your files such a rich source of information for his books. You're very thorough . . ."

Thanks, baby. Chalk it up to my time in army intel. If you didn't write it up right, somebody down the line would get it in the neck. Literally.

I nodded and kept skimming the file. It seemed Jack hadn't just checked out Joey Lubrano's story, he'd also checked out Emily Stendall's. I yawned as I continued to read. "It looks like you investigated your own client? Why?"

Why do you think?

"I guess you didn't trust everything she was telling you . . ."

Bingo.

"But she was the one paying—"

Add an "L" to that word, baby. As it turned out, she was the one playing . . . and she tried to play me.

"I can't see how . . ." I yawned again, felt my eyelids beginning to flag, realized I was finally beginning to relax into sleep. "And I don't see what this has to do with Johnny's case . . ."

Close your eyes, sweetheart, you will . . .

CHAPTER 21

P.I. School

The ability to persuade is central to the investigator's dealing with the subject...those who would persuade must always be prepared to adjust and adapt. Therein lies the challenge.

—*Interviewing and Interrogation* by Don Rabon

"OPEN YOUR EYES, honey."

I was standing by an open window in a shabby, dark apartment. Three floor below, on the shadowy, rain-slicked street, giant Fords and Packards rolled by, the vintage vehicles sporting enough metal to qualify as miniature tanks. Rows of tall, brick apartment buildings lined the sidewalk as far as the eye could see and somebody nearby was playing a haunting big band classic on what sounded like a hissing record player.

"Glenn Miller," Jack informed me. " 'Moonlight Serenade.' "

Wherever I was, it wasn't present day, Quindicott, Rhode Island. "Am I dreaming?" I whispered.

"Yeah, baby."

The voice was no longer in my head but behind me. I turned to find Jack Shepard in the flesh. I took in the length of his tall, broad-shouldered form in the familiar double-breasted suit and fedora, that iron jaw with the scar in the shape of a dagger slashing across it. His hard granite-gray eyes softened when my confused green ones met them.

"Welcome to my world, Penelope."

"What am I doing here?"

"It's the Stendall case." He lifted his chin toward the open window. "Look."

I turned around to peer out the window again. Across the street was a neighborhood pub that I knew still existed in the East Village of Manhattan. A green wooden sign over its battered wooden double doors read MCSORLEY'S OLD ALE HOUSE. The letters were also etched into one of its big, brightly lit glass windows.

"They don't serve dames in there, otherwise I'd get you a cold one." His eyebrow arched and I knew he was teasing.

I smiled. "That's okay, Jack. I'm not much of a drinker anyway, but I still don't understand why—"

I was about to revolve from the open window to face him once more when his big, warm hands rested on my shoulders and turned me back. "Keep looking."

Moments before the damp street had been devoid of pedestrians, but when I turned toward the window again, I saw one of McSorley's battered double doors swing wide. A dark-haired young man emerged on a raucous gust of male laughter. He was wearing a kind of doorman's uniform—black slacks with a green stripe down them. The uniform's cap was tucked under his arm, but he'd removed the short green jacket, which he carried slung over his shoulder. The white T-shirt underneath defined a muscular chest, visible biceps, and broad shoulders tapering to a narrow waist.

"That's funny," I murmured, "from this distance, he looks like Johnny Napp."

"Don't he though," said Jack, "but this kid's name's Joey. Joey Lubrano."

"The young elevator operator who threatened to shut your client's mouth the same way he shut her sister's—by *murdering* her?"

"That's right."

I shuddered as I watched Joey's muscular form move across the dark street. A nearby street lamp cut through the warm, misty evening, shedding enough light for me to see his steps weren't completely straight.

"He looks like he's had a few," I observed.

"I'm counting on it," said Jack.

"But won't that make him reckless? More dangerous?"

"Maybe. But it will also impair his judgment, loosen his tongue, and allow me to manipulate him. You should remember that in a pinch."

"Jack, it looks like he's coming straight for this building."

"No surprise, doll. This is his apartment you're standing in."

"What?!"

"Relax, baby."

"But, Jack, I don't know even what happened in your case. I haven't finished reading the file!"

"And that's exactly why I brought you here. Just think of it as a little on-the-job training."

I suddenly had trouble breathing. This might have been a dream, but it felt very real to me at the moment. I could smell the rancid odor of stale beer from McSorley's across the street, hear the lightly falling rain outside, feel the suffocating warmth of this shabby two-room apartment.

"Are you crazy?" I told Jack. "I won't know what to do or say. I think we should get out of here."

"Take it easy, baby. Just stay behind me. Watch and learn."

"Learn what?"

"For starters, how to conduct an interrogation. Namely, a little information can get you a long way if you use it right."

A minute later I heard a key in the door and Joey Lubrano's powerful form came stumbling into his small, unkempt apartment. He walked into the tiny living room, reached under the stained shade of a stand-up lamp, and turned it on. The pale glow of the low-watt bulb revealed Jack Shepard, relaxing in an armchair, smoking a cigarette. I stood in the shadows behind him, trying not to shake like a kitten at a dog fight.

Joey was young—in his early twenties was my guess—and just as Italian-handsome as Johnny Napp. Dimpled chin, Roman nose, deep brown eyes, and jet-black hair slickly combed. His physique looked even more impressive in the confines of the small apartment. His muscles packed into the white T-shirt and elevator operator uniform. Suffice it to say, I could see why a high-society gal like Mrs. Nolan may have looked twice at her elevator man.

"Hello, Joey."

Joey Lubrano froze, his slightly glazed eyes focusing fast. "What the . . . ? What the hell are you doin' here? And how did you get in?"

Jack took a long drag on his cigarette, stubbed it out on the ashtray beside him. "Your building super was impressed with my P.I. license. Of course, I palmed him half a C note when I flashed him my ticket. That may have helped."

"Get lost."

"Relax, Joey. I just want to talk."

Lubrano stepped forward, his face flushing red, his hands balling at his sides. "Well, I don't."

"Jack," I whispered. "Be careful. He looks pretty angry."

Lubrano looked up, straight into my face. "Who the hell is *she*?"

"Tonight she's my partner."

I stared in shock that the man could see me at all. A part of me hoped that Jack had brought me back here as an invisible bystander. Apparently not. I looked down to find myself in a belted linen suit with a pencil-thin skirt—the same shade of gray as Jack's double-breasted. I felt a small hat pinned to my upswept hair, saw white gloves on my hands—and could only assume that this is what Jack believed a female P.I. should be wearing, if there even was such a thing back in 1946.

"Your partner?" Lubrano snorted derisively. "She's a dame."

Jack's lips tilted in a half-smile. "Ain't she though."

Lubrano's gaze turned nasty, lewd. Slowly, he raked me from head to foot. "Tell you what, dick. Why don't *you* take a hike and leave the broad. She and I can, uh . . . *talk*. And when I'm through giving her what she wants, I'll lay odds she never goes back to you."

Because I blinked just then, I failed to see exactly which of Jack's army jujitsu moves he'd used to render Joey Lubrano helpless. I simply sensed a flurry of movement as Jack exploded from his chair, heard a surprised grunt from Lubrano, then opened my blinking eyes to gawk at the end result—Joey Lubrano's profile kissing the floor, his arms bent back in what had to be a painful position.

"Don't disrespect my partner, Lubrano. It makes me mad."

"Ow! Get off me, dick!"

Jack tightened his grip on the young man's arms. He wailed in pain.

"All right, all right," he moaned. "What do you want?"

"First . . . *apologize* to the lady," said Jack. And when Lubrano hesitated, he tightened his grip once more.

"Okay, okay, I'm sorry. I'm sorry!"

Jack loosened his grip, but only a fraction. "Good boy. Now listen to me and listen good. I've found incriminating evidence in your place—"

"What *evidence*?" spat Lubrano.

"A box of photos. Photos of a naked woman in lewd poses. Photos of a woman that Emily Stendall claims you blackmailed for money and then murdered. Now, after I found those photos, I could have slipped out of here and gone to my client with them—and we both could have gone to the police just like she wanted. But I took a very close look at them, and I'm guessing you have something to tell me, don't you?"

"I don't know what you're talking about," said Lubrano.

"Fine, then I'll haul you out of here and we'll talk it over at the nearest precinct—the one that apparently missed these photos on their first search of your place. How about that?"

"No! I don't want to do that," said Lubrano. "Look, this is all wrong . . . you need to know the whole story."

"Good. And you need to know that after I let you go, I'll be covering you with my rod, so don't try any funny stuff or I'll pump you so full of lead the Parks Department will designate you a metal sculpture. Got it?"

Lubrano quickly nodded.

"Okay, nice and slow," said Jack, smoothly releasing Joey while simultaneously reaching for the gun in his shoulder holster.

"Jack," I whispered after Joey rose and Jack had waved him over to the lumpy sofa. "Why didn't the police find the photos the first time?"

"Baby, didn't you learn anything back at the Comfy-Time Motel? Badges don't always find everything they should—especially when they're not motivated to look very hard. Joey here kept this shoebox under a loose board beneath a throw rug in his bedroom. A good trick, but not an original one."

Joey sat down heavily on the old sofa, rubbing his bruised wrists.

"Okay," said Jack. "Let's take it from the top."

Joey spilled it all. How Emily Stendall had been the one with whom he'd been carrying on an affair. How she'd come up with a plan to extort a great deal of money from her sister, Sarah Nolan. The two women looked a lot alike—they were both about the same height and weight, both had delicate features and pale skin. The biggest difference was that Emily's hair was blonde and Sarah's was jet black.

So one weekend when the Nolans were away, Emily concocted a story for Benny, the routinely half-inebriated doorman, convincing him that the Nolans had left her a key to water her plants, but she'd lost it.

Once inside, Emily shooed Benny away and slipped Joey in. Lubrano took a series of racy photos of Emily— while she was wearing a black wig styled exactly like Sarah's hair. The shots were out of focus on the face, but clearly showed that the photos had been of a dark-haired woman of Sarah's build, in Sarah's bedroom, wearing Sarah's jewelry, and stripping out of her private clothes and under-things.

Then, one night, while Sarah's husband was away on one of his long business trips, Joey charmed his way into Sarah's apartment and actually did sleep with her.

"It was Emily's idea that I sleep with Mrs. Nolan," confessed Lubrano. "She said Mrs. Nolan would feel guilty about it afterward. Then that would give us leverage. She'd be more inclined to pay up because she'd know she wouldn't be able to lie to her husband and claim she'd never slept with me—when she had."

Joey showed up with the photos the next night, demanding a cool two hundred fifty thousand, which would clean out Mrs. Nolan's trust fund. Sarah Nolan broke down and agreed to get the money if he'd just give up the photos and negatives.

"We arranged a night for me to come to her apartment and make the trade," Lubrano explained. "Then Emily and I were supposed to beat it out of town for Miami. That was our plan all along. The money would let us get married and start living the good life."

"But it didn't work out, did it Joey?" said Jack.

Lubrano sighed, shook his head. "The night before we were supposed to do the trade-off, Mrs. Nolan ended up dead. I don't know what happened, but I had nothing to do with it."

"I know," said Jack. "I talked to enough cops that saw you at McSorley's, making bets on dart throws."

"Damn right. I was innocent . . . but Emily was furious. Said it was all screwed up now, that Mrs. Nolan probably offed herself, but we deserved our money and we'd get it, too."

"By blackmailing her husband?" prompted Jack.

"Exactly. But I was scared and wouldn't go for it," said Joey, "I still had the photos and Emily demanded I give them up, but I wouldn't. I told her we should just go to Miami anyways, me and her, but she got nasty and said she wasn't going anywhere with a rube who had no cash and no future and unless I agreed to her plan she'd get even with me good."

"What did you do?" prompted Jack.

"I told her to take a hike, that's what. That broad was good in the sack, but she was all bad out of it, and I'd had it with her."

Jack nodded. "That's why Miss Stendall needed me. She wanted me to get those photos back from you so she could go through with the second phase of the blackmailing scheme—to blackmail Sarah Nolan's husband. And at the same time, she needed to incriminate you."

Joey's eyes narrowed. He leaned forward on the sofa. "Doesn't she know I'd turn on her? The police didn't believe her once, but if they ever did, and I knew for sure I was going down, I'd take her with me. I'd tell all the stuff about her sleeping with me and posing for the photos and our planning the blackmailing together."

"She'd never give you that chance. That's also why she needed me. My bet is she's about to stage a situation between us where I'll kill you."

Joey blinked, confused. "What are you saying?"

"I'm saying Emily Stendall played us. And now it's our turn to play her."

Jack turned suddenly and winked at me. "Any questions, doll?"

My eyes widened. "At least a dozen."

"Let's take P.I. school somewhere else, then," he said, rising. "Excuse us, Joey."

Jack grabbed my hand and kissed it. In an instant, we were no longer in a shabby, two-room walk-up flat. Above us, the chandeliers of Manhattan's elegant Plaza Hotel shimmered. Jack offered his arm and I took it. We glided across the carpet to a small candle-lit marble table in a remote part of the palm-filled lobby.

As we stepped past a gilded mirror, I saw my attire had become decidedly more feminine—my gray linen suit had been exchanged for a deep-green satin dress with a turned-up collar, daring neckline, and matching pumps. My auburn hair was down, falling in perfect waves around my face and looking sleeker than I'd ever been able to style it in my life.

We sat down at the small marble table, and Jack ordered champagne. It arrived in a silver bucket, poured by a white-gloved, black-jacketed waiter into shallow crystal glasses.

"Okay, shoot," he said, after enjoying a long swallow. "Not literally, baby." He winked. "Just ask me what you want to know."

"First, finish the story. What happened to you and Joey and Emily?"

"I brought Emily Stendall some but not all of the

photos. Remember, baby, holding on to some of the evidence is smart insurance in case something goes wrong— like that bullet in Johnny's car."

I nodded silently, the champagne going far too easily down my throat.

Jack continued. "Shortly after she got those photos, Miss Stendall began her blackmailing of Mr. Nolan. She also arranged for me to walk in on her and Joey together. She lured Joey to her hotel room in an apparent ploy to make up with him, but once I walked in, she began to pretend he was assaulting her. 'Let me go. Help, Jack. He's got a gun!' and words to that effect.

"But I was wise to the situation. Told her maybe I should use my gun—on *her*. While she'd been seducing Lubrano, he'd gotten her to admit out loud to everything: the original scheme against Sarah Nolan, and the one against her husband. We'd hidden a microphone in the room, see? The police were next door, listening, with a tape recorder going."

"Okay, first question: How did you know for sure those photos weren't really Sarah Nolan? How could you be sure Emily was telling you lies?"

"I'd been sleeping with Emily. I knew she had an hourglass shaped birthmark on her . . ." Jack's voice trailed off. He glanced around the elegant lobby. "Uh, derriere."

"Okay, I see. You recognized that same birthmark in the photos?"

"Bingo, sister."

"Sister," I murmured, shaking my head. "I never would have suspected Emily, Jack. I never would have thought a woman was capable of perpetuating such a nasty fraud on her own flesh and blood."

"Then you never would have discovered that Sarah Nolan *wasn't* Emily's flesh and blood."

"What?"

"She was her sister all right, but only her *sorority* sister. That's what clued me in early on. When I saw Mrs. Nolan's

birth date was barely eight months after Emily's, I got suspicious, started looking into their backgrounds, discovered
they'd gone to school together. So what lesson do you de-
duce from that, sweetheart?"

I blinked. "Uh . . . I don't know."

Jack sighed. "When you realize that a person is lying to
you—or consciously misrepresenting something—you
want to suspect they have more to hide."

"Oh, sure. Right." I gulped down my champagne in its
entirety. Jack poured more.

"I kept digging and I also discovered that Sarah Nolan's
husband had been Emily's beau for a time back during
their college years."

"So Emily was jealous?"

"She must have been—and angry, too, very angry.
Emily's own family had disowned her by then and her
money was running out. Meanwhile, Sarah had a huge trust
fund and a husband with even more loot. Emily obviously
came downtown to hire me because she thought she'd find a
low-rent dick who'd wouldn't question the story of a woman
like her—with her pedigree and pretty little pout. Especially
not after she started sleeping with me, which was, frankly,
the first thing that got me thinking I was being played."

"That's really why you slept with her? As part of your
own investigation technique?"

Jack's eyebrow arched. "What does your gut tell you,
Penelope?"

"That you're full of it."

"I'll tell you what, doll. Emily Stendall made the mistake of thinking that because my office was shabby that my
sense of justice was, too. But she thought wrong."

"You didn't fall for her, Jack, not even a little bit?"

"Most men stop thinking when a dame's perfume goes
to their head. And I wasn't completely immune. After
we became intimate, I wanted to believe her pitch was
innocent . . . I didn't want to believe she was rotten to the

core. But when I was presented with evidence, I let go of what I wanted and faced the music. I did what I had to do. You hearing me, Penelope?"

I swallowed hard, looked down at the dissipating bubbles in the remainder of my champagne. "You're telling me that Johnny might be innocent like Joey . . . or that he might be as guilty as Emily. And if he is, I have to accept that. Just like you accepted Emily's guilt."

"Yeah, you got it."

I drained my glass. "I don't know if I can do that."

"You're stronger than you think, Penelope."

"I don't see how you can say that. I was such a coward out there . . . in the woods . . ."

Jack reached out, and his fingers began to tuck strands of my auburn hair behind my ear. "The woods are where the wolves live, sweetheart . . . a little fear is a smart thing . . . as long as you don't let it keep you from doing what you need to do . . ."

My eyes met his, and I felt his hand move from my ear to the back of my neck. The light pressure was all it took for me to give in to his kiss, deep and warm and relaxing. I felt the buzz of the champagne and wrapped my hands around his neck. He pulled me hard against him.

"Baby," he growled. "What you do to me . . ."

"Oh, Jack . . ."

"Listen . . ." He smiled. "This joint looks classy enough. Let me get us a room . . ."

"I can't, Jack . . . I have a son . . . and I think . . . I think I'm still married—"

Jack's kiss stopped my words. Then my alarm clock stopped Jack's kiss. With its penetrating warmth still lingering, I opened my eyes to find the morning sun blasting through my open window and Jack's tempting offer faded with the stars.

CHAPTER 22

Casing the Joint

> My head was still booming away and I tried to fix it up
> with a hot shower. That helped, but a mess of bacon
> and eggs helped even more.
>
> —Detective Mike Hammer in *The Big Kill* by Mickey Spillane, 1951

I SAT BLEARY-EYED in church that morning—so tired I
hardly noticed my son's impatient restlessness, so tired my
aunt had to poke me now and again to keep me awake during the pastor's seemingly interminable sermon.

The nightmare discovery in the woods, followed by a
night of Jack's dreams, had me crawling out of bed that
morning with a feeling of impending doom. After the service I said good-bye to Sadie, reminding her to pass
Johnny's letter to Mina when the girl arrived for work.

Stuffed with hot homemade doughnuts and strong
coffee—and milk for Spencer—we left Cooper's Bakery

and climbed into our mud-spattered, weed-encrusted blue Saturn for the trip to Newport. The food helped immensely, and I felt the fortifying sugar rush as I got behind the wheel.

It was a radiant morning, a cloudless azure sky, fresh cool breezes off the ocean, sunlight gold and dazzling. I snatched my seldom-worn sunglasses from the underside of the driver's-side visor to shield my bloodshot eyes from the glare.

"You wore those last year, too," my son remarked, tapping the dash in time to one of those boy band groups on Radio Disney.

"Wore what?"

"Your Hollywood sunglasses."

I smiled. "Maybe I was wearing my contact lenses last year, too."

"Maybe you just want to look like all the other mommies there. They all act like movie stars."

Out of the mouths of babes. "Maybe that, too."

Besides the shades, I was also wearing new clothes specifically purchased for this annual event—white capri pants, a pastel sweater set, and Italian sandals with a matching bag. All were expensive designer quality, which would help me blend into the McClure ranks, but bought at outlet prices, which is all I could now afford. And, frankly, I was grateful to have the long sleeves of the summer-weight sweater. It was warm, but I had some pretty nasty scratches on my arms from running topless through the woods.

Traffic was light and we were making good time as we neared the ramp to the highway. But as we came around a bend, Spencer cried out. "Look, Mom! Cops. Lots of them."

I braked, rolling up behind several other vehicles. Squad cars were parked along both shoulders of the road, bubble lights flashing. Several belonged to the Quindicott police force but the majority were sleek silver Ford Crown Victorias with Rhode Island State Police markings.

For a moment, traffic remained at a dead stop. Several

drivers were rubbernecking at the state police in their gray uniforms and "Smoky the Bear" hats swarming through the wooded area behind the Comfy-Time Motel.

"Move along, move along," called Officer Franzetti as he waved his arms at the traffic jam. The gawkers stepped on the gas and sped away. With no cars behind my own, I stopped next to Eddie and rolled down the window. I tried to offer the handsome police officer my most clueless smile. "What's up, Eddie?"

He motioned my car to an empty spot along the shoulder of the road.

"What's wrong, Mom?" asked Spencer beside me.

"I just want to ask Eddie for some directions, that's all," I lied. From my son's expression, I could tell even he didn't buy that, but I told him I'd be right back. Then I climbed out of the car and approached Eddie.

"What's happened?" I asked.

"The State Police got an anonymous tip last night. A woman caller, alerting them to the fact that a corpse was in the woods behind the Comfy-Time Motel."

Eddie watched my reaction closely. I automatically grasped the buffalo nickel in my pocket for reassurance— the coin that apparently allowed me to bring part of Jack with me beyond the store.

Play it coy, kid, Jack whispered. *Gracie Allen time.*

"Who?"

Play dumb.

I blinked at Eddie in mock surprise, cocked my head. "Really? Was it that girl you told me about yesterday?"

Eddie nodded. "Victoria Banks, age nineteen. She's dead—probably murdered right after she disappeared."

"Murdered?"

"Strangled. And beaten, too. Maybe pistol-whipped."

I shuddered, recalling the horrific wounds I had seen the night before.

"Probably she was killed within an hour of leaving her

motel room, but . . ." Eddie's voice faltered. A shadow crossed his handsome face as he stared at the woods. "I was the one Chief Ciders sent up here to talk to her friends. I told the Chief I thought something bad had happened to the girl, but the Chief . . . well, he couldn't issue an Amber Alert because the girl was over eighteen. And he insisted on waiting twenty-four hours before forwarding a missing persons report to the state police. We couldn't even find her parents. The Newport and Manhattan addresses just had answering machines saying they were touring Europe for the summer."

You get that? asked Jack.

"Sure did," I told him. "Hal lied."

He led you to believe you should simply drop your interest in Victoria's disappearance. Which tells you what?

"Hal McConnell has something to hide."

I could see the torment on Eddie's face. He was blaming himself. I reached out, put my hand on his shoulder. "Look, Eddie. You said yourself that she was probably dead before her friends even reported her missing. You did what you could."

"Yeah," he said softly. "But if I'd gone into the woods for a look-see, she might not have been lying there all night."

I closed my eyes a moment. I felt bad about it, too. "Oh, Jack," I silently whispered. "I wish I could tell him about snagging Vicky's cell phone, just to ease his mind."

Are you nuts? Keep your lips zipped, sister. I mean it.

Just then, a Quindicott Volunteer Fire Department ambulance emerged from the edge of the woods. The red vehicle bumped along the service road at a funereal pace, swaying in the deep wheel ruts I'd followed less than ten hours before. I could tell by the expressions on the State Troopers' faces that the vehicle bore the corpse of Victoria Banks, heiress, and now officially murder victim. Eddie Franzetti went pale as a—well, a ghost.

My heart went out to him.

Jack's didn't.

He's choking on misery. Pump him for information while he's off-kilter.

"But—"

Do it, Penelope. Now!

"Are there . . . are there any suspects, Eddie?"

His big brown eyes blinked, then his face grew more grim. "I shouldn't say anything . . . I mean, it isn't public knowledge. Besides—"

"What, Eddie?"

"I know you're close to Bud Napp."

"We're all close to Bud. He's our neighbor. Bud's been part of the community since forever."

"Just between you and me," Eddie whispered. "Bud's truck is parked back there, too—less than a hundred yards from the corpse. State Troopers have impounded the vehicle and are searching it now for the blunt instrument used on the victim. They found a bullet from a .38 in the cab, which is why they're speculating the girl might have been pistol-whipped. No gun, though."

"So they still think Johnny Napp is guilty?"

"The Staties are looking hard at Johnny's story. Detective-Lieutenant Marsh is in charge of the investigation. He says the facts don't add up and neither does Johnny's alibi."

I recalled my only meeting with Detective Marsh, and it was not a pleasant memory. An imposing giant with square chin, blond stubble, icy-gray eyes, Roger Marsh of the Crime Investigation Unit had also probed the murder of Timothy Brennan at my store last year. Detective Marsh pretty much ran roughshod over me, Aunt Sadie, and my staff. I suddenly felt sorry for poor Johnny. I would hate to be interrogated by Marsh again—especially if I were in custody. Though I was completely innocent of any wrongdoing, Marsh intimidated me so much I was ready to confess to just about anything!

"I heard Marsh tell Ciders that he was thinking of contacting the FBI's Behavioral Psychology Unit—"

"What?!"

Officer Franzetti waved an oncoming car down the road, gave me a sidelong glance. "Yeah. They're talking like Johnny's a real, live, serial killer . . ."

IN LESS THAN an hour, we arrived in Newport and were cruising down Bellevue Avenue, past American castles built at the turn of the last century by the Vanderbilts, Astors, and other merchant prince types. Most of those great Gilded Age elephants were museums now, open to paying tourists and available for private party bookings—such as the magnificent beaux arts mansion that had hosted the New Year's Eve ball where Bethany Banks had been murdered.

Not all of these grand houses, however, were open to the public. Throughout the town, even along the famous oceanside Cliff Walk, some historic homes had been set up as bed and breakfasts while others, including Windswept, the McClure family manse, had been maintained or rebuilt as primary or secondary residences for both the old- and new-money families who owned them.

Windswept stood on a promontory overlooking the rocky shores of the Atlantic Ocean, surrounded by acres of rolling grass and manicured trees. A grim gray edifice of weathered granite and dark wood, the mansion had been built by the McClure family patriarch well over a century ago, and she wore her age well.

As I rolled up to the gate, a uniformed security guard collected my invitation, then checked off my name on a clipboard. The ten-foot-tall iron bars of the crested gate swung open electronically. We drove for a moment and I soon spied heavy stone turrets and slate-shingled spires looming above tall oaks. A long red banner flapped in the wind from the tallest flagpole. Suddenly Jack whistled in my head.

Wow, babe. You never told me you used to live like the Queen of England.

"Impressed, Jack?" I asked silently. "Don't be. I never lived here."

Well, you married royalty by the looks of these digs.

"I always thought of Windswept as a modest dwelling. After all, it's smaller than San Simeon and has fewer rooms than the Taj Mahal."

Cute, doll, but bitter doesn't play right when it comes out of you. Leave the world-weary cynicism to mugs like me.

The surroundings grew more festive as we approached the main building. Laughter and music floated on the fresh ocean breeze along with the smoky scent of mesquite barbecue. On the great lawn, tents were scattered about. Swarms of children ran and played, chaperoned by an army of party planners dressed as clowns, cowboys, and cowgirls.

A man with orange hair, a red nose, and a polkadot jumpsuit waved me into a parking area that was already crowded. He looked a bit surprised to see a battered Saturn with weeds stuck in the fenders rolling into an area crowded with mirror-shiny Mercedes, BMWs, Porsches, and Rolls-Royces, but I noticed he did offer me an extra-big smile.

On the seat next to me, Spencer plastered his face to the window.

Hmm, lots of fun—for the curls, bows, and knickers set. Where do the grown-ups romp and play?

"See that big yellow tent down by the tennis courts? That's the bar—though I think my sister-in-law Ashley prefers to call it a 'salon.'"

Yeah, I've noticed rich gin-suckers employ euphemisms.

"I will be avoiding that place like the proverbial plague. But speaking of employment, Ashley must have hired an army for this event. As usual, she's outdone herself in the excess department."

Can't wait to meet this dame.

"With luck you won't have to."

I pulled into a nice shady spot in the shadow of two Cadillac SUVs nearly the size of Buy the Book's floor-space. I grabbed my Italian leather bag (bought at outlet prices) and slung it over my shoulder. Spencer burst through the door and raced toward the great lawn.

"Whoa, hold it, mister. Let's stick together."

"Aw, Mom."

"Come on, what do you want to do first?"

Spencer didn't hesitate. "Paintball."

I frowned. "I'm still not sure you should be participating in that sort of thing. You're too young, and it sounds dangerous."

"Come on, Mom!"

Yeah, come on, Mom. Let the kid play cops and robbers. And for heaven's sake, don't coddle him like a China doll or he'll turn into another overly sensitive, depressive snob, just like your ex.

Jack's observation stalled me, and I realized that if my late father and brother Pete had been here with me, they probably would have said the exact same thing. "You know . . . you could be right."

"What did you say, Mom?"

"I said you're right, Spencer. Let's go find that paintball stand and sign you up right now."

Spencer's smile would melt the ice caps. "It's this way, Mom. I saw the tent as we were driving up."

My son led me to a large khaki-colored tent crowded with kids. Inside, I approached a tall man in camouflage fatigues and black boots with a nametag on his combat suit that read *Captain Bob.* He offered me a polite grin, then addressed Spencer.

"Are you here for the junior competition, recruit?"

"Yes, sir!" Spencer barked, perfectly in character.

"And what's your name, soldier?"

"Spencer, sir."

"We'd better hurry, the junior event starts in twenty minutes, and we've got to get *Lieutenant* Spencer here suited up."

Ten minutes later, Spencer stood proudly before me. Paint gun in hand, he wore a clear face mask, coveralls, rubber galoshes, knee guards, and a helmet. My little trooper.

Captain Bob could see the look of trepidation on my face. "Don't worry. These kids are firing the equivalent of water balloons filled with paint from a distance of fifty yards—the trees and grass are going to take the most punishment."

"Can I watch?"

Spencer was horrified. "Mom!"

"Afraid not, Mrs. McClure. No one goes into those woods without protective gear. Anyway, there are more chaperones than soldiers out there. The officer here will be just fine."

"What next?"

"Well, the lieutenant here joins the rest of the squad in the woods. You head back to the party. Meet your friends, have a drink, and get something to eat." Captain Bob glanced at his watch. "We'll be back to this tent in about two hours."

I gave my son a final hug and a kiss before I sent him off to paint war. Then I left the tent and emerged in the brilliant sunshine, fumbling in my bag for my "Hollywood" sunglasses. I turned away from the glare to face the mansion—or rather, a small area beside it, which was the family's private parking area. I recognized the McClure family's Mercedes, and my sister-in-law's white BMW. The car parked next to them was also familiar—a sleek black Jaguar with a white and blue decal on the trunk.

My heart stopped. "Jack, that's the car! I'm sure of it. The car that almost ran over Angel Stark."

Careful, doll. I know what you're thinking.

"But Jack, shouldn't I check it out?"

Sure. I just want you to be careful.

I looked around. There were plenty of people nearby, but everyone seemed to be going about their own business.

Just waltz over to the car, Jack said. *Walk like you own the place and nobody will look twice. Trust me.*

I got all the way to Ashley's BMW without anyone noticing, walked right past it to the black Jag. Up close, I realized the odd decal was a parking tag for a Newport country club, the splash of blue a leaping marlin.

I peered through the windshield—hopefully without appearing to do just that. Leather seats, sporty, wood-grained interior, stick shift, GPS, combination radio and CD player, cell phone in the dashboard, all the bells and whistles. No guns, bludgeons, whips, or chains in sight.

Luckily, the door was unlocked.

I reached out and grabbed the handle on the passenger side. I closed my eyes and lifted the latch, waiting for a car alarm to blare, for everyone to look in my direction, for a security team to surround me and escort me off the premises where the Newport Police would take me into custody.

Miracle of miracles, the door opened soundlessly. I climbed inside, sank deep into the leather bucket seat.

"What now, Jack?"

Case it good. Toss the glove compartment, check under the seat, behind the cushions—

"Will do."

I found nothing on the dash or under the seats. Inside the glove compartment, however, I discovered a leather case containing the Jag's registration and insurance information, and a batch of business cards. All bore the same name. I fingered one of the cream-white linen paper, gilt scripted cards that read *Mr. Donald Morgan Easterbrook, Jr.*

I pocketed one card, stuffed the rest back into their pouch, then shoved the case into the glove compartment. I was about to peer under the dashboard when a silhouette abruptly blotted out the bright sun.

"Breaking and entering and grand theft auto. Have you fallen on hard times, Penelope?"

I looked up. Kiki McClure-Langdon stood beside the car. Behind her stood the owner of the Jaguar, her fiancé Donald Easterbrook, Jr. His photograph in Angel's book didn't do him justice. From the top of his perfectly coifed head to the broad span of his muscular shoulders, the prince of the Newport jet set was more than just John Kennedy, Jr. handsome, there was a sizzle of hot Latino blood, courtesy of Easterbrook's wealthy Brazilian mother, that rendered him breathtaking.

I turned away, flushed red with embarrassment. Just as I was certain the situation could not possibly get worse, it did. Coming toward us was La Princessa herself: my sister-in-law, Ashley McClure-Sutherland.

CHAPTER 23

Angels and Demons

With his strong face, his athlete's build, and the Gary Cooper manner, [he] projected what psychologists call the halo effect. People with the halo effect seem to know exactly what they're doing and, moreover, make you want to admire them for it. They make you see the halos over their heads.

—Tom Wolfe, *Hooking Up*, 2001

"GOOD GOD, JACK, what do I do?" I silently asked, trying not to lose it.

Guess, he answered in my head.

Swallowing a lump of sheer terror, I attempted to feign cool Jack Shepard control, then stepped out of the Jaguar, shut the car door, and faced Kiki. Meeting her stare, I flashed a (thoroughly fake) confident smile and levelly told her, "Sarcasm doesn't suit a woman who tried to run down Angel Stark on the very night she was murdered."

Kiki winced, then looked at her fiancé—worry and confusion suddenly invading the typically superior expression of her ice-blue gaze.

Beautiful, doll. Keep going.

"Oh, you were quick," I said, "but not quick enough. There were witnesses to that incident on Cranberry Street. And I think the police will find it a neat coincidence, your staying at the same inn on the same night as Angel Stark— who just happened to turn up dead on that very property the next day."

A sudden gust stirred long blonde strands of Kiki's hair and the gauzy blue fabric of her sundress. Her already pale features turned snow white. Her pink painted lips moved, but no sound emerged.

Florid-faced, Ashley McClure-Sutherland pushed past her cousin and stepped between us. "This is ridiculous," she cried. "How dare you invade my home and intimidate members of my own family. My God, Penelope, you're nothing but trouble. My family's curse."

It was a vicious remark, but I refused to be baited by my sister-in-law. I bored in on Kiki instead.

"Did you know Victoria Banks has also been murdered?" I asked. "It happened within hours of Angel's demise, and she was strangled in the same manner—just like her sister Bethany."

Kiki literally fell against her fiancé. Ashley appeared to be struck dumb, for perhaps the first time in her life.

Pour it on thick, doll. They're on the ropes, Jack coaxed.

Finally, Donald Easterbrook spoke. "Where did this happen?" His rich baritone seemed unruffled by my revelations.

"Victoria's corpse was discovered in a wooded area outside the motel in Quindicott this morning."

I locked eyes with Kiki again. "I watched the State Police haul her dead body to the morgue on my way to Newport."

I paused to let the words sink in. "Don't you find it odd that Victoria's murder occurred so close to Quindicott, where *Kiki* chose to stay the night?"

Out of the corner of my eye I noticed that our confrontation was beginning to attract attention. Kiki shifted her gaze from her fiancé to Ashley, then back to me.

Reaching a hand into the pocket of my capri pants, I grasped that old buffalo nickel. "Jack? I have to get them to talk to me. What more can I say?"

Threaten them with the cops, baby. Do it loudly.

"So let's call the police," I said with a raised voice. "Because if you don't talk to me *now*, you can talk to the police when they arrive."

Donald Easterbrook's dark eyes flashed, but he quickly masked his annoyance with a smile. His strong, tanned hand closed on my arm.

"If you want to talk, let's do it inside," he said smoothly.

He released me before I could yank my arm free. With Ashley flanking me, I followed Donald and his fiancée through a side door into the mansion.

Ashley caught up with Donald, spun to face him. "I don't think this is a good idea." She glared at me. "Not at all."

"This won't take long, Mrs. Sutherland. We'll go to the library," said Donald.

I half expected Ashley to butt out, but she angrily followed the rest of us into Windswept's bookroom. The large two-story space was lined with polished oak shelves. Aging, gilt-edged books filled those shelves, and high-backed, green velvet upholstered chairs, ornate book stands, and Tiffany lamps were scattered about the waxed and polished hardwood floor. One corner of the room was dominated by a large Victorian standing globe with brass fittings. Sun streamed through high windows, warming the room, which smelled faintly of dust.

"Sit down, Mrs. McClure, won't you?" Donald said with a chivalry that surprised me, considering the circumstances.

Ask for a drink, advised Jack.

"But I'm not thirsty," I silently told him.

Baby, wise up. Alcohol loosens tongues, remember? Ask for some yourself. Pretend to sip yours. Chances are, Prince Donald will join you—and do more than pretend to sip.

Jack was right. I boldly asked for a cognac and got one. Donald went to a small bar in the corner and fixed a round, including Kiki, Ashley, and himself.

I sat rigidly in one of the high-backed green velvet chairs. Ashen-faced Kiki sat in an antique love seat opposite me. Ashley chose to pace the hand-woven Aubusson area rug. Finally, Donald Easterbrook sat down on the love seat next to his fiancée. He leaned forward, dark eyes studying me. For a moment we faced one another in silence.

Despite the malice radiating from my sister-in-law, and the rage in Kiki's eyes, I felt no such hostility from Donald. I read somewhere once that anger and animosity often spring from a lack of confidence. Donald Easterbrook had no such deficit. Poised, polite, and self-assured, he seemed in control of the situation. Though half the age of my sister-in-law, Donald had handled Ashley better than I ever could. And by dragging us into the mansion, I realized he'd handled me well too.

It was Donald who broke the silence. After a long sip of his cognac, he asked, "Why do you think Kiki killed Angel Stark?"

"It goes back to Bethany's murder," I replied. "Someone in your circle murdered Bethany Banks. Angel said as much in her book, and I believe her."

"Someone *else* was arrested for that crime," said Donald.

"And he was acquitted," I pointed out.

"*Released* because of legal technicalities," he corrected.

"He was an innocent patsy and you and I both know it, Mr. Easterbrook. You have more of a motive for murdering Bethany than Johnny Napoli. She was your fiancée and was cheating on you when she rendezvoused with Johnny that night."

"So why do you suspect Kiki?" Donald pressed.

"Three reasons. The first is that she had a better motive than anyone else. After Bethany's murder, Kiki became engaged to you."

"We'll let that go for a moment. Tell me the second reason."

"Angel's book made a lot of people angry. Some of them were mad enough to confront her. Her publicity manager told me a doctor she identified as a pill pusher to your set nearly assaulted Angel in a Manhattan bookstore. Victoria Banks almost attacked Angel in my own store the other night. And someone driving the black Jaguar outside tried to run down Angel Stark an hour later."

"Your point?" Donald asked.

I shifted my gaze to Kiki. "You were in my store the night Angel gave her reading. You were staying in the same bed and breakfast as Angel, when you could just as easily have been staying here at Windswept."

"Kiki had car trouble," Ashley cried. "She got stuck in Quindicott!"

"Nice story, but I don't buy it," I replied, my eyes never wavering from Kiki's. "I think Kiki confronted Angel in her own time—after the book signing, back at the Finch Inn. And I think that's when Kiki murdered her. She was the only person in your circle besides Victoria Banks who was anywhere near Quindicott that night. And I think Vicky Banks is now off everyone's suspect list."

"But you're wrong!" Kiki cried. "I saw Hal there, too. Hal McConnell."

I blinked in surprise. "Hal McConnell was at Angel's reading? I think I would have remembered that."

Kiki shook her blonde mane. "Not at the store. I saw Hal at the Inn, later that night."

I leaned forward. "When?"

Kiki shrugged, bit her lower lip. "I don't know, maybe one in the morning. Certainly after midnight."

"How can you be sure?"

Kiki took a breath. "Because you're correct about one thing. I was there to confront Angel. I wanted her to stop harassing us, to leave us out of her life, her books. I was there to stop her lies."

"What lies, specifically?"

Dead silence descended. Kiki's lips became tight, Donald put his arm around her shoulder. A grandfather clock in the corner ticked louder than Big Ben.

"Okay," I finally said. "Kiki, tell me more about your encounter with Hal that night."

Kiki swept her hair back, took a fortifying sip of cognac. "I went to Angel's room at eleven o'clock. I knocked, but she wasn't back yet. I tried again at midnight, but she still hadn't returned. I tried to sleep but couldn't. Maybe a half an hour later, I heard a car park, and voices, too. I got dressed and waited for Angel to come up the stairs. After a long time I went down to the front entrance. No one was in the lobby and I went outside, onto the porch. That's when I saw Hal in the parking lot and I called out to him."

"Are you sure it was Hal?" I asked.

Kiki nodded, "I'm positive, because he came up to the porch steps and I spoke to him. It was Hal all right. Polo shirt and all." She rolled her eyes. Donald gave a slight amused grunt.

"What am I missing?"

Donald shrugged. "It's just . . . well, since he was, like, twelve years old Hal has bought like twenty Polo shirts every summer, and that's what he wears all season. It's become kind of a joke among us. Hal and his ubiquitous Polo shirts."

"You're sure he was wearing a Polo shirt the night you saw him at the Finch Inn, the night Angel was killed?"

"Sure," said Kiki. "I saw it under his open windbreaker, so wrinkled and ratty it looked like he'd pulled it out of his trunk. Hal used to be a neat freak, but I hadn't seen much of him since Bethany died. I guess things like that can affect you in a lot of ways."

I thought of Hal's change of hairstyle—brushing the longish hair forward rakishly around his face instead of neatly back off his face as I'd seen it styled in all of his photos. I remembered the way he'd dressed when he'd come to the bookstore the morning after Angel's and Victoria's murders—well-dressed for a summer Saturday in an impeccably tailored blue blazer, his buttoned-down shirt crisp and white, his silver-and-blue striped tie perfectly knotted in a snug Windsor.

I took a closer look at Kiki then. Her gauzy blue sundress revealed ample amounts of toned, tanned flesh— from her throat, shoulders, and arms to her long, lean legs. Her skin appeared flawless. Not one scratch or bruise that I could see.

"What did Hal say to you?" I asked.

"Not much," said Kiki. "I called him over, and he said he was just passing through and wanted a room but the place was full. Said he was going to try the motel by the highway, or just go home. But I knew it was crap."

"Why?"

"Because I'm sure he was looking for Angel, too," insisted Kiki. "He kept eyeing her rental car in the lot, like he was waiting for her to show up."

Donald spoke next. "Mrs. McClure. You did say that Victoria's body was found at that motel, didn't you?"

I nodded.

"Well there you are. Hal was at both murder scenes. And he attended the ball where Bethany was murdered as well. Surely Hal is the better suspect?"

"Except for one thing. Hal McConnell loved Bethany

Banks. Angel Stark said it in her book, and Hal told me as much himself."

"Unrequited love, Mrs. McClure," said Donald. "Look around at all these books. I'm willing to bet a goodly number of them tell stories of unrequited love and the tragedy that can be caused by such frustrated emotions."

"Oh, but Hal's love was no longer unrequited," I replied. "In the last few months he'd been seeing Victoria Banks. They shared an affection. Why would Hal murder a woman who returned his affections?" I shook my head. "Anyway, you're both forgetting the black Jaguar parked outside. I doubt Hal was driving it. But someone was and that someone tried to kill Angel Stark."

"You forget that the black Jaguar belongs to me," said Donald, a cagey half-smile crossing his face.

"Are you telling me you were in Quindicott last night?" I asked.

"That's exactly what I'm telling you, Mrs. McClure. I drove here from Connecticut last night. I happened to breeze through Quindicott for gas. I saw Angel in the street, and we had words. So you see, Kiki had nothing to do with that encounter."

"What kind of words did you have exactly?"

"I told her she made a big mistake publishing her book, that's all."

I studied Donald's attractive, confident features, thinking there was more to this. Although Angel Stark had admitted no such thing in her book, Hal McConnell claimed Angel had been sleeping with Donald.

Remember what I showed you, baby, said Jack. *A little information can take you a long way in an interrogation if you know how to use it. So use it—fast.*

"I know you and Angel were sleeping together," I said as casually as I could manage. "But *when* exactly did you stop?"

"Right before Bethany was murdered," Donald blurted out.

Kiki's jaw dropped. "Donny, shut up!"

Donald stared at me blankly.

Good work, baby. A deer in the headlights. You've got him admitting to something he didn't want to. Keep him talking, he's probably dying to spill . . .

"So you didn't love Angel?" I asked. "Or did you?"

Suddenly, Kiki went from outraged to curious. She stared at him expectantly.

Donald's eyes widened even more. "Of course I didn't love her! Angel and I were hot and heavy for a few months. The sex was great. That's all."

"Did Bethany know?" I asked.

Donald shrugged, looked down at his cognac. "I think Bethany found out near the end, but she never threw it in my face if she did. I mean . . . we weren't married yet . . . wild oats, you know . . ."

"Sure," I replied. "And she decided to sow some oats, too," I replied. "And get even with you in the process. Like having a fling with a member of the catering staff right under your nose—and the noses of all your buddies—a low-class stud she knew and you knew, too, because he supplied drugs to your crowd."

Donald scowled. I'd hit a nerve. He shifted on the love seat, took yet another long hit of cognac. "That may be true," he said, his eyes beginning to appear slightly glazed from the alcohol, "but the guy . . . he never had sex with Bethany . . . he never laid a finger on her."

You've definitely got something here, said Jack. *A point of pride. He's still jealous that his girl wanted to sleep with Johnny-boy. So press that button. Hard.*

I cleared my throat. "Is that what you think? That Johnny didn't have sex with Bethany? Well, that's wishful thinking, but that's not what I heard from the police."

"Hey, whatever you heard is wrong, okay," said Donald, his voice finally betraying tension. He pointed his finger at me. "That guy, he *was* a patsy. I know. Because I know who set him up. The same person who killed Bethany Banks."

"Oh my God!" Ashley lunged between us, wide-eyed. "Don't say anything more," she cried.

"Why not, Mrs. Sutherland?" Donald replied, the pointing finger turning into a dismissive wave. "What does it matter now anyway? Beth's dead."

"Sit down, Ashley," I barked. To my amazement, she did.

"It was *Angel* who killed Bethany," said Donald. "I know because I saw Angel leave the room right after the murder. Bethany went down there to have her fling with that waiter. I got wind of it and went down to stop it. But by the time I got there, I saw that Angel had already strangled Beth. She'd killed her before that Johnny person even arrived."

"Why?" I asked, not yet ready to believe him.

"She was high that night," said Donald. "And she was crazed because . . . well . . . she wanted me to dump Bethany and marry her instead. She made this declaration to me in private . . . but that was absurd. Angel Stark was a crazy slut and I told her so. She slept with every guy I know. She was just wild oats, a party girl, not someone you'd marry . . . not someone in my position, anyway. Angel lied about Beth in her book, you know? Bethy didn't sleep around. Angel was describing *herself* . . . a convenient fuck."

I looked at Kiki. Her legs were curled up under her like a gawky adolescent. She was biting her pink lips.

"You know all this, don't you, Kiki?" I asked.

She gave a tense shrug. "Of course."

My gaze swung back to Donald. "I gather Angel wasn't happy with your decision."

"That's an understatement. Angel claimed she was going to tell the world about me cheating on Bethany, and I threatened Angel right back. I told Angel to keep her mouth shut or I'd turn her in for dealing drugs."

My eyebrows rose at that. I knew Angel used drugs, she'd said so in her first book. But this was the first I'd heard about her *dealing* them. "Why should I believe you?"

"Because its true," Kiki blurted out. "Angel's been dealing drugs in our circles for years. Johnny Napoli was a Johnny-come-lately to that little business."

"Where's your proof . . . for any of this?" I asked.

"I was an eyewitness . . . I *saw* Angel leave that storage room," Donald replied. "Her silk jacket was ripped, her face was flushed. When she was gone, I went inside and . . . I found Beth, lying there, not moving . . . I didn't want to believe she was dead at first, you know? I tried to see if she was breathing, but she was dead all right . . ."

He stopped talking, seemed lost in his own thoughts. He sipped more cognac and I pressed. "Why didn't you tell the police what you saw? Why didn't you tell them everything?"

Donald sat back, shrugged. "Klaus von Bülow."

"Excuse me?"

"O. J. Simpson . . . Michael Skakel . . . The media and private investigators crawl into every nook and cranny of people's lives when there's a high-profile murder trial. We didn't want that. None of us. Bethany was already dead. Nothing could bring her back . . ."

My eyes narrowed on Donald. He was an attractive charmer, but I knew he was holding back. "It was more than that, wasn't it? Did Angel threaten you somehow?"

Once again, Donald shifted uncomfortably. "After I had gone down there . . . you know . . . and saw Bethany like that . . . my mind started racing. I put it together that Angel had done this . . . I ran back upstairs, found Angel coming in from outside. Her torn silk jacket was gone . . . her long white gloves were gone . . . I pulled her into an alcove." He shook his head. "I could have strangled *her* right then and there. I told her we were going to call the police together, but she told me if I called the police, she'd testify that I had

killed Bethany. That she'd seen me do it . . . I knew it
wasn't an idle threat . . . I had already touched that belt and
Beth's body . . . I was afraid there would be evidence
against me . . ."

"You got scared?" I coaxed. "You panicked?"

"Angel told me that Johnny Napoli was about to go
down to have sex with Bethany, and he would be the one to
discover the body and the police would discover it was his
belt . . . she said the police would pin it on Johnny . . . I
knew she was right . . . and I wasn't thinking clearly . . . so
I went along with it . . . when the chaos started, after the
body was discovered, I made sure people *saw* me go in the
room and touch Bethany's body—the grieving fiancé, you
know? So the police would be told I had touched her after
her murder. Everything went like Angel said, the police
took the catering kid away and we all went home fast . . ."

"And when you considered coming out with the truth," I
said, "your family raised the nightmare specter of those
celebrity scandals? The Klaus von Bülow case and the
Michael Skakel and O. J. Simpson trials?"

"Right," said Donald.

"And then Angel wrote that book."

Donald shook his head. "When I saw her in the street, I
really cursed her out. It wasn't enough she killed Bethany,
now she wanted to cash in on it."

"What did she say?"

"She just laughed in that way she does," said Donald.
"She was such a bitch. She jacked up her usual threat level.
This time she told me to keep my mouth shut or she'd
come out with evidence that I had been cheating on
Bethany with Kiki and that Kiki and I killed Bethany together. It was just a bluff. I knew it, but it made me crazy,
and I told her to go to hell."

"Your story is very detailed, Donald. But why should
I believe you?"

"Because Kiki and I still have Angel's torn silk jacket

and white opera gloves from that night. There's blood on the jacket and gloves, so it probably has traces of Bethany's DNA."

I couldn't believe my ears. "You're joking."

But Kiki shook her head. "I also noticed Angel had ducked outside. Donny saw Angel come in downstairs, but I actually watched her from an upstairs bedroom window. She'd stuck something behind some statue in the garden. And when she came back, she wasn't wearing her jacket or gloves any longer. I'm sure she expected to retrieve the clothes later, but I went out, took them, and threw them in my car. I thought it was a good idea to hold on to that stuff."

"You forgot about the other pair of gloves," said Donald. "They were in that bundle, too."

"Whose gloves?" I asked. "Kiki's?"

"No," said Kiki. "Bethany's."

Donald explained. "Angel had taken Bethany's opera gloves off her corpse. One can only assume she wanted to make sure there was as little physical evidence left behind as possible."

Kiki nodded. "That's why there was no skin under Bethany's fingernails from their fight."

I blinked in astonishment. The two of them would make a formidable couple, I concluded.

"There's still something you aren't telling me," I said. "When exactly did you two start your romantic relationship?"

Donald and Kiki exchanged glances. It was Donald who spoke. "By New Year's Eve I was through with Angel, and I was getting tired of Bethany's endless demands and tantrums. Kiki and I became close over the holidays and hooked up."

"Kiki said she saw Angel from an upstairs bedroom," I noted. "But those Cliff Walk mansions are essentially museums. The upstairs rooms are supposed to be off limits, even during private parties. So I'm guessing Donald was with you up there, Kiki? And that accounts for the 'mysterious' hour Angel claimed in her book that Donald was missing from the party?"

"Yes, he was with me," she admitted. "The whole idea that the rooms were off limits is what made it so"—she shrugged—"interesting. Donny and I hooked up in one of those museum bedrooms, then Donny went back to the party first. I waited fifteen minutes before coming down to the ground floor again. You know, so people wouldn't see us coming down together."

"So, if this is all true, then who murdered Victoria Banks?"

"It wasn't me," said Donald. "I liked Vicky. After Bethany was gone, the Banks family wanted me to stay in touch—to help them get over their loss. I did. Vicky and I got to be friendly . . . When Hal wasn't around, we talked."

"How close did you get?" I asked.

"Close," said Donald, glancing nervously at Kiki.

"Close enough to tell Vicky Banks that Angel was the one who killed her sister?"

"Maybe . . ."

"No wonder that poor girl was gunning for Angel. It wasn't Angel's book at all—it was your telling Vicky that Angel got away with killing her sister that drove her over the edge."

"I didn't kill Vicky," Donald replied. "I have dozens of witnesses that will tell you I never left this house since Friday night when I drove through Quindicott and spotted Angel."

"No, you didn't kill Vicky with a *rope*," I said, "but you told her things you never should have, just to ease your own guilty conscience. Things that sent a young and impressionable girl over the edge. Keep that physical evidence safe, because you're going to need it to prove your story."

I stood and faced Ashley, whose expression was nothing short of shock—whether it was from the startling truths she'd just heard or the fact that I'd stood my ground and shook those truths loose, I couldn't say.

"Thank you for your gracious invitation," I told my sister-in-law. "Now I'll collect my son and we'll be leaving."

I arrived at paintball headquarters in time to witness the junior team being rewarded for their efforts. Every little solder got a plastic medal, complete with a red, white, and blue ribbon. Spencer's eyes were bright when he rejoined me a few moments later.

"It was so cool, Mom. Captain Bob led us on a commando raid and we 'achieved our objective.' "

"I'm proud of you, honey," I said sincerely. "Mommy achieved her objective, too."

CHAPTER 24

Judgment Day

They were careless people, Tom and Daisy—they smashed up things and creatures and then retreated into their money or their vast carelessness . . . and let other people clean up the mess they had made. . . .

—F. Scott Fitzgerald, *The Great Gatsby*, 1925

Planning is for the poor.

—Robert Evans

AFTER TAKING SPENCER out for ice cream, then stopping by the bookstore to make sure Sadie and Mina had things in hand, I drove my Saturn over to the Finch Inn, but not up the tree-lined drive. Instead, I parked on the side of the street and cut the engine.

I pulled out Victoria's cell phone and dialed the Inn's

number. Fiona answered on the first ring. We exchanged pleasantries, then I got to the point of my call. "Is the security camera you installed over the front entrance still working?"

"You bet," Fiona replied. "I haven't had a lithograph, framed portrait, or antique lamp disappear since, either."

"Do you still have the surveillance video from the night Angel disappeared?"

"Sorry, Pen. The State Police confiscated it the next day. I never even had a chance to review it before they swept it up in their investigation."

"But if there was something to see, would the camera pick it up?"

"Sure," said Fiona. "The camera moves back and forth, from side to side—covers the entire porch and the front door. If there's something to see, the State Troopers will see it."

"But only if they know what to look for . . ."

"Something's up, isn't it, Pen?" Fiona's voice was palpable with excitement.

"Not sure yet. I'll let you know." I quickly ended the call before prosecutor Fiona could begin her cross-exam.

Though it was nearly six o'clock, the late summer sun was still above the horizon and a few hours of daylight remained. I would need it to prepare for what Jack had suggested on the way back from the McClure's. I climbed out of the car and walked up the Inn's tree-lined drive. Instead of going up the steps to the Inn's main house, I followed the wooded path along the pond, which led to Fiona's still-under-construction restaurant. The scent of salty sea was heavy as a damp, warm breeze whipped across the inlet.

Even down by the water, the day was still sticky and uncomfortably warm, yet I suppressed a shiver. The body of Angel Stark had been dragged from this very spot, and I doubted I would ever banish the sight of her murdered corpse—or Victoria Banks's, for that matter—from my mind.

Living with the dead, said Jack. *That's the world you're in now, baby. Get used to it.*

"Jack, do you believe Kiki and Donald's story? That Angel killed Bethany in some kind of jealous rage?"

Yeah, doll. It all fits. I'd already suspected Angel of being envious of Bethany from that little bit of self-serving prose she read in your store. What convinced me that Priss Kiki and Prince Donald were on the level about Angel doing the dirty deed was their claim of evidence. Angel's silk jacket—

"Right, like a certain presidential intern's blue dress . . ."

Blue dress? Want to drive that by me again, sister?

"Never mind."

Anyway, physical evidence like that will back to the hilt what they're claiming, so you better count on it existing if this next step fails.

I nodded, understanding and agreeing. Angel had been more than a careless, eccentric author. Obviously, a sick, jealous, unbalanced monster had been lurking behind the bohemian-style designer clothes and false-revelatory prose.

So you've got Johnny down to two counts of murder, Jack said. *You still have to prove who killed Angel—*

"And Victoria. I know."

Donald has a solid alibi for that night. But Kiki doesn't.

"No. But there's something else she doesn't have."

I could almost hear Jack smiling when he said, *That's right, doll. You tell me.*

"Defense wounds." In the warm car, I had already removed my long-sleeved summer-weight sweater and threw it over my scratched-up shoulders. "If Kiki had needed to hide scratches or other defense wounds," I told Jack, "she would have worn something with long sleeves to the party, just like I had. But that slight gauzy sundress of hers revealed nothing but perfect skin. Not one bruise, not one scratch."

Right, baby. You're on a streak. Don't stop now . . .

I approached the construction site. The restaurant was still a fleshless skeleton, stark in the waning afternoon. The brick foundation rose chest-high. Wood-frame walls and supporting steel beams were still exposed. Work had stopped here since the grisly discovery, and close to the water, ribbons of yellow plastic crime scene tape fluttered on the warm breeze.

"We're here, Jack. What do you think?"

Piles of wood were stacked about, most under canvas. I wove my way around support beams and unfinished walls that would soon be dining areas and a kitchen.

It'll work. But you need something even higher than these walls.

I spied a tall pole, planted just beyond the perimeter of the structure, and probably used by the builders for surveying. "Found it!" Glancing around the area, I also discovered a tall ladder propped near a parked yellow forklift and backhoe.

"I think it'll work, Jack."

Then roll the dice before your subject skips town. Make that call.

I flipped open Victoria's cell phone. On the display screen, I highlighted the phone number of her last incoming voicemail message—just as I had yesterday. The party answered on the third ring. I recognized Hal's voice.

"Still have Victoria's cell phone, I see," he said, the touch of weariness in his voice making him sound older than his years.

"Yes," I replied. "And I'm about to turn it over to the police so they can match the calls stored in its memory against your own phone records."

The silence was deafening.

"Hal, I know you lied to me. About Victoria's father being in town, and about where you were the night Victoria vanished. It's time we talked again." I paused. "Nine o'clock tonight. At the construction site near the Finch Inn. And don't even *try* to tell me you don't know where that is."

I hung up before he could reply. With a sigh, I consulted my ghost. "Jack? Do you think he bought it?"

You have to assume he did. Now you've got to work fast to get it all ready.

"I know. Lots to do. And no time like the present."

Jack grunted. *So to speak.*

A FEW HOURS later, I was pacing the Finch Inn construction site, watching the sun drop below the horizon and a black velvet shroud slowly smother the summer blue sky then pierce it with starlight as sharp as daggers.

Behind me, that tall wooden pole I'd spied earlier stood firm as the wind increased, blowing through the trees with an ominous intensity. The inlet's sea water continued its lazy incessant lapping against the dark bank.

"We're all set," I murmured to Jack as I checked my watch for the fifteenth time in as many minutes.

Maybe not.

Seeing as how I had a potential murderer on his way to meet me, I tried not to react with total alarm when I asked Jack, "What the heck do you mean, maybe not?!"

I've been mulling everything over, and it seems to me there's still a piece missing in this puzzle. The piece. Angel's gun. The one she tried to give to Johnny. Remember why Johnny raced to the border in the first place? Angel was trying to blackmail him into killing someone for her— now who do you think that someone was?

"Donald Easterbrook?" I guessed, "for almost running her over? Or Kiki, for stealing Donald away? Or . . . Victoria Banks?"

Victoria had threatened Angel very publicly at your bookstore—

"And, according to Vicky's roommates, she'd sent Angel threatening e-mails, too. You know what e-mails, are, right, Jack?"

What do you think? I've been watching you tap away on that typewriter box for a year now. Anyway, that means there's even more evidence to show Victoria Banks had an intent to harm Angel Stark—which would have given Angel a motive to go after Victoria. Seems to me, Angel was worried how far Victoria would go with her threats . . . and that night, when the girl actually threatened her in public, Angel decided to rid herself of the little Banks pest before she got around to getting rid of Angel.

"So what about the gun then?"

We know from Kiki's claim that Hal was here late last night looking for Angel—and he lied about it to you, so he's trying to cover up his tracks. If he killed Angel, like you and I both think he did, he might have taken that gun from her. And he could be packing right now.

"Gee-zus, Jack, what a time to share this with me!"

I quickly used Vicky's cell to call Eddie Franzetti. He was the only person on the Quindicott Police force whom I trusted with this information. He'd been through this with me before, when he helped me capture Timothy Brennan's killer.

"Sorry, Mrs. McClure," said the desk sergeant. "Eddie went up to Providence with Johnny and Bud Napp. Tomorrow Johnny's going to be arraigned for murder, and the Staties wanted him close for a perp walk in the morning. I guess Bud wanted to go along to support his nephew."

"Dammit!" (I couldn't help myself.)

"Is anything wrong? Is there anything I can help you with?"

"No thanks, Sergeant."

Call it off, doll, Jack said when I hung up. *If he's armed, you may be setting up another crime scene here.*

A stone rattled on the path. I turned at the sound. Hal McConnell was approaching me, a frown creasing his handsome features.

"Sorry, Jack," I silently told the ghost. "It's too late. We'll just have to make do with the resources at hand."

I surveyed the suspect. He wore khaki pants that flapped in the summer wind. A yellow polo shirt, buttoned to the top, peeked out of his buttoned blue blazer. Once again, he wore an outfit too heavy for the warm, sticky weather. Hal stopped a few yards away, eyes level with mine. The warm breeze blew his forward-swept hair back, and for the first time I saw the angry bruise, confirming what I'd suspected. He'd suddenly changed his hairstyle for one reason—to cover a defensive wound.

"Well?" Hal asked, sliding his hands into his pants pockets.

"I spoke to Kiki Langdon earlier today," I began. "She told me she saw you the night Angel was killed, in front of this inn."

Hal's half-smile turned sour. "I see now that Newport's code of silence is selectively applied . . ."

I shook my head. "Hal, listen to me. The security camera above the Inn's front door would have photographed your whole encounter with Kiki. The State Police have that evidence now—and they'll care about it once I tell them what to look for and why."

Hal swallowed. His hands came out of his pockets. He rubbed the back of his neck, like he was thinking fast.

Good, honey. You surprised him with the camera. He didn't know about it.

"So I talked to Kiki that night? So what?" he finally replied. "It's not illegal to stop by an inn . . . I'll just deny having anything to do with Angel's murder."

"There are things the police don't know yet, Hal. Like the fact that Angel was the one who murdered Bethany, and Bethany's little sister, Victoria, discovered that fact."

Hal blinked. I'd caught him off guard again.

Keep going, baby.

"Yes," he slowly admitted. "It's true. Vicky knew. Donald told her . . ."

"Easterbrook?"

Hal nodded, sighed, folded his arms tightly across his chest. "It wasn't enough to have Bethany. He started on Victoria, too . . . Before Bethany's body was even in the ground." A bitter expression crossed his features. "Donald has a hobby, Mrs. McClure, getting girls into bed . . . not that it's a crime. With him it's more of a compulsion . . . maybe it's in his blood, part of that Brazilian meal-ticket his father married, or maybe he's just phenomenally more successful at it than the rest of us so it comes off as out of control, but . . . there it is."

"You must be furious with Donald then. He slept with both of the women you loved."

Hal laughed at that, a broken, brittle sound. "You think I loved Bethany? Once maybe. But by the time she was murdered I hated her so much I probably could have killed her myself."

"But not Victoria."

"No. Not her. But then there was always more to her than Bethany. She quickly regretted getting involved with Donald. She . . . she was starting to love me, I think."

Okay, baby, you got him where you want him. Spring your theory. Only make it sound like you already know for sure, like he's not telling you anything you don't know. Lie, baby. Lie good.

I swallowed my nerves. "And then, of course, Angel killed Victoria. I know that, too, Hal. I found the evidence."

His expression darkened. "I heard the whole thing over

the cell phone. We were talking, Vicky and I. Suddenly Vicky said something like 'what are you doing here,' and then I heard another voice. Angel's. She said something like 'you want to threaten me *now*?' That's when the connection broke."

"You were in Newport when this happened?"

Hal shook his head. "I was already in my car, on my way to that fleabag motel on the highway. After the connection broke, I floored it. When I pulled into the parking lot, I saw Angel getting into a parked car. I thought Vicky might have been in that car, too, and I followed it."

"So you came here to confront Angel."

"I got here right as she pulled up. Of course, Vicky wasn't in the car. Not in the backseat, not on the floor, not in the trunk. By that time, Vicky was already dead in the woods. But I didn't know it at the time. I demanded Angel tell me where Vicky was, what had happened."

"And did she?"

"Angel was high, I think. She laughed and ran down this path. She thought it was a big game. She had some yellow rope draped around her neck, told me how she'd grabbed a few pieces of it off the back of that kid Johnny's pickup, just so she could frame him a second time."

I closed my eyes a moment. "Jack, did you hear that?"

Yeah, baby. Remember the kid's testimony in the bookstore—he'd said he'd been so upset trying to get away from Angel he'd flooded the engine in the parking lot. It wouldn't start for a few minutes.

I could hardly believe it was that simple. "That must have been the moment Angel grabbed the lengths of rope," I silently agreed. "But Johnny had been so focused on the truck's stalling, he never saw her do it."

"Angel's hands were still bloody when I confronted her," Hal continued. "She was still holding the gun she'd used to beat Vicky unconscious. She pretended to tighten the piece of rope around her neck so she could show me exactly how she'd killed Vicky. It was a big game, a big taunt to torture me. That was Angel's kick, you know? Making people squirm. She'd gone to the motel, called Vicky from one of the motel's pay phones to lure her outside, then forced her at gunpoint into the woods. There were no bullets in her gun, she told me she'd thrown them in Johnny Napp's face when he'd refused to help her. So she beat Vicky unconscious with the butt and strangled the life out of her with one of the pieces of rope she'd taken."

His gaze, which had gone far away as he recounted that night, suddenly focused on me. "Angel was a monster and had to be stopped. And I was going to stop her. That's all I could think. I just snapped . . . slapped her and cursed her. She fought me, but I took the ends of the rope she'd draped around her neck to taunt me and I started to choke her. Angel fought hard. I know what she wrote about me in that book—she called me childish, sentimental, weak, had no respect for me. She never thought I had it in me . . . but I wouldn't stop . . ."

My throat suddenly felt like it had been stuffed with cotton balls. I tried to clear it.

Steady, kid. Hang in there.

"So that's why you were wearing the jacket and tie when I met you at the bookstore?" I asked. "And why you quickly threw on a wrinkled, dirty windbreaker from your car's trunk after you got back to the parking lot. To hide the scratches?"

"Yes, Mrs. McClure, and why I'm wearing this jacket now."

"And you knew your skin and blood might be under Angel's fingernails and on her body. So you threw it into the water hoping to destroy any such evidence."

"Yes. For all I know, it didn't," he admitted.

"For all I know, it did," I said.

Hope flashed behind Hal McConnell's stare, followed by suspicion. "Why am I here, then? This *is* blackmail, isn't it? You want money, don't you?"

"Not blackmail," I said. "Blackmail is impossible. Look up."

Hal lifted his head. "See that box on the pole behind me, the wires leading out of it, to the bushes over there?"

His eyes traced my map. Hal nodded.

"There's another security camera up there. If you killed Angel right here, as you said you did, then the murder was caught on camera and that recording is also in the hands of the State Police."

Hal's eyes dropped. He reached one hand into the pocket of his sport jacket. "I guess I'll need this then . . ."

As I watched, Hal drew a bloodstained handgun out of his pocket. Before he could raise the weapon, Seymour Tarnish burst from behind a pile of canvas-covered wood on the site, waving a baseball bat he kept in his ice cream truck and yelling—

"Don't try it, buster. You might be able to shoot me, but you can't shoot everyone!"

Milner Logan stepped out from his hiding place behind the chest-high brick foundation, weaponless, though his muscular physique was imposing enough. From behind Hal McConnell, Mr. Koh emerged from his hiding place behind a bush, a long branch in hand. Finally, Fiona Finch, my aunt Sadie, and J. Parker Brainert stumbled out of their own hiding places. Poor Brainert was cursing that he'd stepped his loafers in a pile of goose dung.

Hal McConnell quickly realized that they'd heard every word.

"Yes, Hal. They are all willing to testify to the things you confessed if they have to."

Hal shrugged, turned the gun handle first and handed it to me. "I wasn't going to shoot you. There are no bullets in the gun," he said. "It's just another piece of evidence I wanted you to have."

Suddenly, Hal's face and body seemed to completely relax.

I stared at him, puzzled. "You look relieved."

"It's all going to come out now," he said. "All of it. No more wall. No more code of silence. They'll never forget Bethany now. Or Victoria . . . and they'll all pay for hiding the truth."

I took the gun and he met my eyes.

"But, Hal, the truth won't set you free," I said softly. "You'll have to stand trial."

"It's okay, Mrs. McClure. I'm ready. Unlike Angel, I have a conscience."

EPILOGUE

I have a secret passion for mercy ... but justice is
what keeps happening to people.

—Ross McDonald

"I HAVE A surprise for you, Jack."

A surprise for a ghost? Don't that beat all.

It was late Monday evening, chilly for early October,
and I was alone in my bedroom, getting ready to turn in. I
pulled the combination alarm clock/CD player out of the
shopping bag and began struggling to free it from its foam
prison.

"It'll just take a few minutes to put together," I promised.

Baby, in case you haven't noticed, time is all I got.

Today, I had finally found the time to drive to All
Things Bed & Beautiful. Besides the alarm clock/CD
player for myself, I'd gotten Aunt Sadie a new comforter

and Spencer a set of Spider-Man sheets. He was sleeping on them now. But Sadie wasn't under her new comforter. She and Bud Napp were, once again, out on the town—which for Quindicott meant pizza at Franzetti's and a drink at Donovan's Pub.

For weeks, Jack had insisted that Sadie and Bud's nights out were "dates." I had disagreed, thinking a man of Jack's time just couldn't grasp how a man and woman could be platonic friends. But then last week, I caught Bud kissing my aunt by the door, and I finally had to admit that maybe Jack Shepard knew a thing or two more than me about human nature.

Any news yet on the McConnell kid's fate? asked Jack.

"Yes, as a matter of fact . . ."

After discovery by both sides and much haggling by Hal's legal team, the district attorney's office had agreed to let Hal plead guilty to manslaughter. There would be no trial. And the sentencing had just come down earlier this very afternoon—which was probably also why I felt the need to take a drive.

"The judge gave him seven years in a minimum security facility," I informed Jack, "and he'll be eligible for parole in four."

Sounds like a cakewalk.

"Not for somebody who's used to the freedom wealth brings. Of course, I hear he'll be doing an independent graduate studies program out of Brown University while he's in prison. Egyptology, I think—"

You don't say? Guess that makes sense. I never saw a cell that didn't have some sort of hieroglyphics scratched into it.

"Don't make fun, Jack. I feel bad enough as it is."

Why, for Pete's sake?

"You know why. Hal McConnell wasn't really a murderer. He was just trying to protect Victoria that night, and—"

Don't say Angel drove him to it, doll. Murder is murder. A life was taken and can never be given back.

"But Angel was a murderer herself, two times over."

That's what the law is for, baby, to mete out justice. You did what you set out to do, didn't you? You got your Johnny-boy off.

"I know . . . and Bud is grateful beyond words. So am I, Jack. To you."

Can the sweet sap, doll. Pour it over your pancakes.

I laughed, then went back to trying to set the right time on the digital display of my new alarm.

"Really, Jack, I mean it. If you hadn't suggested faking that security camera on the pole that night, I don't know if I'd have figured out how to get Hal to . . . you know, uh, give up the ghost, so to speak . . . no offense."

Funny, I never thought I'd see an ice chest get so much mileage in the P.I. game.

"Seymour Tarnish's ice cream truck came in handy on that score . . . and Milner Logan was great in actually climbing the ladder and getting it up there. Not bad for a bunch of—what did you call them?—cracker-barrel yahoos."

Yeah, sure. Whatever you say, baby. So what's happened to that Johnny kid now, anyway? I haven't seen him around in weeks.

"Oh! That's right, I never told you. He went to culinary school. Bud's helping him with some of the tuition, and Fiona is lending him the rest. She said once he graduates, he can work off the loan at her new restaurant—assisting the head chef, which she hasn't exactly found yet. But I'm sure she will before the Finch Inn restaurant opens for business this Christmas."

I wouldn't make book on that, sweetheart.

"On what?"

On some hoity-toity chef leaving the bright lights of his big city restaurant job for this little podunk burg.

"Quindicott is a charming and quaint little town, Jack Shepard. Repeat after me. Quaint is good."

Baby, the only good thing about this town is you.

I was unwrapping a new CD when the words sunk in. I completely froze, unable to believe my ears. "Jack? Did you just go sappy on me?"

Yeah, honey. Savor it while you can.

"You know, Jack, seriously . . . I never asked you: What did you think of my work . . . as a P.I.?"

Not bad. For a dame.

I smiled. "Thanks."

But you've got a helluva long road to travel, sister, so don't let it go to your head.

"I won't. But I'll tell you what, I'm pretty sure this will."

I pulled a bottle of chilled champagne out of my tote bag. A minute later, I was popping and pouring the bubbly into a shallow glass—okay so it was a cheap plastic party glass and not fluted crystal, but the champagne was real.

Finally learning how to let your troubles make a getaway, I see.

I smiled and hit the play button on the new CD player. "And here's a little something for you."

What's that?

He didn't have to ask twice. The CD of Glenn Miller's greatest hits immediately began to fill the room with 1940s' big band classics, starting with that haunting standard, "Moonlight Serenade."

Hey, that's the tune somebody played the night we braced Joey Lubrano.

"Aw, Jack, you remembered. How romantic."

He laughed and so did I. Then I leaned back on my bed, closed my eyes, and sipped champagne. After two hours, I had (mostly) forgotten how bad I felt about Angel Stark and Victoria Banks and today's sentencing of Hal McConnell. I had finally learned how to relax with my ghost. I was so relaxed, in fact, I began drifting off and almost didn't hear Jack talk to me one last time.

I'll see you in your dreams, baby, he whispered. Then I felt the cool kiss of his presence temporarily recede, back into the fieldstone walls that had become his tomb.

Don't Miss the Next

Haunted Bookshop Mystery

The Ghost and the
Dead Man's Library

Hard-boiled private eye Jack Shepard didn't have much use for books—at least, not when he was alive. Scholarly tomes never helped him persuade a clammed-up booze-hound to spill, nail a fakeloo grifter, or make a hatchetman grab some air until the coppers showed. So, of course, he has little interest in the crate of dusty old volumes that arrive at the Rhode Island bookshop he's been haunting for fifty years. On the other hand, young widow Penelope, her aunt Sadie, and their book-loving friends in the Quindicott Business Owners Association (a.k.a. the Quibble Over Anything gang) are *thrilled* with the delivery. The rare leather-bound library of Edgar Allan Poe limited editions had been willed to Buy the Book by an elderly admirer of Sadie's. The dead man's library is so valuable that Pen and Sadie are immediately inundated with astronomical bids for each and every volume in the set. Everything appears rosy, until Pen and Sadie begin to sell off the books one by one . . . and one by one each buyer dies. The police don't believe Pen's "literary" theory—that these deaths are linked to the rare book purchases. In fact, the police don't believe these deaths are murders at all. Pen, of course, knows differently, which means it's time to persuade her hard-boiled haunter to stop resting in peace, start cracking some clues, and make sure this twisted Poe freak kills "nevermore."